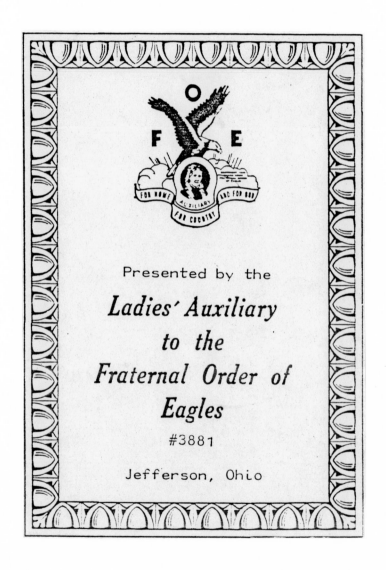

Presented by the

Ladies' Auxiliary
to the
Fraternal Order of
Eagles

#3881

Jefferson, Ohio

THE RANSOM

Also available in Large Print
by Grace Livingston Hill:

Amorelle
Blue Ruin
Found Treasure
The Enchanted Barn

THE RANSOM

Grace Livingston Hill

G.K. HALL &CO.
Boston, Massachusetts
1990

Copyright 1933 by J. B. Lippincott.

All rights reserved.

Published in Large Print by arrangement with
Munce Publishing Co.

G.K. Hall Large Print Book Series.

Set in 18 pt. Plantin.

17.95

LT

H646 r

Library of Congress Cataloging in Publication Data

HIll, Grace Livingston, 1865–1947.
    The ransom / Grace Livingston Hill.
        p.   cm.—(G.K. Hall large print book series)
    ISBN 0-8161-4911-9 (lg. print)
    1. Large type books.   I. Title.
[PS3515.I486R36   1990]
813'.52—dc20   89-48662

CHRISTOBEL got out of the car and went into the house alone. She had asked them to let her out. She did not want to go to the station with her stepmother's parents, and was glad that her father had not insisted upon it.

It had been all she could stand to drive from the cemetery with them. It had made her feel like screaming. They were a pair of incompetent weak-faced jelly-fishes, she reflected as she slowly mounted the marble steps of her father's pretentious home. It was all wrong, people like that being mixed up in any relationship with her wonderful father! How did it ever happen that he had got into such a mess? She tried to think back to the days when her father first met her stepmother, but it was all very vague, an indefinite part of her childhood, although she distinctly remembered her own mother, and the soft feel of her kisses, and her arms hugging close.

These aliens, her stepmother's parents, angered her. What right had they to come into a family affair and have to be thought about and planned for and taken to the station just when the dreadful, ostentatious funeral service was at an end?

Of course, they were Charmian's parents. That had to be considered. And as one looked at their shallow old faces, one could see vague resemblances to the vivid beauty that had been Charmian. Charmian! What a name to give a woman who had to at least pretend to be a mother. Yet that old mother's face made it perfectly natural that her daughter should have been named Charmian. Just a silly weak woman with a petted under lip and a slightly retreating chin; she had never grown up though her body was withering like a little old garden rose that was turning brown at the edges. Light hair, bleached to a yellow gray. Weak blue eyes that took in everything even from behind the impressive black veil.

"She didn't miss a thing, even with tears in her eyes," thought Christobel grimly. "I s'pose she did feel bad, maybe. She was her own daughter, and of course she ought to. Still, she hadn't seen much of her for several years. It couldn't weigh on her very heavily. I don't believe anything ever weighed on her but herself anyway. She looks selfish!"

Would Charmian have looked like her mother if she had lived to be an old wrinkled woman like that? Christobel went on idly meditating as she hunted in her hand bag for her latch key.

Charmian had been vivid, gorgeous, even in her coffin. It had seemed as if she must be but playing a part. There was that affected smile she always wore when in company, her lips delicately pursed, her eyebrows placid, the long lashes lying on the rose petal cheeks. Christobel could vaguely understand why her father had married her.

Yet looking at her as she lay there almost smothered in those myriads of flowers, Christobel had not been able to forget the look of those coral lips when they had told her that she was to go away to school; the lifting of those exquisite eyebrows in haughty disapproval at Randall her young brother when he made a noise; the unloving, prideful expression of the whole face of the spoiled beauty who had become her mother in the early days of her baby sorrow over the loss of her own precious mother.

Seated in the carriage opposite this Charmian-mother's mother, Christobel had found herself tracing the same selfish lines exposed in the old face, that she had never been able to forget in the face of the daughter. Oh, it was plain to be seen why the dead woman had grown up silly and petted and spoiled.

And the old father. He had a weak chin and watery eyes that had looked around on the strange city streets with an indifferent air. If he had any character of his own he had long ago taken the easiest way and given it up to his pettish wife. Yes, in a way they both looked like Charmian.

Christobel drew a long breath and tried to wipe them out of her memory. They were not her grandparents anyway. She had always been eager for grandparents and had looked forward with some interest and not a little curiosity to their coming to the funeral. But these shallow old people had merely explained her stepmother, set her into her true background, confirmed the feeling Christobel had always secretly had about her even at the first when she was trying to obey her father's earnest solicitation to love this new, queer, too-giddy mother that he had found to fill the empty place.

Oh, well, that was that, she reflected as she fitted her key into the lock and opened the great door with its bronze fittings.

Christobel didn't like that door, nor the

big stone lions that crouched on either side of the entrance. They seemed too ostentatious. She didn't like the big house with its high ceilings and modernistic furniture. It had nothing of home about it. It had been her stepmother's choice. Christobel wondered if her father helped pick it out, and whether he liked it.

Every vacation when she had come home for a few days to have a new outfit and be hustled off to some girl's camp, or get ready to go back to school again, the house had seemed less and less like a home, and more and more like a furniture display in a great department store. There wasn't a thing in it that one could feel like loving and keeping.

Christobel closed the door softly as befitted a door whose mistress had gone out of it never to return, and went and stood in the great doorway of the reception room on the right.

She stepped softly within the heavy hangings of the silver cloth backed with velvety black, and took in the whole barbaric effect of silver and black and startling splashes of scarlet that made the room look like some strange alien fantastic world. Weird lights in odd places, angular pyramidal mirrors like flashes of bright sabers; queer, box-like furniture that gave one an odd sense of being in a dream and finding the world upside down. It was not like a home at all, this great uncanny room.

This was the place that Charmian had made about herself, a world of unrealities, and now she was gone out of it all! Here were the things she had brought together, but she had had to leave them all and lie in a bed of roses and be put away under the ground.

Where was she now? Was that all of her?

Some of the teachers at school had openly said that there was no other life than this. But Christobel had never been willing to accept that theory. She had always thought of her own mother as being somewhere, in some definite place, watching her perhaps, and surely waiting for her to come some day when she was an old woman.

But now, this other woman, who was not in any sense a mother, who had insisted upon being called Charmian by the children of her husband, who had packed them off to a school in almost babyhood, and made a strange alien world of home, where was she now that she was gone out of life?

Was there any one for her to be with? Or was she all alone? Did she have to wait somewhere for that unpleasant old weak-chinned father and mother whom she had never noticed much on earth? Oh, life was a queer tangle! A problem that could never be solved till one went out of it.

Of course there were people who could throw all that off and just not think about it. Eat and drink and be merry. Most of her school mates were like that. They laughed at her when she asked serious questions. They said "Why worry? You can only be alive once!" and danced gayly on.

But Christobel had never been able to do that. She had made merry with the rest, had been fairly feverish in trying to have every minute filled with something bright and gay so that she would not have time to think. But underneath there had always been that question, that wonder, that hope that would not be stilled; yes and that fear too, that this life was not all that she ought to be doing about it, though she had not an idea in the world what it was she might do. Nobody else seemed to be worrying about it. Not even death seemed to stir many of them seriously. They hurried to get the funeral over and get back to life, gay, bright, breath-taking life! Charmian had been that way too.

She had hated funerals. She had hated even the mention of funerals.

Though Christobel had spent very little time with her stepmother in the ten or eleven years Charmian had been married to her father, she seemed to know a great deal about her likes and dislikes, her fears and contempts. Every contact with the handsome stepmother seemed graven deep into her sensitive heart. For instance, she never would forget the bored drawl of her voice the night she crept from her lonely little bed, put to sleep unkissed. Christobel had come weeping to find her father who had always remembered the good nights before, only to discover Charmian in the midst of a discussion about sending Christobel and her brother Randall off to school.

"But they are only babies yet," she heard her father say in a shocked voice.

"That's it," Charmian had drawled insolently, "I can't be bored with babies, certainly not some other woman's babies. That wasn't what I married you for."

In the midst of the awful silence that had followed those words Christobel had crept trembling to her little bed and wept herself to sleep. But she had never forgotten

Charmian's voice, nor the white angry hurt look of her father's face.

Another time later, when she was at home for a few days, Charmian had showed a great fear. The cook had been sick, terribly sick, and the doctor had sent for Charmian telling her the servant was dying. Charmian had looked at Christobel, then only about thirteen, and wrung her hands together, and cried out:

"Oh, I can't go, Chrissie! It would make me ill. I never could bear sickness, and I'm afraid of death. You go, that's a good girl."

And Christobel, with a great wonder, and a growing contempt, and a secret dread, went. For very shame for Charmian Christobel had gone and held the hand of the dying cook, patting her cold wet brow, holding up the hand that had tried to make the sign of the cross at the last moment.

Now, as Christobel looked about the great grotesque room, forcing herself to walk softly, as if still in the presence of the dead, entering the little inner room which had been Charmian's special sanctum, she was summing up all her impressions of her stepmother, and wondering what there could be for her in that other life to which she had gone—if there really was another life.

9

White velvet here in this inner room, white velvet lining to the silver draperies, white velvet rug, marble and onyx in the floor and tables; white-shaded white-pedestaled lamps of alabaster, wildly lovely, with a glow like hidden fire in their white, white depths; white velvet draperies at the windows about a frostwork of hand made lace. Could anything be more exquisite, pure, simple, lovely, like driven snow? Crystal flowers in great costly sprays of cunningly placed mirrors, voluptuous bits of statuary, modern to the last degree, the only bit of color a lank slim devil of a doll in sumptuous taffeta of palest green and rose, lolling with abandoned air over a white velvet chair. The room might have been a lone iceberg at the North Pole, with a faint image of sunset in the sky, so white and lonesome it looked.

Yet in all that whiteness there was not a suggestion of purity, nor holiness. It rather seemed like something lovely gone astray, dishonored, put to a wrong use.

Christobel shivered and wondered at her vague thoughts. She could not reason out all these things, she was too young and inexperienced, yet she felt them, like balls of ice against her young consciousness, and the tears stung to her eyes, and made a lump in her throat.

Charmian had made all this around herself, for herself to enjoy. And suddenly, without warning, just a sharp pain in the night, and some power rushed her out of it all, rushed her to the hospital in terror, through a frantic operation that was too late, and herself, her little petted self, had been snatched away from the white velvet life she had planned. Planned, not because she liked things white and pure and sweet, but because she delighted to take a precious costly thing and desecrate it for herself. That was the great thought that hovered crushingly over Christobel's overstrained consciousness. Where, where, *where* had Charmian gone? Almost she felt a passing pity for the woman she knew had hated her.

Sudden distant voices in the other part of the house brought the girl back to the present. She turned swiftly, and moved noiselessly over the deep priceless rugs, back to the shelter of the heavy draperies into the wide hall. Those were the servants' voices and she did not wish to be caught here looking into Charmian's particular sanctum as if she were curious.

The voices were in the dining room, diag-

11

onally across the wide hall, but the silent empty house carried the words clearly. Indeed the voices were not hushed. It was evident from the clinking sounds that silver and crystal were being placed upon the table and sideboard. Probably the dinner table was being prepared for the evening meal.

Christobel was not very well acquainted with the servants in the house. She had been only the day before summoned home from boarding school to attend the funeral, and the servants were all new since her last homecoming. Charmian had a way of changing her minions often.

"Well, and now I wonder what'll be coming next?" said a voice with a decided Irish accent. Christobel wondered if it might be the cook, only what would the cook be doing in the dining room? Her province was the kitchen.

Then it sounded as if the butler entered and put down a tray of glasses on the sideboard.

"Oh, *now*," giggled the parlor maid unmistakably, "I suppose we'll have a spell of Mrs. Romayne."

"What's Mrs. Romayne got to do with it?" asked the lofty voice of the butler who was new in the house and had not got the ways of things yet.

"Oh, you don't know Mrs. Romayne yet, do you Hawkins?" giggled the parlor maid knowingly. "Wait till you see. She'll have very much to do. She's come back from Florida especially to look after things. She called up this morning when they were all out and said she'd be in this afternoon after the service. Oh, you'll find out. She'll meddle in every blessed thing. She's that kind. You ought to have heard her nosey questions this morning."

"But who is she?" demanded the butler.

"Oh, she's a pretty widow lady that's crazy about the master," responded the parlor maid. "Wait till you see. Honey on her words, and a laugh like a young bird."

"Is the master fond of her?" asked the butler cannily.

"Who can tell?" chirped the parlor maid. "What difference would that make anyway?"

"All the difference in the world," said the butler wisely.

"Ah, but you don't know the lady, Hawkins," giggled the girl. "She's clever, that woman is. She knows what she wants and she gets it. I've seen her like work before."

"Well, it's likely to be some one. I'll look her over. If I don't like her I'm leaving," announced the butler.

"Whist! There's Marie comin' in from the funeral," warned the cook. "Better not talk before her. She's a sneak. She'd likely tell the master if it served her own interests. They certainly had a long service. I hope the proud lady is well buried and deep."

Christobel in her shelter of the silver draperies shivered. There was something uncannily harsh in the tone of the woman. She felt as if she ought to walk out and rebuke her, yet what could she say? She shrank from having anything to do with them. She would wait a moment until they were all gone back to the kitchen. They evidently did not know she had come in. She had no position in her father's house yet. The spirit of Charmian still lingered in those grotesque rooms.

"Hi, there, Marie!" challenged the parlor maid. "Have a pleasant funeral? What was she like? Was there a lot of flowers?"

"Oh, sure," said the lady's maid loftily, "a grand funeral. And she looked lovely as life."

"Say, Marie," asked the curious furtive voice of the cook. "What come o' them fur coats she got up the day she was took sick? Did she keep 'em?"

"Sure she kep' 'em. She was just crazy about 'em. I'm goin' up now an' try on that sable wrap. If there's time before the family gets back I'll come down an' show ya."

There was a sound of the swinging door into the butler's pantry.

"Do that," encouraged the cook. Evidently the butler and parlor maid went out. "An' say, Marie, if ya happen ta come acrost that there string of purple beads she useta wear, just bring 'em along. I'd like 'em fer a sowveneer! You do that fer me, an' I'll say nothin' about what I know! See?"

"Awright," agreed Charmian's maid, "I s'pose you know those beads are real amethyst. They're worth a lot. But I ain't goin' to do a thing till after Miss Christobel goes back ta school. She's got eyes like a cat, that girl. She'll likely go back ta night ur tamorra, and then I got clear sailin'. The master'll leave it ta me ta put things in order. He doesn't know what she had. He'll never miss anything."

"But there'll be the bills!"

"Naw, he won't pay any attention now. He'll just pay 'em and be done. It's only women would know. An' if Miss Christobel is gone who's goin' ta know?"

"There's another woman hankerin' ta get

15

in our missis shoes," warned the cook. "That Roymane lady is come up from Pam Beach. She called up this mornin'. What you do you better do quick."

"My land!" said Marie in dismay. "Has she come? Well I'll stay in ta night and get things well outta sight. Then let her snoop!"

"Well, ef you're goin' ta show us that fur wrap you better get a hustle on. They'll likely be comin' back from the funeral right soon an' you don't wanta be masqueradin' round in no dead lady's cloes."

"All righty! I'll hurry!" said Marie and turned toward the back stairs.

But Christobel had flown, stealthy as a cat, up the velvet shod front stairs, up the hall away from her own room to the spacious apartment that had belonged to Charmian.

She opened the door and slipped her hand inside taking the key out and fitting it into the outside of the door, and while she did so she cast one frightened glance into the rooms that had been her stepmother's. All soft pinks and blues in satin and luxury, a bedroom beyond done in lettuce green, and the door wide open into the strange weird bathroom where all the fixtures, even the bathtub were done in black, with the floor in black and crimson tiles.

16

Christobel shut the door softly and locking it, removed the key and fled swiftly to her own room, just in time to escape Marie as she came from the back stairs.

She heard Marie go forward to her mistress' apartment, try the door, even rattle it, stand in wonder a moment, and then turn away and go swiftly past her door and down the back stairs again. She could hear suppressed excited voices downstairs when she opened her door, but that was all.

Christobel stood an instant trembling in her room wondering what she should do next. She did not feel at home anywhere in that house. She did not even feel at home with her own father, for always, even when he had come to the school to visit her in these later years she had seemed to feel the presence of Charmian with him, as if she were so much a part of him that she would somehow know just what had passed between father and daughter. She had long ago sensed that Charmian was jealous of every word, every kiss, every look even that passed between her husband and his children. And now as she stood clasping that key in her cold hand she could not be sure whether she had done right or not, whether perhaps she had not been meddling in something where her father would not want her to interfere. Still, it had been all too evident that those servants were planning to spoil her stepmother's possessions, and surely she had been right in stopping everything by a locked door until her father came to say what should be done.

Softly she stole to her door again and tried to listen but the voices which had been rather loud and startled as if the four downstairs had been accusing one another, suddenly hushed as another sound broke, the rattle of a latch key in the front door. Then there was a soft scuttling back into the kitchen and only the quiet of a gentleman's well ordered household as some one entered the front hall.

Christobel slipped out into the hall and looked cautiously over the banister, hoping her father had come, but a sudden rush of heavy young feet brought the knowledge that it was only Randall her younger brother. She drew back into her own doorway till he reached the upper floor and then met him face to face on the way to his own room which was at the back end of the hall and next her own.

"Oh, hello, Chris, is that you? Where's Dad? In his own room? I gotta see him right away. I gotta take the next train back ta school. We got a big game tamorra an' I gotta be there. I'm cheerleader."

Christobel was aware of the soft opening of a door at the foot of the back stairs, for the door squeaked a little on its hinges, and she drew her brother cautiously within her own room and closed the door.

"Rand, you can't do that! You can't go right away without taking time to see Father. That wouldn't be decent."

"Aw, whaddaya mean decent? Dad couldn't expect me ta stay. I got my school duties, see?"

"No, Rand, you can't go off like that. We've got to be here when Father gets back. You can't go off. I tell you you *can't!* Somebody else can take your duties. Tomorrow is Saturday. They wouldn't expect you to be back yet. It would be only respectable to wait over Sunday."

"Aw—, Chris! Whadda *you* havta say about it anyway? The funeral's over isn't it? Gosh, I'm glad it's over. I don't see what they have such terrible things for anyway. All that bunk, reading and praying and yammering, and all keeping still so long. When you're dead you're dead aren't ya? What good did that do Charmian? A lot she ever cared

19

about such bunk! I don't want any yammering over me when I die."

"Don't Rannie!" said Christobel putting her hands over her eyes and shuddering. "Don't talk about dying."

"Aw well, I'm not going ta croak yet a while. Say, Kid, got any money? Lend me ten ur fifteen? I'm dead broke, and I been over my allowance so many times lately I don't likta ask Dad fer any just now."

"What do you do with all your money, Rand? Dad gives you a much bigger allowance than most boys get. I know for the girls at school tell me what their brothers get, and it's rarely half as much as yours."

"Aw well, that's my business, isn't it? If yer going ta preach I'm done. I havta take it from Dad, but I don't from you. Are ya going ta lend me twenty-five ur not? I ask ya?"

"I haven't got it, Rand, honestly I haven't," said his sister looking even more troubled at the increased demand. "I had to get a present for our principal on her birthday. All the girls were in it and they wanted to get something really nice. It took all I had. I had to ask the office to lend me money for my carfare here."

"Good night!" said the boy fretfully,

"Then I'll havta pawn my watch, and I hate like the dickens to do it. Dad's been awfully white about getting me a new one when I smashed the last and I don't want him ta notice it's gone."

"Look here, Rand, you'd better tell Father everything. You'll just get into a mess if you don't. Dad would rather have you come across with the truth I'm sure. And you oughtn't to trouble him just now when he's going through all this."

"All this?" said the boy wonderingly. "You don't think he *cares* do ya? Why, she never cared anything about him! She just bled him fer money all the time. I know that fer a fact. I saw a few things that time I was home with a broken leg. You can't tell me!"

"Rand, for pity's sake, stop talking like that and be decent. If you think so keep it to yourself, at least for a while. Hark! There's Father coming in now, and there's some one with him. We'll have to go down, Rand. Father will expect it."

"Good night!" said the boy under his breath peering down the stairs into the lighted hall. "It's that old uncle of Charmian's. Now he'll have ta stay ta dinner and I won't get ta see Dad at all. Say, Chris, I'll slip down the back way and snitch a bite in the kitchen,

21

and then pawn my watch and get back ta school, and you tell Dad I hadta get back on that train, and that I'll write him and explain. Say I'm sorry and all that—"

"I'll do no such thing!" said Christobel angrily. "You're not going away without Father's permission! Go on downstairs and behave yourself like a decent son of the house. Yes, Father, Rand and I are here! We're coming!" she called as she saw her father lift a tired face toward the two as they stood together at the top of the stairs.

"Aw you!" said Randall as he moved sullenly down the stairs after his sister into the full light of the hall.

As she passed down the stairs she caught a glimpse of Marie coming furtively, warily from the back hall with an anxious look on her face, and a bunch of keys in her hand.

2

THE dinner table was a stiff affair, the young people scarcely speaking except when necessary, the two men carrying on a desultory conversation about politics and the prospect of a war in Europe, in all of which neither seemed much interested. But finally when the table was being cleared for the dessert course and the butler had for the moment left the room the unwelcome guest disclosed the true cause of his coming.

"H'm!" he said clearing his throat. "I am wondering when my dear niece's will is to be read?"

"Will?" said the head of the house lifting his eyebrows in a question. "My wife left no will."

"No will?" said the old man with a swag of his head in disapproval. "That makes it most awkward, doesn't it? How careless of her. Well, then, just when is the estate to be divided?"

"Estate?" The younger man lifted his chin a trifle haughtily and looked at his guest as if he had been an old black crow come to pick his bones. "There is no estate," he said coldly. "My wife owned no property whatever."

"Oh, but surely she owned this house. She told me several times that she bought it. She said it was hers."

"It was hers only in the sense that I bought what she selected. Charmian was absolutely penniless when I married her, and she had nothing except as I gave it to her. I did not give her this house simply because I found that she was utterly unfitted either by character or by education to manage business affairs."

"Indeed!" said the uncle severely. "I was led to believe quite the contrary. I understood that she had been most successful in her investments. That she had an uncanny way of always knowing where to place her money, and that her gains had been phenomenal."

Mr. Kershaw lifted his head now and looked the old man steadily in the eyes, speaking more severely than Christobel had ever heard him to to one older than himself. He was by nature a most courteous man.

"I am sorry to have to inform you, Mr. Madden," he said, "that every investment my wife ever made, and every attempt of hers to play the market turned out to be my heavy loss instead of her gain. My wife lost heavily in several ill-advised ventures and had so involved herself with my money that I was obliged to make good. If you wish to confirm my words you may consult my lawyer who is even now trying to straighten out a mess that came from her great desire to roll in wealth. I have nothing further to say in the matter."

The butler had returned with dessert and

the baffled old man subsided into his coffee and pastry. Christobel and Randall eyed their father speculatively in the light of what he had just said. For the first time in their lives it occurred to them that their father might have had some rough sledding in his career that had always seemed to them a charmed path of success.

"Gee! Was Charmian like that?" meditated young Randall, and told himself he was glad he hadn't pawned his watch. Dad might have noticed and felt hurt about it, seeing it was a good one and his last birthday present.

But Christobel had suddenly remembered the key that was in her possession and the overheard conversation, and was trying to plan what she should do about it. Ought she to tell her father?

An oppressive silence was beginning to settle over the table when Mr. Kershaw broke it in a businesslike tone.

"By the way, Mr. Madden, what time did you say your train was leaving? Randall and I have an errand down town presently, and we could drop you at the station."

"H'm!" said the old uncle gathering the last delicious crumb of pastry on his fork delicately. "I didn't say. I was not altogether sure I should leave to-night. I didn't know but business might detain me—" He paused and gave place for an invitation to remain as a guest of the house. Christobel and Randall exchanged quick glances of apprehension, but as if he read his children's thoughts Mr. Kershaw looked up quickly and answered:

"Well, whatever you say. If you prefer it we can drop you at your hotel instead of the station."

The old man swallowed his mortification and decided for the station, and with relief to all the meal was ended at last.

"I want you to get your coat and hat and come with me Randall," said his father in a tone that made the boy look at his father with sudden apprehension. He wondered anxiously if Dad had had a letter from the school, and hurried off to get his coat.

"Anyhow, we're getting rid of this old geezer," he whispered to his sister as he passed her on the stairs. "Some sucker he is. I wonder Dad didn't pitch him out of the house. Some nerve he has asking about a will!"

Christobel had a chance to speak to her father for just a moment as he came from his room with his coat on and his hat in his hand.

She had reconnoitered and knew that the

servants were all in the kitchen at their dinner, yet she stood half hesitating whether she ought to tell him or not.

"What is it, daughter?" he asked kindly as he came into the hall and saw the trouble in her eyes. "Something you want to see me about? I won't be very long. Is it anything in particular? Will it wait?"

"Why, I guess so," she said looking with troubled eyes across the hall to Charmian's door. "It's just that I happened to overhear the servants talking. Maybe I was mistaken. They might have been joking, but it didn't sound like it. It seemed as if they were planning to go through her things, and—I locked that door. Was that right?"

"Certainly, that was right. I should have thought of it before. They are all practically new servants but Marie, and I never did trust her. What did they say?"

"I couldn't hear it all," said Christobel with a worried tone. "They spoke of two fur coats, new ones, a sable and an ermine."

"She had no such coats," said the father looking puzzled.

"I thought from what they said they had been sent up on approval. They gossiped about what you would say when you would see the bill. And they spoke about a chain of amethysts, purple beads the cook called them."

Christobel noticed a startled look in her father's face.

"I should have looked out for things. No telling what she—" he said and then checked himself. "I mean I'm glad you locked the door."

"But Father," began Christobel again, "I'm afraid Marie has another key. I saw her coming this way carrying a bunch of keys as we were going downstairs to dinner. Perhaps I ought to have told you right away, but I didn't like to before Mr. Madden."

"Well," said Kershaw looking troubled, "never mind. Suppose you just stay around near and keep your eyes open while I'm gone. I'll get back as quickly as possible. I wouldn't go now only I must get rid of this old man, and there is a matter of business I must attend to to-night, a telegram or two that will have to be sent—and I want Randall with me," he added as if to explain not leaving him behind with his sister. "You sit in this room if you like and read or something. Or downstairs wherever you like, but just keep your eyes and ears open. I don't imagine they'll dare to do anything much, not with you in the house, and perhaps not anyway."

Christobel walked idly up and down the hall for a few minutes after they were gone. She tried to shake off the awesome feeling of death that still seemed to hover about the proximity of her stepmother's door. She reasoned with herself that it was silly and childish to be afraid of just rooms with nobody in them, but somehow that memory of the still tenement of clay that had been her sharp young stepmother's would pass continually before her eyes.

So she turned into her father's room.

Curiously she looked about her. She had seldom been in this particular apartment. She did not know the furnishings. There was a strangeness about the whole atmosphere, as if it were merely a stopping place for a momentary waiting. Not as if there were any attempt to make of it a home where a human soul had comfort and resting. Poor Father! A great pity swept over her for him. What had he had in life anyway? Those revealing words about property that he had spoken at the table had stirred her deeply for him. What had he had in any of them except a channel to take his money from him? She and Randall had never been at home much.

Money and more money they had always been crying out for, and he had always given it freely, with only occasional troubled questions as to how it was spent. He must have been that way with Charmian too. Charmian had always had luxury after she became Mrs. Kershaw.

Christobel found herself wondering if her father had a great deal of money. She had never thought about it before; she had always taken it for granted that the wealth had been unlimited. Yet there had been a certain oppression, a look of almost fright when she had spoken of those valuable fur coats, that he all too evidently had not known about. These were hard times. People everywhere were losing money. Some of the girls had had to stop school at Christmas because their parents had failed and had no more money to keep them in such an expensive school. Had the great depression come anywhere near her father? Was that perhaps why her father's hair had silvered at the edges so much since the last time she had seen him?

She switched on the lights and looked around her. There was no evidence of failing fortune in the furnishings of the room, but Charmian would have seen to that. The house must come up to her standard of luxury in every detail. The handsome leather chairs and davenport, the curious tables of metal and tile, the extremely modern lamps and queer triangular ornaments. They did not speak of a restful homelike atmosphere for a tired man when he came home from business.

But Christobel was young to think of such things. She merely felt them vaguely. The room did not rest her. It somehow repelled her. She turned away and was going to her own room, but some unformed thought came to her and drew her to the door of the inner room, her father's sleeping apartment. Ah! All was different here. The furniture was old and plain, a walnut bed and bureau, a chiffonier of indifferent pattern, a Brussels carpet on the floor that looked as if it had seen wear, and yet somehow spoke to the girl dimly of the past. Where had she once traced her finger over that pattern of autumn leaves on a gray ground and thought it lovely? Could it be when she was a little, little girl?

And then a picture in a cheap little frame caught her eye. Why, that was her mother's picture up there on the chiffonier. Could this be her father's refuge from the world? Did he still cherish her mother's memory?

Christobel went and stood before the picture. It was not the photograph of her mother with which she was familiar, the one her father had had put in a little locket long ago when she first went to school. Nor yet the miniature he had given her later on her six-teenth birthday. That had been sweet, but unreal. This old faded photograph had about it a simple air of reality that went deep into her heart. The faint smile on the shadowy picture recalled the dearest thing that life had ever held for her, and drew her so that she took the picture and pressed it to her lips again and again, and found a tear upon the glass that she had to wipe off. Ah! This was the mother she had almost forgotten, yet for whom her hungry young heart had been cry-ing out through the years.

At last she put the picture back in its place and turned away, reverently, as if the place were sacred. Somehow she felt that she would be nearer to her father now because she had caught this glimpse of the place in the great house where he truly lived.

Suddenly she wondered if she ought to have come in, and stepping out closed the door carefully. What mattered that outer richly furnished library, since there was this inner shrine? What mattered the whole house? She could breathe more freely now since she knew this plain quiet spot where her father really lived.

She came out of her father's apartment, went down the hall to her own room, and stood at the window looking out with unseeing eyes at the roofs and chimneys of the square. A moment later some one tapped at her door.

"There is a lady downstairs who wants to see you Miss Christobel," said Marie, handing her a card.

"To see me?" said Christobel wonderingly. "Oh, it must be for Father, I'm sure. I know so few people in the city."

"You are the lady of the house now," snapped Marie coldly, critically, as if with a kind of ill-hidden contempt that she did not know it herself without being told.

"Just a child!" said Marie contemptuously a moment later down in the kitchen. "She notices nothing. She couldn't have locked the door. It wouldn't occur to her. I must have locked it myself and mislaid the key. But where I could have put it I do not understand. But come, now is the time. Mrs. Romayne is here. She will keep Miss Christobel quite a time with her pussy ways and her flattering talk. Sucking in, that is

33

what she is here for! Come on. The butler has gone on an errand for the master."

With a sinking of heart Christobel looked at the card. Mrs. J. Rivington Romayne. Wasn't that the name of the woman the servants had been talking about? Romayne? The woman who had called on the telephone? The woman they had said would get her father? She gave a little shiver of dislike and hesitated. Should she go down? Did she have to?

But of course as no alternative offered she was forced to go. There was however a hostile light in her eyes as she entered the smaller reception room to the right of the hall and stood for an instant between the draperies looking into the dimness of the rich furnishings of the room.

A soft movement sounded from the dimmest corner like the going of silken garments, and a breath of exquisite violet perfume stirred in the air. Then Mrs. Romayne stood before her, pausing just an instant under the light of a tall alabaster floor lamp that threw a mellow flood of amber about her head.

Mrs. Romayne was exquisite. Even Christobel's hostile eyes could not help seeing that. Lovely dark hair in rich waves close to a shapely head, large soft dark blue eyes shining with sympathy, small delicate lips, not too red, smiling just a little in eagerness. Barely an instant she lingered in that flood of soft light and then moved forward and took Christobel into her arms gently, with what seemed like rare tenderness, yet the girl resented it.

"Oh, you precious little girl," said the older woman, as she emerged from the somewhat prolonged kiss which she had pressed upon Christobel's unwilling lips with a fervor as if she had the nearest right. "I have so longed to come to you, to get you in my arms! To mother you! Of course I could not under the circumstances. But as soon as I knew that she was gone I felt that now the way would be open for me to get nearer to you."

Christobel drew back disturbed, and looked at her. Who was this woman who presumed to be so loving? Why should she feel this way? It seemed all wrong that she should resent her so much, yet she could not help it. She did not know just what to do. She did not want to be rude to one of her father's friends—if she was her father's friend.

"Won't you sit down?" she asked coldly,

wishing there were more light in the room that she might see her caller clearly. There was something oppressive and almost intoxicating in the dim darkness and the exquisite perfume. She drew a deep breath, looked about for the electric button, and discovering it switched on a flood of concealed light all around the edge of the ceiling that gave a more normal look to the visitor.

"Oh my dear!" said Mrs. Romayne in a sweet voice. "How lovely you are! Come, let us go over here and sit down together on the couch where we can have a real heart to heart talk."

She slipped her arm around the shrinking girl and drew her over to a deep couch in a far corner where her face would again be in shadow from a tall screen that stood near by.

Christobel did not want to go with her, did not like that compelling arm about her, but there was something irresistible about the woman, as if beneath the sheath of delicate flesh she were made of iron. Christobel felt suddenly helpless in her grasp, and loathed herself for yielding. Yet the quiet courtesy in which her costly school had reared her, somehow forced her to obey. She settled uneasily down on the edge of the couch as far away from her caller as she could get without actual rudeness.

"Now. Tell me all about yourself, dear," murmured the too sweet voice. "You can trust me absolutely with everything. You can talk as freely as if I were your very own mother, darling child! I know your young heart must just be bursting. Of course, you have your father, but a young girl always needs a woman in whom to confide. I shall be so glad to be that confidante. I have always wanted a daughter. You will find me filled with the utmost sympathy. All your lonely years. Just cry on my shoulder if you want to. It will do you good and I shall so enjoy comforting you. Just tell me everything, little Chrissie!"

Christobel drew herself suddenly, sharply away from the soft, manicured, beringed hands that were caressing hers.

"Why there's nothing to tell!" she said coldly. "I have no need to cry on anybody's shoulder."

"What a brave little girl she is to be sure!" said the sugared voice, and the soft hand reached out again for the girl's hand. "You don't quite trust me, do you? But you needn't be afraid. I'm your father's closest friend. I shall understand all about everything."

A sudden constriction came in Christobel's throat. Was this true? Was this woman of the honeyed words in her father's full confidence? Well, perhaps it was so. As she looked at the graceful form with its clinging black lace draperies, the delicate hands, with the sparkle of jewels, the white throat with a single bright gem hung on a cobweb-like thread of platinum, the patrician tilt of the lovely chin, the bright assured eyes, she could well believe it might be true, and her heart sank.

Was it true then, what the servants had said, and was another woman coming to stand between herself and her beloved father?

Why was it that she hated the thought so? Why couldn't she yield herself to the love that this woman's lips were professing? She had yearned for love, yet somehow this love did not ring sincere. Oh, her heart was tired and storm-tossed! She wished she did not have to think anything about this woman. She wished she would go away and leave them to themselves, at least for this one night. She wanted to think of her father in the light of that plain little room upstairs where she had seen her mother's faded photograph as if it were the dominating feature of the room.

She wished she had not had to grow up and decide all these unpleasant questions.

But perhaps she was hard. Perhaps she was foolish to have paid any attention to servants' gossip. Perhaps it had influenced her natural judgment more than she realized. Surely she must be courteous to this friend of her father's whether she was an intimate friend or not.

So she summoned words to her inexperienced lips. She was so unused to dealing with anybody but the other girls, or a disinterested teacher now and then.

"You are very kind," she managed to say, yet knew that her tone was cold and aloof. "There really isn't anything to tell you. We have been very much occupied all day you know. There have been relatives here of course—"

The woman looked startled.

"They are not in the house now?" she asked quickly, and looked toward her velvet evening wrap lying on a chair at the other side of the room.

Christobel caught at the thought.

"Well, not just now," she said guardedly. Was it wrong to let this woman think that perhaps some of them might be coming back? Indeed, she did not know how many more relatives might turn up during the evening. There had been a number at the funeral. "Suckers" Randall had called them under his young scornful breath.

"You mean—relatives of hers? Of Charm—this is, of your stepmother's?" asked the visitor alertly, and there was a touch of curiosity, one might call it impertinence, that put Christobel on her guard. She drew herself up a tiny bit haughtily.

"Of Mrs. Kershaw's, yes," she said briefly.

The lady's eyes narrowed speculatively.

"Who were they, dear? Any one I know?"

"Her parents of course," said the girl growing resentful at the questions, "an uncle, and several cousins. I really do not know if you knew them."

"Were those Snowden girls here?" went on the prying sweet voice. "Of course I saw them at the funeral. But were they here in the house? Are they staying here?"

Young as she was Christobel could not help seeing what the woman was trying to find out, and she shut her lips determined not to give out any more information; but suddenly, before she could think how to give an answer that told nothing she heard stealthy sounds overhead, or thought she did, and her father's suggestion that she keep her eyes and ears open came to her. It certainly sounded as if some one, or perhaps more than one, were walking about overhead. And this room was directly under Charmian's apartment.

She started up and sprang to her feet.

"Oh," she said, "I've just remembered something Father told me to do—about the servants—I'd forgotten!—And it must be attended to at once. Will you please excuse me a moment?" She hurried from the room.

She went cautiously, with swift step, her senses alert. Yes, there certainly were footsteps coming along the upper hall, coming from the direction of Charmian's room she was sure, as she paused an instant to listen, with one foot on the lower step of the stairs. They were hurried footsteps, and muffled as if in stockinged feet. There seemed to be more than one person!

There was a swift shadow crossing the head of the stairs above the second landing, and then another, making a wide grotesque shadow on the wall at the side of the first landing, as if a woman with her arms full of something were passing. And then came a second, and a third, each hurrying faster than the last, almost pushing one another along.

Christobel with swift catlike tread sprang up the stairs, reaching the top just in time to see the last of the three shadows vanish through the doorway that led into the back hall. She had distinctly seen the last figure, and was sure it was Marie. Her arms had been full of garments of all kinds lying across a big pasteboard box. Then the leather swing door that was arranged for silence swung back, caught in something bright and scarlet like a flame, swung open again till a hand snatched at and pushed back the hindrance and the bright thing fell back and lay on the floor while the door swung shut.

Christobel stood still, her hand instinctively going to her heart as if to hush the noise of its beating. She waited a full minute it seemed to her, then she tiptoed softly to the door and picked up the bright flame, hurrying forward to her father's room with it, trembling so that she scarcely dared to look at what she held.

She went into her father's room and flashed on the light holding out the garment. Yes, it was as she had thought, a scarlet dress of exquisite velvet, transparent and supple as a serpent's empty skin, and bearing on one shoulder a gorgeous jeweled pin. It was light as a feather and slippery like a living thing. When she held it out Christobel could see her stepmother in it, as she had seen her at Christmas time when an unexpected indulgence had allowed her to come home for part of the holidays. Not that there had been much Christmas about it or home either, for her father had been busy at the office most of the time, and her stepmother had been going out to parties till all hours. But she had seen her in this red velvet sheath ready for the Christmas party, her white shoulders gleaming with a dazzling almost unearthly beauty against the quivering ripples of the velvet, her great eyes flashing like two dark jewels in the startling penciled and shadowed whiteness of her make-up. And quickly there came another vision, of that same proud woman lying dead, the scornful jewels of her eyes closed forever, the long curled lashes lying on a still white cheek.

Christobel shivered, and dropped the velvet thing as if it had been a snake. Dropped it into a chair at the back of the room out of sight and went out of the room shutting the door behind her. It would be safe there until her father came. Oh, if he would come soon! What ought she to do about the servants? Undoubtedly they had made away with other things, and perhaps it would be too late to trace them when he came. Oh, why did any one want those things anyway? The things that had been Charmian's. Her father would not be able to do anything with them. Still— there were those two fur coats. Valuable. Not paid for yet and might be returned. She must do something. Oh, if her father would only come! Yet—there was that woman downstairs. How could she tell her father anything about it with her there? How could he do anything? Her heart resented taking another woman into their family confidence. Somehow she must get rid of her. How could she do it without being actually rude?

As she stepped into the hall she wondered why the light at that end had been turned out. It had been brightly burning she was sure when she went down to meet Mrs. Romayne. She remembered looking up that way and noticing that the front hall shade was up.

Then down on the floor in front of her stepmother's door she saw something gleaming, like little twinkling lights, and stooping found it was a scarf of gauze with tiny rhinestones set in a pattern about its border, a lovely trifle that reminded sharply of its gay selfish owner.

Christobel tried to pick it up, but found it

was shut in the door, and taking hold of the knob she found that the door was not locked. It was then she discovered a bunch of keys dangling from the key hole. They had not locked the door after them! They had left the keys behind! Then they must be intending to come back!

3

CHRISTOBEL folded her hand softly about the jingling keys and held them still for an instant trying to think quickly what was best to do. Here was she who had never had anything to do with her father's house, or Charmian's things, who had been practically pushed out of her father's house to grow up among strangers, having to take control in a great crisis like this.

She wished she did not have to tremble so. Why did she care what happened? Only she did so want to do just the right thing! Ought she to send for a policeman? Only then it would all get in the papers, and Father wouldn't like that. And after all, what proof had she? Only a series of shadows on the wall, and a velvet gown and scarf. This bunch of keys? Well.

Then she drew the door shut and locked it with her hand still folded about those noisy keys, and hurried back into her father's room where she stuffed the keys quickly down under one of the big leather cushions of the first chair she came to.

The next move was to get downstairs before it was discovered that she had come up and get rid of that unwelcome caller.

And none too soon. She thought she heard the cautious swing of the upper hall door as she reached the first landing, and no fairy could have trodden more lightly. She got herself down to the small reception room as quietly as a thistledown, and drifted over to the visitor with an ingratiating smile, even as she kept her ear attentive to the cautious sounds above.

"I wonder, Mrs. Romayne," she said sweetly as she approached the couch where that lady was awaiting her, and meanwhile taking in all the luxurious fittings of the room with appraising eyes, "if you would be good enough to excuse me for the rest of the evening, and let me see you another time perhaps? You see I promised my father to look after a matter for him during his absence, and I find it is going to take more attention than I thought."

"Oh, my dear!" said Mrs. Romayne springing lightly to her feet and showing great eagerness. "Do let me help you. That is just what I came for. To be of use. What is it? I have nothing whatever on my program for the evening. I had set aside everything else to give this evening to you and your dear father, and I shall be so pleased to take any responsibility. Of course it must be hard for you. Why, you are scarcely more than a child."

"Thank you, Mrs. Romayne." Christobel wanted to freeze up but she forced herself to be gracious. "You are most kind and thoughtful, and I appreciate your sympathy but this is something that an outsider could not possibly do. It is a personal matter—"

"But I am not an outsider, Christobel dear," laughed the lady good-naturedly. "I am an old old friend."

"Thank you," said Christobel keeping her voice steady although she was quite at her wits end and ready to cry in her vexation at this persistent woman, "but this is a matter that even a personal friend could not attend to. I really must ask—"

But the lady interrupted.

"My precious child, do let me do *something* to help, please, *please!*"

Christobel in her desperation wondered what to do. Then suddenly an idea occurred to her.

"There is one thing," she said hesitating, "but—it's really too much to ask I'm afraid."

"Oh no, my dear. I'll be glad to do *anything*," persisted the lady.

"Well, then—I'm afraid it will be a lot of trouble to you, but if you are going anywhere near, and going soon, I would be so glad if you would take a message from me to some one."

The woman's eyes narrowed speculatively, but she kept insisting that it would be no trouble at all.

"And I could bring you word again," she said brightening.

"Oh, there won't be any word to bring," said Christobel quickly. "It's just that I would like some message to get to my old nurse early to-night, that is *soon, right away!* You see I always go to see her when I come back to the city. She was my nurse when I was a child. And she counts on my visits. And I'm not sure I can get time. Father hasn't told me when he is planning for me to go back to school, and if it should be early in the morning I couldn't get to her before I left. You see she works, and she has to go early. Would

48

you mind driving to her rooming house and telling her *personally*—you know I could send a servant but it wouldn't mean the same as sending a friend—" Christobel in her eagerness to be rid of her caller was outdoing herself in cunning. "Would you be so good as to tell her that I hoped I could come to-night, but it isn't going to be possible, and I'll try to make it tomorrow night if I stay here over Sunday. But if I don't come she'll know it was because I couldn't. I'd be so grateful—. I won't forget it."

"Why, of course—" said Mrs. Romayne unenthusiastically, "I'll do it gladly. Only—wouldn't it be better if you wrote? I could send my chauffeur, and then perhaps I could help you here."

"Oh, no," said Christobel in alarm. "I would rather not do that. She—she might be hurt! She—well, you could explain how it is that I had something to do for Father—and—well, if a lady took the trouble to call it would mean so much more to her. I wouldn't have suggested it only you were kind enough to offer—" she ended lamely, a pretty distress in her face. She felt like a young hypocrite, but she was in a fever to get rid of her guest. She was sure she heard soft footsteps again overhead, and she was trying to think what she ought to do next. Mrs. Romayne was slowly, almost reluctantly putting on her wrap. One could see that she did not want to go.

"Well, my dear, part of my errand this evening was to ask you and your dear father—and your young brother of course too if he is still here, to come and take dinner with me tomorrow night. I think it will be so lonely for you here and it may help to tide you over the first day."

"I couldn't promise, Mrs. Romayne, I don't know Father's plans you see. We haven't had a minute to talk together since I came. Not a minute alone I mean."

"Well, when will your father be back. Soon?"

"I can't tell how soon," said Christobel in despair.

"Suppose I come back in about an hour and we all talk it over together? That would be lovely, wouldn't it? I'll come."

"Oh, no, please, Mrs. Romayne. Not to-night," said Christobel almost in tears of despair. "We would rather be all by ourselves to-night if you don't mind."

"Oh, well of course," said the lady with the least bit of a quiver of hurt in her voice, and a drooping appeal in her attitude. "I

50

thought it might be kind of homelike to have a woman around this first night. Not so uncanny. It's always uncanny after a funeral I think. Don't you really want me to come? I could stay all night with you just as well as not, dear child."

Christobel barely saved herself from a shudder at this.

"Not to-night, Mrs. Romayne," she said with a new-born dignity.

So at last the lady withdrew, taking the address of Maggie the nurse, and promising to let her know by telephone what had been the result of her visit.

Christobel apologized for the absence of the butler and let her guest out of the door herself with as much sweet apology as she could muster, then watched with relief from the dark window of the big reception room to see the car drive away at last into the night. Then she turned and tried to think what to do next. She could distinctly hear scurrying feet abovestairs.

Slowly she walked toward the stairs, slowly, quietly, went up. As she went she tried to reason.

The servants were all too evidently in a panic over the absence of the keys. Had she been wrong to take them away? Perhaps she had only precipitated trouble. They would have time now to secrete whatever they had taken. Ought she perhaps to call the police station? Oh, if her father would only come! He had spoken of having to stop in his office for some papers. Would it do any good to call him there?

She was halfway up the stairs by this time, and then to her great relief she heard her father's latch key in the door and turning she flew down to meet him.

Her face told him that something had happened, and with a cautious look around and up the stairs he drew her within the curtains of the small reception room. Randall stood beside them his eyes growing large with excitement as Christobel talked.

"A lady came to call!" said Christobel trying to keep the tremble out of her voice.

"A lady?"

"Yes. A Mrs. Romayne. She said she was a very dear friend of the family," and her eyes sought her father's face with a quick anxious questioning.

"Yes?" he said watching his daughter, with a face that showed no emotion whatever.

"She asked for me," said Christobel, hurrying on with her story. "We were sitting in this room, over there on the couch, and I

52

heard sounds in the room overhead. It seemed like people walking hurriedly in their stocking feet. It kept up for several minutes and I remembered what you told me to keep my eyes and ears open so I excused myself for a minute to go and see what it was. But I heard the steps coming along the hall as I started up the stairs, so I went very cautiously. Looking up I saw three wide shadows like three women with a lot of things in their arms, moving fast across the wall just above the first landing. But when I got to the top of the stairs I could only see the back of one of them passing through the swing door to the back hall. I couldn't tell surely which one it was because the hall was pretty dark, only the light at the head of the stairs left burning, but I think it was Marie. I thought she had dark hair, but she had so much in her arms I couldn't be sure. She had a very large suit box piled high with clothes, and one slipped off the top, and stuck in the door. I guess she didn't know it for she went right on, or perhaps she had heard me coming and was afraid. Anyway she dropped the dress—it was red velvet with a diamond pin on the shoulder—and I went softly and picked it up. It's up in your room now. And then when I came out I saw something glittering in the dark, and it was a little scarf with jewels on it, but it was shut in the door and when I went to pull it out I saw the door was not locked and there was a bunch of keys dangling from the lock.

"I didn't have much time to think what to do. I was afraid they were planning to come back for more things. So I locked the door as fast as I could and came right downstairs again. But I heard those footsteps again up in the hall just as Mrs. Romayne was leaving, only they were gone when I started up again, and then I was so glad to hear your key in the lock."

She finished with a catching of her breath almost like an excited sob.

"Where are the keys?" asked her father.

"Under the cushion in your big leather chair upstairs," said Christobel. "The scarf is up there too."

"Dad, don't you want me ta call the p'lice?" asked Randall excitedly.

"No son, we'll handle this I guess. At least don't get the police in on it till we see what really has happened. You go very quietly through into the kitchen and stand at the foot of the back stairs. Lock all the back doors and take the keys out, and just wait. Don't let anybody get by, see? Probably, there's nothing much to it. They'll just likely be frightened. But one of them might try to get away with something valuable. It has been done before. Chris, you go upstairs as usual and shut your door loud enough to be heard so that if anybody is listening they'll think you have gone into your room, and then you slip quietly back and stay inside my room till I call you. Now, are we ready?"

Christobel ran upstairs quite naturally, went down the hall humming, and suddenly remembered that humming was not a thing people usually did in a house where there had been a death. She stopped the humming but she gave her well-conducted door a bigger slam than it had probably ever had before, and then she tiptoed noiselessly back to her father's room.

Mr. Kershaw had found the keys and Charmian's room was already unlocked, the door standing wide, and the room ablaze with light. The hall light was also turned on.

Mr. Kershaw stood in the open door and beckoned her to come with him.

"See if you can find those fur coats," he whispered, and Christobel, feeling that she was entering forbidden ground, went excitedly through her stepmother's wardrobe.

The wardrobe was a good-sized room of

itself, and there were rows and rows of gowns on hangers all about the room, many of them carefully covered with muslin covers, or bags of flowered chintz. But several dresses were dropped upon the floor, and some bags and covers thrown carelessly aside, as if some one in great hurry had been there. One delicate evening frock of soft material like a delicate pink cobweb was trailed along the floor near the door as if it had been dropped and overlooked. But nowhere, either on shelves or floor or in the outer room, were there any suit boxes such as would be used to send a fur garment from the store. It did not take long for the two to discover that both the fur coats, if there were such coats, had been taken elsewhere.

Mr. Kershaw looked sharply around the place, and stooped to pick up a bit of yellow paper. There it was. The slip that came with the sable coat. Twenty-seven hundred dollars! He silently held it out for Christobel to see and then stuffed it into his pocket.

"All right! That's enough. Now you go over into my room out of sight. If I should whistle you can call the police department. You'll find the number at the top of the front page of the directory right there on the telephone table. Otherwise keep still till I call you."

Christobel stepped into her father's room and waited in the dark. She was very much excited, but suddenly she realized that she was very happy too. For she was doing something with her father at last. It wasn't very much perhaps but she was in his confidence, working with him just as any other girl might have done. It made her glad. It made her so glad that she felt a hot tear steal out under her lashes and roll down her cheek, but all alone in the dark room she smiled it away, tossing the hair back from her hot forehead. Oh, it was great to be working with her father even in a sordid little thing like catching some thieving servants.

Suddenly Christobel heard her stepmother's bell ring, the bell with which she had always called her maid.

There was silence for a long moment and then the bell rang again, and after an instant there came hurried footsteps, and Christobel looking out from the shelter of the dark room saw Marie halt outside in the hall, and look with frightened eyes toward the wide open door of her former mistress' room as if she expected to see a ghost.

Then Mr. Kershaw spoke.

"Marie, where have you put the two fur coats that my wife purchased a few days before her illness?"

There was a moment of frightened silence and then Marie spoke in a little choked voice. Christobel could see her hand go nervously to her throat.

"Oh!" she said, and then trying to make her voice sound assured, "Why, I'll get them. I took them over to my room and put them under the bed. I just couldn't rest easy at nights knowing they were over here and I was responsible for them. I didn't want to bother you at this time, Mr. Kershaw."

Mr. Kershaw eyed her sharply.

"You may bring them at once," he said severely. "I'll go with you and carry the boxes back myself."

"Oh, but no, that's not necessary!" protested the frightened girl eagerly. "I can carry them quite easily."

"I prefer to go," said the master of the house calmly, "and while we are there we'll just bring back the other things that belonged to Mrs. Kershaw. There are a number of dresses gone—" he pointed to the confusion reigning on the floor of the wardrobe whose door stood wide open. "And some jewels!" He snapped a jewel case shut.

"Christobel!" he called raising his voice. "You may come too."

"Oh, but Mr. Kershaw," said Marie anxiously, "I just took a few things over to give them a cleaning and mending so that everything would be in good order in case you wanted me to pack them away."

Marie was clever. She was regaining her confidence. She almost smiled at her master. But Mr. Kershaw did not smile. He seemed to be looking straight through her. He stalked gravely along with her, keeping time with her quick nervous feet as she hurried to do his bidding.

Marie made one more stand at the swing door.

"You just wait here, please, Mr. Kershaw," she said in suave tones, "my room's not in such good order as I'd like it to be when you see it. These have been busy days you know—" and she tried to put across another smile. "I'll bring everything to you."

For answer the householder held open the door for her to pass. Christobel followed like a silent shadow behind, giving her brother a signal as she passed the top of the back stairs and saw him looking up in wonder.

So Randall Kershaw came nimbly and silently up and joined the procession into the short side hall that led to the servants' rooms.

It was quite a surprise to the cook and the parlor maid arrayed as they were in some of their dead mistress' garments. For the cook had stuffed herself into a delicate evening affair of thread lace over a pale rose lining, and her bulk had promptly split the frail French seams from neck to hem. But the cook had not discovered the discrepancy yet and went sailing up and down the little hall, one hand waving a pink ostrich feather fan back and forth, the other fingering joyously a long chain of amethysts that hung about her fat red neck. She had her head behind her watching the train coming after and admiring herself like a child, and thus she came face to face with the master of the house as he stood at the entrance to the hall.

Then she let forth such a scream as might have aroused the neighborhood. It brought the parlor maid out of her bedroom door, arrayed in Charmian's black velvet and the short white evening wrap of ermine. She stood there guiltily, too frightened to even scream, and while they faced their master, caught red-handed, Marie dived like a shadow into her own door and brought forth the sable coat, holding it out with one hand, and its big cardboard box in the other.

"It's here, all safe," chirped Marie in a high unnatural voice. Then she turned upon her two confederates.

"And you all, what are you doing with Mrs. Kershaw's things? Parading around like so many children? What business had you to be touching the things I brought to my room to clean I'd like to know?"

"I was only tryin' it on ta see how I wad look," whined Mary the cook. "I've allus hankered fer a black lace dress. I just wanted to see how becomin' it might be! And anyhow it's tore!" she said, suddenly getting a view of herself in Marie's mirror through the doorway. "Mrs. Kershaw give this ta Marie because 'twas tore, and I knew Marie wouldn't mind. It's Marie's dress, this is, Mr. Kershaw." Mary felt that she was doing well, not only providing an excuse for herself, but getting in well with Marie, for now the dress would be Marie's.

But the master was not deceived.

"Take it off!" he demanded. "Go in your room and take that dress off. But first, take off that necklace and give it to me."

"Aw, but Mr. Kershaw," protested Mary

glibly, "this is me own string of beads that Mrs. Kershaw give me fer a keepsake."

"You can't put anything like that over on me," said the master of the house sternly. "Hand them to me at once. That is not a string of beads. Those are valuable stones, and you know it. Now, go into your room and take off that dress, and bring it to me with everything else you have taken that belonged to my wife. No, Clara, you can't go until you have given me the ermine wrap, and then you may go and take off the velvet dress."

He put out a heavy hand and caught the frightened parlor maid by the arm, stripping the lovely satin lined wrap from her shoulders and handing it to Christobel.

He turned back to the huddled servants. Marie stood sullenly in her doorway and Clara and the cook were crying abjectly. "Now," he said sternly, "you may bring me everything you have taken from my wife's apartment. If there is a single thing missing your rooms will be searched and you will be prisoners until it is done. Randall, call up the police station and ask them to send a couple of officers over here at once. Let them wait downstairs until I call for them."

The three frightened women scuttled out

of their rooms and hurried out of their borrowed finery, hastening to get together every scrap of anything that had ever belonged to the house. They even burrowed deep into their trunks and brought forth things taken months before and so long hidden that they had been forgotten.

"We meant no harm," twittered the cook as she produced a handful of small jewelry purloined from time to time when she happened to be left alone in the house.

"Bring everything!" said the master of the house sternly. "Your rooms will be thoroughly searched and if there is found a thread of anything that does not belong to you you will be imprisoned."

With a moan of mingled hope and fear the cook bounced back into her room and looked for more ill-gotten gain, and presently a goodly pile of dry goods, jewelry, even table linen and silver were assembled in a heap in the outer hall, and when the three burly officers arrived and stalked past the subdued women, they stood humiliated in a row, the parlor maid and the cook weeping convulsively, Marie with her sleuth eyes cast down, and a sullen look on her pretty, clever face.

"Now," said Mr. Kershaw when the officers had searched each room carefully and found only a few questionable things which the women said they had "forgotten," "I'll give you three just half an hour to pack what is left and get out, and the officers will remain on guard outside your doors while you are doing it."

They began to whine and plead, to promise all sorts of things for the future if he would only let them stay. All but Marie. She knew that her work was over in that house, her mistress dead. She had planned a big scoop on a large scale with her confederates, had failed, and now all she wanted was to slip away into the unknown and begin a new life in a new place. She cast withering looks of scorn at the other two who wept copious tears as they packed, hurrying with trembling fingers and furtive glances at the watching officers. She had only resentment and contempt for them. If it hadn't been for their careless clumsiness she might have got away with her own story. But those two had to appear all decked out! They had not been careful at all in spite of her warning after she found the keys were gone; and after the eerie ringing of the bell from the apartment of a dead woman. They should have known and been on their guard. There was vengeance in Marie's eyes as she packed.

When the half hour was over the police-men escorted the three crestfallen women out of the house, with orders to see each to her own place wherever that was, in the taxi-cab that had been ordered, and they departed bag and baggage.

Then the three Kershaws stood in the front hall of their deserted home and looked at one another. They felt closer to each other than they had been for the past ten years.

4

IT was the father who first recovered his equilibrium.

"There remains the butler!" he said with a sad smile, the first breaking of a gloom that had been on his face since his children had come back from school, "we might as well make a clean sweep of it and get rid of him too, though I'm sure I don't know what good it will do. Their successors will proba-bly be just as bad if not worse. I suppose I ought to have had them all arrested."

"D'ya think Hawkins was mixed up in this mess?" asked Randall, keen for another sensation.

"Perhaps not," said his father, passing his

hand wearily over his eyes. "He wouldn't likely have cared for fur coats and velvet gowns except as merchandise with a possible profit, but no doubt he has helped himself to some of the stores in the cellar. I guess there was plenty!" and he sighed heavily.

"Shan't I go up and put out those lights?" asked Christobel practically, hoping to turn her father's attention and wishing she knew how to lift some of the burden from his shoulders.

"Oh, I'll do that," he said. "I had forgotten."

"We'll all go," said Randall. "Better give a once-over to the rooms again. There might be something hidden away they've forgotten."

So the young people followed their father up the stairs and back to the servant's rooms again.

It was after they had been carefully over the closets and bureau drawers again, and had put out the light behind them, that Kershaw paused in a new kind of dismay before the heap of his dead wife's clothes lying in a quivering mass of velvets and chiffons and fur.

"We oughtn't to leave these things here I suppose," he said looking at them helplessly with a sad distaste. "I don't know why I made such a fuss about it after all. I suppose I might as well have let the poor things take them. Nobody would have cared. If it hadn't been for the principle of the thing. I can't bear to be robbed even of something that is of no further use to me."

"Let's put 'em back!" said Randall energetically, stooping over the heap with a wide basket-ball reach and scooping up a great armful. "You get the rest, Chris, an' we'll stow 'em away."

The father gathered up the little white ermine coat that Clara the parlor maid had shed, and touched its whiteness half pitifully.

"Wait, Rand," cried his sister, "you're dragging that sable coat and it's got to go back, hasn't it Father?" She looked half frightened toward her father wondering if he would consider her words presumptuous.

"Why, yes," he said brightening, "I suppose that will be possible, if it is a recent purchase. Both of those furs can be returned. That ought to be looked after to-morrow morning. Could you call them up Chrissie and ask them about it? Here. Here's the sales slip. But—Oh, I forgot! Perhaps you ought to be going back to school in the morning," he said with another of those deep sighs. "I haven't had time to think about anything yet." And again that look of depression came over his face and made it look almost ashen.

"No, not to-morrow," said Christobel, "of course not. To-morrow is Saturday anyway. Come, let's get these things put away. What are you going to do with them Father? Pack them away somewhere, or give them to somebody, or sell them? If you'd like me to I'll attend to that for you and you needn't bother any more about it."

They had reached the door of Charmian's rooms now and Randall had flung it wide and dumped his armful down on a chaise longue. His eager breezy youth seemed somewhat to dispel the gloom from this room where one was so conscious that the inhabitant had gone out never to return. Randall had little reverence for anything. He dashed in where any angel would have feared to tread, but on this occasion it was a relief to them all.

"Now, where d'ya want this junk put? Gimme the hangers, Chris, an' I'll stick 'em in." Christobel handed him a bunch of hangers from the rod in the wardrobe, and he proved himself not so awkward in putting them into the dresses.

"You mustn't be so rough with those delicate laces and chiffons, Rand," warned his sister coming to the rescue.

Mr. Kershaw was forcing himself to go about the room.

"I don't think you ought to be doing all this, Chrissie, little girl," he said suddenly with a new tenderness that made the girl's heart leap. "There are some friends I suppose who would look after it for us, though I'm not sure whom I would want here. I didn't care much for some of the people who have been coming to the house. There would be Mrs. Romayne. I suppose she would come in, but your stepmother never liked her. It seems rather crude."

"No, Father, don't get anybody. This should be my work," said Christobel suddenly filled with longing to get all such matters out of the way before that perfumed woman of many words should come around. "I'll not mind doing it at all. But—don't you know what you want to do with them? Of course those coats. Here, I'll fold them in their boxes and they'll be ready to go back. But the rest. There are some lovely things here Father. And they ought to go to some one. Aren't there people who would like them?"

"Yes, plenty!" said her father sternly, "but they are not the sort of people I care to please. I would rather burn them all. They are of another world. A wild sort. No, I don't know anybody I would want to have them. You couldn't use any of them yourself I suppose? No. I wouldn't want you to. They are not your type of things. I would rather you had things of your own that fitted your character."

Christobel was silent a moment thinking this over.

"No, I would rather not have them!" she said gravely, trying to keep her utter distaste for them out of her voice.

"Well, then, why don't you send them— or some of them at least—to her mother? Wouldn't she like to have them?"

The father looked at her thoughtfully.

"I hadn't thought of her. What could she do with them? Take that for instance," and he touched with his toe the lovely red velvet that had poured itself in a brilliant pool on the floor. "How would Mrs. Harrower look in that?"

Christobel's lips almost quivered into a smile to think of the meek, petted little old

70

woman, with her faded eyes and hair and her indifference to the world in general, arrayed in that sophisticated frock.

"She could sell it," said Christobel practically. "It is a lovely frock and imported, I guess. There are places where they pay good prices for such things. I know because the girls at school get most of their evening dresses at such places. They'll get a dress that originally sold at a hundred or two sometimes for forty or fifty dollars."

"Well, Mrs. Harrower wouldn't know how to make any such deal, and I'm not sure under the circumstances that I care to assist her financially any more than I have been compelled to already. If you can discover anybody who will buy any of these things you have my permission to sell them. Just pick out a few plain things that you think the old lady might like and put them into a box and we'll ship it to her. For the rest I don't care what you do with it. Come. Let's get out of here. Suppose we go over into my place and talk things over."

Mr. Kershaw snapped out the lights and locked the door and they went over into his big room.

The children stood about almost embarrassed for a moment. They felt so little acquainted with this new father who was so much more friendly that he had ever been before. Then as he turned on a low reading lamp that made a pleasant dimness in the room he came toward them and flung an arm about each of them and drew them toward the wide leather couch.

"Come, let's sit down and get acquainted," he said with a sudden effort as if he were longing to get somehow nearer to them.

Christobel nestled down with her head on her father's shoulder, and even Randall seemed not averse to being drawn close also. They sat there in utter silence for a few minutes, a kind of peace coming over them after the troubles of the day. Then the father spoke:

"I hate to have you go back," he said. "We ought to stay nearer together, see more of each other." His tone was almost shy.

Then after a minute Christobel spoke.

"Father, why do I have to go back? Why can't I stay here with you? This is my last year. The rest of the semester isn't going to be much but getting ready for commencement, rehearsing plays, and writing essays and all that. What good is it anyway?"

"Oh, but—" objected the father, "why, of

course you need to graduate. It's the thing to do."

"But why, Father dear?" she urged.

"Well," said the father trying to think of some suitable reason, "everybody has to graduate. They graduate and then they come out. One of your stepmother's reasons for buying this great house was that it was almost time for you to come out and we should need an outfit like this to do it properly. And of course it might look rather queer to come out without first graduating. People might think you couldn't pass your examinations or something."

"What people? Why do we care what people think? I have passed my examinations. I got good marks too. Why should I have to go through all the rest? I'd much *much* rather stay with you," and she snuggled down closer and nestled her hand in his.

He gave her hand a warm pressure, and felt a strange sweetness to have her so close after all these years of estrangement. It almost unnerved him to think she cared to be with him. He had thought of her as having grown away from him.

"And Daddy," she went on earnestly, "why do I have to come out? I'd much rather stay in. What do people come out for?"

"Well," began the father, "the world seems to think it is a necessary act."

"Did my mother come out?" she asked suddenly with a sweet shyness in her voice.

The father was still a long time, and then he answered in a moved voice.

"No."

"I'd like to be like her, Father, if you don't mind," she said in a low voice.

He drew her closer, and said with a fervent gentleness:

"There's nothing in the world greater that I could desire for you, Chrissie dear."

"Then may I?" she asked eagerly.

"May you what?" said the startled father.

"May I stay at home with you, and not go back to this last semester of school, and not do any coming out ever at all?"

He was still a long time and then he said:

"Well, daughter, this is a new thought to me. I'd have to think it over."

"I'm sure my own mother would want me to stay here with you," she breathed earnestly.

He turned his lips toward her and kissed her forehead very gently.

"I'll think about it little girl."

"I wouldn't mind staying too," said Rand gallantly, "only I guess I'd havta go back fer the rest of the term. I'm cheerleader ya know, and it's rather late ta get a new one. We've been practising a lot fer the spring games."

"Well, yes, son, it wouldn't be quite right to desert them just now, would it? And anyhow you have those examinations to take over again, that we were talking about to-night. It wouldn't do to leave school with a blot on your scholarship. We'll ship you back sometime to-morrow I guess, but we'll try to make some plans to be nearer each other after this term is over. I've been thinking a lot about it. We'll see when we get things here straightened out."

"Father," said Christobel after a moment of silence, "do you think a lot of this house? Did you buy it to stay in always like a sort of ancestral home?"

"I did *not*," said her father decidedly, and a smile melted over his tired face. "Why, little girl, don't you like it?"

"Well," said Christobel slowly, "I suppose it's all right, only somehow it's so big and strange. I don't know whether I could ever get used to it. There doesn't seem to be any really useful *homey* rooms in it. Maybe that's only because I'm not used to it. But it doesn't seem like the home we used to have when I was a little girl before we went to school."

"Gee! Where'd we live then?" asked Randall suddenly raising his head from the soft cushion and entering into the conversation. "I don't just remember that time. Wasn't there a big tree and a swing in a side yard?"

"Yes," said Christobel eagerly, "and a flower garden. I had a garden and you had a garden, and you used to pull the plants up every day to see if the roots were growing any more."

"Gee! I remember! And I usedta skin the cat on the toppatha swing frame. Where was that, Dad? Somewhere in the city, wasn't it?"

"Yes. It was over on the other side of the city, quite a long distance from here. It used to be a suburb then, but it is within the city limits now."

"Is the house still there or has it been torn down?" asked the boy.

"Oh, it's still there. I still own it," answered the father sadly.

"Is it rented?" asked Christobel.

"No, it's never been rented. Somehow I never quite wanted to rent it. I always thought perhaps I'd go back there some day.

But of course I don't suppose I ever shall," he ended with a sigh.

"I wish we could," said Christobel wistfully.

"Say! Gee! So do I!" said Randall rumpling his father's hair that was beginning to show threads of silver in its blackness.

"You do?" said the father, a pleased surprise in his voice, and then more quietly, "Oh, but you wouldn't if you saw it. It's all built up all around. There are a lot of plain little houses in rows down in the next block where there used to be meadows and a sunset." His eyes took on a retrospective look, as if he were again watching one of those sunsets.

"Oh, I remember," cried Christobel. "Mother and you and I used to go down in the meadow and watch the sun go down, and once I remember you wheeling Rannie in his baby coach."

"Aw, get out," said Randall half pleased. "You remember a lot! You're not so much older than I. Only a little over two years. I guess I remember that too. I remember throwing sticks down in a little creek that went through the lower part of the meadow, and there was an old cow and a dog that came to drive her home."

"Yes, and you were afraid of the cow," laughed Christobel. "And Mother called you little soldier!"

"Say! Weren't you ever afraid of cows?"

"Yes, she was afraid of cows, too, when she was a tiny girl," said the father with a pleasant look of reminiscence in his eyes. "There was a day when that cow stood before her and mooed at her and she puckered up her face and roared so loud she frightened the cow. Your sister turned and tried to run, but stubbed her toe on a stone and was so scared she held her breath for fear the cow would walk over her. Mother had to pick her up and hold her close and kiss her a long time before she would stop sobbing."

"Why, I remember that," said Christobel softly, nestling close on her father's shoulder and speaking with a deep joy in her voice, "I remember—the feel of her arms around me!" and there was such yearning in her voice that her father was greatly stirred.

He laid his hand tenderly on her soft hair beside his face.

"Poor little girl!" he said gently, "without a mother all these years!" And then he gave another of those deep dreadful sighs that hurt Christobel to hear.

"Never mind, Daddy," she said and put

her small hand up and stroked his face softly, "We've—got—you now."

And then there came back to her the memory those terrible words of the cook about that awful Mrs. Romayne and she put her hand down quickly in her lap and wondered if they really did have him permanently, or was Mrs. Romayne going to get him away from them?

And then the telephone rang sharply like an intruder into their intimate talk.

Mr. Kershaw gathered himself reluctantly from the couch and answered it. A woman's high-pitched sweetly modulated tone responded.

"Yes? Hello? Oh, Mrs. Romayne? Yes. It was very kind of you to call. I am sure my daughter appreciated it. Yes, she said you had been here."

He drew his brows in an effort to remember what Christobel had said about the visit, and the sweet full tones flowed on.

"Oh. . . . Why, no," he suddenly responded. . . . "Why, I'm not sure. . . . She probably did mention it, but I've had a number of things to attend to. . . . We have only just begun to talk. . . . I have been otherwise occupied all the evening. . . . Dinner tomorrow did you say? . . . Well, I would hardly be able to make it myself. . . . It's most kind of you. . . . But perhaps Christobel—You see Mrs. Romayne I have some things to look after for my son before his return to school. . . . What? . . . Oh, you said dinner Sunday—" he frowned. . . . "Well, Christobel might. It's most thoughtful of you.—Yes, I suppose you're right. It is a little dismal for a young person of course. . . . Just a moment Mrs. Romayne, I'll speak to my daughter."

The father looked up to see a look of dismay on his daughter's face.

"Oh, no, no, Daddy, please," she said in a low tone. "I'd so much rather be with you alone, you and Rannie."

There was a light in her father's eyes as he took up the instrument again.

"Well, Mrs. Romayne, I guess we'll just ask you to excuse us this time. We appreciate your thoughtfulness of course, but we have so many things to talk over, and the time is short. Some other time perhaps you'll be good enough to ask us. . . . Oh, that's very kind. But just now I think it will be impossible."

Christobel watched her father's face as more honeyed words were poured into his ear. He had a very pleasant smile on his

80

face. Was he sorry not to go? Or would he perhaps prefer to go alone after they were back in school? She tried to put away the thought but the poison of the cook's words had entered into her soul, and she could not quite get back the sweet freedom of their quiet intercourse when he came back and sat down with them on the couch again.

"I declare I believe I'm hungry!" he said as he put an arm around each of them. "I wonder what had become of that butler? Can he have cleared out, or is he taking the night off as well as the evening? If he were here we might ring him up and have a tray up with sandwiches and ginger ale or something like that. Rand, go ring the bell."

"Oh, Daddy!" said Christobel springing up eagerly, "don't call the butler. Couldn't we all go down in the kitchen and find something? I know how to make cocoa. It would be fun!"

"Let's," said the boy, springing up and pulling his father to his feet as if he had been another boy. "There might be olives and celery. There were some left from dinner. I saw them."

"They're probably not left now," laughed the father. "I believe we had a bunch of crooks in the kitchen."

"Well there'll be more in the pantry perhaps. There'll likely be crackers and jelly and cans of things. We have suppers like that at school. Some of the fellas raid the kitchen sometimes when the matron's out for the evening, and we have great suppers. I can scramble eggs."

It was on the tip of his father's tongue to ask Randall if he had been on the raiding parties, but remembering some of his own early escapades, and seeing the boyish look in his son's eyes he grasped his hand and followed, letting the raiding parties pass for the moment. There was something wonderful to this tired silent lonely father in being with his long alienated children again.

So they all tiptoed quietly down to the kitchen looking cautiously about for the butler as if they had no right in those precincts and might be scolded if they got caught.

Like three children they raided their own kitchen, a great tiled place with looming gas range, wide gleaming sink, electrical apparatus galore, and equipment enough to feed an army.

"Where would the cocoa be kept?" asked Christobel opening cupboard doors and peering behind boxes and glass jars and tins.

"Well, I'm sure I don't know," said the

bewildered father. "This never was a kitchen that I had much to do with," and he made a wry face.

"I'll find it," chirped the girl with an excited laugh.

Randall was snooping around in the pantry and store room. He discovered the electric refrigerator, a mammoth concern almost big enough for a garage.

"Gee! Here's olives!" he shouted. "And celery too! And a whole roast chicken with only half the breast gone! Gee! This is great!"

He appeared in the doorway bearing the platter in one hand and a bottle of olives in the other.

"And here's the cocoa," said Christobel triumphantly. "Now, I wonder if there is any milk? We could use condensed milk you know."

"Two bottles in the 'frigerator!" shouted Randall going back on the search again. He handed out a bottle.

They rifled the china closet of some of the priceless dishes that Charmian had purchased for her de luxe dinners, and spread their repast on the kitchen table with the eagerness of children, the man of the house entering into the spread with avidity, and joking with his children as if he were only an older brother. As they sat down to their impromptu supper Christobel thought in her heart like a chime of sweet bells, "Oh, I'm so glad Mrs. Romayne isn't here! I'm so glad we've got our father to ourselves!" If only there wasn't any Mrs. Romayne in the future. Oh, how could she ever stand it to go back to school after this beautiful little time together and think she would be separated from her father again by another woman?

Later, when they had cleared away the things and gone at last to rest, she crept into her bed with the thought that Mother would have enjoyed seeing them all together again. Mother was the only woman that would have fitted in with their little time together. Oh, if Mother could only come back to them!

5

QUITE early the next morning Christobel woke up and looked about the unfamiliar room.

It was not a room where she had ever slept before on any of her former visits to her father's home. Charmian had always relegated her to one of the smallest guest rooms on the third floor back whenever she had happened to be in that house for a day or two en route to some other parking place. This room was one of the best guest rooms, and her bags had been dumped there on her arrival the day before the funeral because the bed happened to be made up for a weekend guest whose visit was cancelled on account of Charmian's operation.

Christobel did not feel at home in this room, although she admired the beautiful things in it. It seemed even more like a picture room than the rooms downstairs. There were lovely curtains of delicate lace like frost work with an inner sheath of palest green taffeta ruffled elaborately. There was a bedspread of green taffeta to match, and the delicate color was carried out with variations of ivory lace in frills and insets in the covers of the bureau, the lamp shades, the shields for the wall lights, the cover to the dressing table and the very upholstery of the bench of the dressing table. Ivory and green were the fittings of the dressing table, and the private bath beyond showed the same colors in tiles and bath towels. Christobel liked it, it seemed so restful. Yet she did not feel at home in it. There was something too fussy about it all. The hair brush and other toilet articles on the bureau had edges of filigreed gilt, and there were ruffles, ruffles, ruffles, and frills everywhere, and tiny silk rosebuds sprinkled over the lace and silk till it was almost bewildering, and much too ornate.

To Christobel, contrasting it with the monotony of a boarding school room that had not had the special attention of a loving mother it seemed rich and beautiful, but not her ideal. She felt like a little cat in a strange garret.

She lay there a few minutes with her eyes half closed letting the green shimmer from the lovely curtains fill her gaze with their restful light. There seemed something pleasant about waking up and she was almost afraid to try to think what it was lest she be disappointed and life would turn out to be the same empty dull perspective filled with many uninteresting duties that didn't get one anywhere and went on and on indefinitely.

It seemed that somehow there was a burden lifted from her, and suddenly it came to her that it was the funeral. That was over. That had been something to dread. That had been something to *greatly* dread. That solemn finish of a life that had never been anything to her but a distress.

Christobel had not felt enmity toward her stepmother. In a way she had admired her young vivid personality, could have been interested in her if she had not come between her and any sort of life or love of her own. Yet she had not rejoiced with any triumph when word came that she had been so suddenly blotted out in the midst of her gay activities. It had rather been a frightening thing to have her dead, to have to see her so.

Christobel was glad that it had been God who had taken her away, and that she had not been asked if she would like to have Charmian gone. It had truly never occurred to her to wish that she might die. Now that she felt the great relief of her absence she was glad that she had not been tempted by any such wish.

She thought back over the years when she used to cry herself to sleep at night with loneliness, and longing for some one to really love her. Oh, yes, her father had loved her, but he had been so hampered and tied by Charmian, that it seemed as if even on the rare occasions when he ran away from home to see her for a few hours at the school, they were both held from speaking out freely and saying the things they would have said, by the very fact of Charmian being back in the city in the big house that was called home, and yet was not a home.

Christobel drew a deep breath of relief and

put the subject away from her. She was not glad that Charmian had had to die to get out of all their lives, but she was glad that there was a new era opening before her. Glad, glad, with a thrill she had not felt since she was a little little girl, that her father was hers once more. For a little while at least. Oh, if there were only some way of keeping him. Of not having another stepmother come in the way between them as those awful servants had suggested. Oh, did men always have to marry again? No, there was Betty Bates' uncle Harmon. His wife had died when Betty was only a tiny girl and he had been true to her memory ever since.

But Christobel could remember back to the day when her father brought Charmian home; how he had explained that she needed a mother because her own mother had died, and that he had brought her a lovely one. And Charmian had looked her over coldly and said, "I am glad she has curls. I hate children with straight hair." Perhaps her father felt that he was doing it for their sakes. She was sure he had. If in some way she and Randall could only make up to him for the lack of Mother then he wouldn't be so lonely. Perhaps he wouldn't want to marry again. But she could see how hard it was going to be to get away from that Mrs. Romayne if she determined to marry him and mother them all.

The thought of Mrs. Romayne brought back last evening and her long conversation on the telephone. But Father hadn't seemed to want to go and take dinner with her himself. Perhaps he didn't care anything about her—yet! If there were only some way to get him away where Mrs. Romayne couldn't ever find them!

Then she recalled the blessedness of sitting with her head on her father's shoulder as long as she wanted to, and putting a shy hand up and touching his hair and smoothing his cheek, without any sharp sneering Charmian to say:

"Get up you great girl! Don't get mushy over a mere father! You're too big to kiss and maul him. For pity's sake go to bed!"

Oh, how deep those words had cut when she had first heard them! Were all stepmothers like that? Christobel thought not. Marta Sharpless had a sweet stepmother that sent her lovely presents and kissed her and came often to school to see her. No, it must be just like buying something. One took it for what it looked like in the store. One couldn't tell how well it would wear. And Charmian hadn't worn well. Father hadn't been to blame. Somehow she could feel that Father had suffered too! He hadn't been happy. Even Father had seemed relieved last night to be all alone. Just they three! Not even a servant! And then Christobel sat up sharply in her luxurious bed and remembered.

There wasn't a servant in the house and there would be no breakfast unless she got it. Women always looked after those things. Would she know how? She had never a chance to do more than make cocoa and toast in school. Oh, yes, she could scramble eggs. What could they have for breakfast?

She sprang out of bed and began to dress rapidly, trying to remember what she had seen in the refrigerator last night. She would love to get a beautiful breakfast, fruit and cereal, and toast and coffee, chops, hot cakes—But there would not likely be any chops in the house, and she wouldn't know how to cook them if there were. How did one make hot cakes?

She had seen a package of bacon, but how again did one cook bacon? She didn't even know what it looked like before it was cooked.

And coffee. Could she make coffee?

She hurried softly downstairs listening as she went on tip toe.

The house seemed great and empty in the early morning. She hadn't stopped to see what time it was until she came into the big gloomy kitchen and the electric clock said only half-past seven. Her father did not usually eat before half-past eight or nine. But then it might take a very long time to get a first meal ready. She was glad she had come down.

She shivered a little as she looked around and rolled up her sleeves out of the way. Now that she had come into the kitchen with two swing doors shut behind her she rather dreaded to go back to the front of the house again. It seemed somehow as if the shadow of death was in the corners of the rooms, the rooms that Charmian had made for herself and her friends. But of course that was silly. That was something she must get over.

She went to a great cupboard and swung open the door. There were a lot of pasteboard boxes up on the shelf. They had labels. She selected a cereal that she had always liked pretty well at school, though they seldom had it. She looked inside at the curious fine little grains. Was that the way they looked before they were cooked? Made out of wheat! How did they get them into such cute little pellets? Machinery probably. What a lot of interesting things there were in the world that she had never known about!

She turned the box around in her hand and studied the label. Ah! Here were directions for cooking. She drew a deep breath.

Two cups of boiling water to one of the cereal. The water must be on the jump when the cereal was poured slowly in.

She studied the directions carefully, reading them over twice and then hunted out a kettle and a cup and measured her water for boiling. It was all most absorbing.

While the water was boiling she investigated the refrigerator again, got out the bacon and eggs, and found the coffee. She was delighted to discover that a can of coffee also had directions for making.

Suddenly she heard footsteps outside the back door, and stepped back into the pantry out of sight. Had that butler come back? She didn't want to meet him alone. He might not like it that she was in the kitchen. Then she remembered that it was her father's kitchen and she had reason to be there. There was no sense in her trembling this way at every little thing. She suddenly felt that she wanted to cry.

But there came a thump at the back door as if something had dropped on the door step, and then the footsteps ran away back to the street again.

Christobel mustered courage to open the door, and found milk bottles, cream, a loaf of bread and a dozen rolls lying there. That must have been the baker with the bread who had frightened her. And no telling when the milk came.

Happy as a child playing dolls she brought in the bread and milk. And now to her delight she found the water bubbling away gayly, and went about following directions for making the cereal. It was most exciting, for at a certain stage the whole mass rose up threatening to overflow the saucepan and the inexperienced cook burned her finger and got a shot of hot steam in one eye before she managed to turn the gas lower.

The coffee was another problem, and while she made it two good slices of toast began to burn and lift up a smell that was fairly choking.

In the midst of it all while she was trying to keep the next batch of toast from burning, and at the same time hold a blistered finger under the cold water faucet, the door swung open from the pantry and there stood the haughty butler looking at her with a cold disapproving eye. He had evidently let himself in silently with his own latch key at the servants' entrance.

Christobel felt herself begin to tremble. But then she remembered that her father was upstairs and there was no cause for fear. Only somehow the old habit had fallen back upon her.

"Where's the cook?" asked Hawkins sharply with not as much respect in his voice, she fancied, as there had been yesterday. His eyes were bleary, and he had a sullen look upon his face.

"Just a minute," she managed to say calmly, "I'll call my father. Watch that toast please till I get back."

She darted through the door and up the back stairs before he could say more, knocking excitedly on her father's door.

"Hawkins is downstairs, Daddy," she whispered at the key hole, and then to her relief she heard her father coming instantly to the door.

He was putting on his coat as he came, and seeing her perturbation he smiled at her.

"Where? In the kitchen?"

"Yes," breathed Christobel, "he frightened me. He is very cross."

Her father went swiftly down the stairs and into the kitchen but Hawkins was already on his way up the back stairs, walking stealthily. She saw him push open the swing door and look toward her for a second, as she stood in the upper hall, then glide stealthily toward the servants' part of the house. Something in his manner alarmed her. Softly she crept to her brother's door and called him.

"Rand! Come quick! Daddy may need you! Hurry! The butler is back and he looks ugly. Daddy may want you to call the police."

Something in her tone must have reached down beneath the deeps of sleep in which Randall was involved, for after the first sleepy "Wotchawant?" she heard him roll out of bed and plant his feet firmly on the floor. A moment more and he was at the door enveloping himself in a bath robe made of all the colors of the rainbow, and shuffling his feet into slippers.

"W'ere's he at?" Randall was frowning, his hair sticking in every direction. Randall's hair was straight and sharp and black and thick.

Christobel choked back the excitement that

almost made her voiceless and managed to tell what she knew in a throbbing whisper.

"Aw-wright! Just you stayyere! Don't get excited, see? I'll handle this!" he said loftily.

Christobel saw him march with a heavy frown toward the swing door, and was suddenly frightened lest something would happen to him. Perhaps she shouldn't have called to him at all. He was such an excitable kid! And then a strangling smell of burning toast came to her nostrils and she fled to the kitchen in panic. Her toast was burning again. Hawkins had not attended to it! Her cereal too perhaps. Her nice breakfast that she had worked so hard to get!

Hawkins was coming back from the door of his own room as Randall encountered him. He looked at the boy with fight in his eye, and Randall gave him back a glance of battle.

"Hey! Who's done what with my property?" demanded the irate butler sticking out his jaw at the son of the house in a most unbutlerlike manner.

"Whaddaya mean coming back ta the house and talking like that?" spoke up Rannie in a lordly manner. "Where were you las' night I'd liketa know? You're half stewed now ur ya wouldn't dare talk like that. What you got ta say about anything, running off all night? My father give ya permission ta go?"

"You shut up! It's none o'yer business," returned the angry servant. "I want my property. Have ya got it hid somewheres? You show it up mighty good an' quick ur I'll show ya where ta get off. You're nothin' but a kid that nobody cares anything about anyways. Get outta my way!" And he lurched toward Rannie threateningly.

Rannie waited long enough to buck his head down and back tossing his forelock out of his eyes, while his fingers with one swift movement gathered the silk tassels of his loud bath robe and stuffed them into his pockets. Then he made a quick dive straight into the knees of the butler, toppled him neatly and unexpectedly onto the floor, and calmly sat down on his chest, pinioning the arms of the drunken man in a fierce young practiced grip that was like iron.

"What's all this?" demanded Rannie's father suddenly appearing on the scene.

"Tie 'is feet up, Dad!" directed Rannie calmly, tossing his long lock out of his eyes. "He's half-stewed. He ain't fit ta have 'round." And then to his sister who had only waited to turn out the gas under her cooking and flown back to the scene of action, "Chris, you call up that p'lice again and get him ta remove the débris so I c'n get dressed. Good night! This is some household I'll say! Dad, han'me that towel on the rack there in the bathroom. I gotta tie this sucker's hands."

Christobel cast one glance at the prostrate Hawkins and flew to the telephone.

"But Rannie," said the father as he lost no time in securing the towels, "what's happened? Are you sure—?"

"Tie those feet first!" yelled Rannie. "Talk afterwards."

Mr. Kershaw stooped and tied a firm knot about the kicking feet, then straightened up, as Hawkins suddenly lifted up his voice and screamed, "Help! Help! Murder!"

"He's half stewed, Dad," said Rannie calmly from the breast of the struggling man. "Can that noise, Hawkins. You won't get anywhere doing that! Dad, he pulled a gun on me. See! There it is over there in that corner. Doncha touch it Dad. Ya might wanta get the finger marks. Say, Dad, you certainly had one buncha crooks running the house!"

In amazement the father stood over his young roughneck son and watched his strong young paws tie the knots firmly. His boisterous child could do something, it seemed, even if he was always in trouble in the school where he had spent his last four years.

"But, I don't understand!" said the father bewildered. "Do you mean that he tried to shoot you?"

Then there arose a protest from the half sobered butler who looked anything but dignified lying there in front of his bedroom door.

"Nothing like that, Mr. Kershaw," protested Hawkins, "I was just putting the gun in me other pocket. It's not loaded at all. Just look in it an' see!"

"Doncha touch it, Dad. Wait'll the cop comes."

Where did this young man get the worldly wisdom to be so cautious the father wondered in passing? He had no idea how many mystery stories Rannie had absorbed within the covers of his algebra and Latin Grammar during study hours. Rannie was well put up in all the technique of crime, even if he couldn't pass in Latin and mathematics.

"It's not necessary to send for the police, Mr. Kershaw," proclaimed the prostrate butler now, in his most butlerish tones, trying to be convincing in well-feigned dignity. "If you'll just persuade this crazy kid ta let me up I'll open the gun meself an' let ya see. It's only an old gun I carry fer self-defense, sir, but I never carry nothing but the gun, sir. It's only a fake, sir."

"Lie still!" commanded the master of the house.

"Indeed, sir, yer only making trouble fer yerself," pleaded the butler. "I'll be obligated ta sue ya fer this ef ya don't let me up before the p'lice comes. I've done nothing at all but come up seeking me own property, and I found it gawn! It's me that should send the p'lice fer you, Mr. Kershaw, taking a honest man's clothes outta his room, and making a clean sweep of it. Not a thing left. Just tell me what have you done with me clo'es an' I'll pack them up an' get outta yer house. I never was treated like this in a place before. I tuk ye fer a gentleman, Mr. Kershaw."

"Yes?" said the master. "And I took you for an honest servant, but I've found out that I was mistaken."

"I'm as honest a man as you'll find," said the butler fervently. "Call yer parlor maid. She'll tell ye. She's known me since she was a small child. Call Mrs. Kershaw's maid, Marie. She's me own niece."

"Unfortunately they do not happen to be

within calling distance," said Kershaw, noticing with satisfaction that a pair of heavy footsteps were coming up the stairs.

Then the two big policemen who had been there the night before came tramping down the hall and stood at Hawkins' feet, and the honest(?) butler quailed as he met their eyes.

"Oh, there you are, McBride," said Kershaw. "Thanks for coming so soon. We're not needing this man's services here any longer, perhaps you can just relieve us of his custody. You'll find his baggage down in the servants' dining room, minus a good deal of the family silverware which he had carefully stowed among his effects. I thought I'd just look around a little last night before he returned, and discovered that he had not been letting the grass grow under his feet while he was with us. He's been in the house only about a fortnight but I imagine we'll find there are other things missing when I get a chance to look over the list of things that are out of the bank. I haven't investigated farther yet. Of course if the man can return what he has taken away it would be well to be easier on him," he added with a knowing look.

The officers nodded gravely, and bent to snap the handcuffs on their prisoner.

Rannie released from his position on Hawkins' chest arose and pointed to the gun in the corner.

"Better take that with ya," he said with a boyish swagger. "He says it isn't loaded, but it hasn't been touched yet. He pulled it on me just before I lunged at him, but when he fell it slid off there."

The officer gave the boy a keen look, another at the gun, a swift glance around to reconstruct the scene as it must have been enacted, and then pulled out a big handkerchief and picked up the gun in it. Carefully he opened it and showed them a bullet inside, and without a further word he folded the gun in his handkerchief, slipped it in his pocket and walked his prisoner away to the car waiting at the door.

With the sound of the closing front door the three who stood not far apart in the entrance to the servants' hall, drew sighs of relief.

Then Rannie, with a voice of patronizing admonition addressed his father.

"Doncha realize what that guy was trying to do, Dad?" he said with the air of a wise parent addessing a small child. "He wanted ya ta pick up that gun and getcher finger prints on it, an' then he was figuring ta try an' prove that *you* pulled the gun on *him*, see?"

His father smiled a weary, half-amused smile.

"I guess so, Sonnie," he said, "but what I want to know is, how many times a week did you go to the movies while you have been in school, and just what kind of mystery stories have you been reading? I wonder if that won't account for some of the complaints I've been having about you lately?"

Randall's face grew suddenly red.

"Aw, well, ef that's how ya feel about it I wish I'd let the poor fish get away with it," he said in quick anger.

"No, Rannie, you did good work," said his father. "I was glad to see you were no coward. You certainly were equal to the occasion. I was just wishing you could bring the same keen alert action to your school work that you did to getting Hawkins tied up. That's all. Think about it, Kid."

Rannie dug the toe of his bedroom slipper into the hall carpet and looked sullen.

Christobel came out from her hiding behind the swing door.

"Well, that's all of them, anyway!" she said with a deep breath of relief. "There can't be any more people coming in with keys."

"Not exactly all," said Kershaw thoughtfully. "The chauffeur hasn't been heard from yet. I wonder—" and he walked to the back window and looked out toward the garage.

"I don't think he had a key to the house," he said meditatively, "but—there's no telling!" and a frown gathered on his brow. "I guess the whole bunch are a crooked lot. They probably figured that nobody would be watching last night and they could get away with almost anything. They are probably all lined up together. I should have told the police to search the garage. The chauffeur sleeps there, and no telling what he's got stowed away handy to take with him. I guess I'd better put it in the hands of the police right now before we have any more unpleasant experiences."

But as he was starting toward the telephone the bell rang.

The brother and sister stood together listening, all excitement for what might be going to happen next. They heard their father's quick sharp questions. "Who? . . . Where is he? . . . Which hospital? . . . What car was it? . . . You don't say! . . . You say it was all smashed up? . . . You say you have what's left of it? . . . What? . . . Liquor? . . . You don't say! . . . Not to my knowledge! . . . You say he was not killed? . . . Seriously injured? . . . Yes. I'll be down inside of an hour. . . . Yes. . . . Thank you for calling, Chief."

He hung up the receiver and turned back to the children.

"Well, you won't be troubled by the chauffeur coming in on you this morning!" he said, trying to make light of it. "He took a joy ride last night with a cargo of liquor on board. I guess he and the car were both pretty well tanked up from what they say. He went over the stone wall just above Dybert's curve, broke his leg and an arm or two, a few other minor troubles like concussion, and incidentally smashed up the new limousine that Charmian had just bought. We certainly have made a clean sweep of it so far as servants are concerned."

He stood for a moment looking down at the floor, his lips closing in a thin line that seemed to speak volumes if one could only understand. Of course his children sensed it, but they could not know that he was going back a few weeks to the time of the hiring of these new servants, and remembering how he had protested against it. Charmian had turned away tried and true servants for these because she said they were more up-to-date, complaining that the others did not understand the requirements of the service of the day.

Well, Charmian was gone, with all her mistakes. It was no use to grow angry over what might have been. He turned with another of those deep sighs that so wrung Christobel's heart.

"Well, Rannie, get your clothes on and let's go somewhere and get breakfast. Hurry up, son."

"Breakfast is all ready," declared Christobel triumphantly.

"Ready. Why, who got it?"

"I did!" said Christobel with sparkling eyes. "Only I'm afraid it's all cold by this time."

"Why, you great little girl you!" said her father stooping to kiss her forehead, and for a moment losing that careworn expression that had become almost habitual with him.

"Hurry Rannie!" Christobel called happily, "I'll go down and get it on the table!" As she ran lightly down the stairs the cloud of gloom and heaviness seemed to her to lift from the big alien house.

Christobel lighted the gas and the cereal

began to bubble once more. She connected the toaster putting in another set of bread slices. It seemed a really happy moment when her father and brother walked into the kitchen.

They all ate as if it were a picnic, and lingered, hating to break up the pleasant family feeling. But presently, after there could be no longer any excuse for sitting there, the father drew back his chair.

"Now, I've got to go to the police station, and get this gang off my mind. Then I'll attend to that car business. I may even have to go to the hospital and see that slippery chauffeur. What are you two going to do to amuse yourselves?"

"Aw, Dad! I'm going with you!" said Rannie rising determinedly. "That's where I belong."

"But you see your sister doesn't want to go to the station house. It's no place for her, and I don't exactly like to leave her alone in this great house. No telling how many friends that crooked bunch have who might come snooping round."

"I'm not afraid, Father," said Christobel gravely, giving a quick fearful glance around the big kitchen. "I've got these dishes to put away and those clothes to pack you know," and she half shuddered at the thought of going into the departed Charmian's private room alone. It was silly of course, but it seemed a terrible task. Something of the feeling that had come over her in that white velvet reception room began to settle down over her spirit now. She had a feeling that Charmian would not like her to be having her way in this big house that had belonged to her, and with her own garments. So it was a great relief when her father spoke.

"No," he said decidedly, "you're not to stay here alone. We've got to get some one to stay with you. What if you call up Mrs. Romayne? She has offered to do anything for you that you want. I know she will be entirely willing."

Christobel caught her breath and felt the blood rushing away from her lips and cheeks back into her heart in a wild throbbing. Distress showed plainly in her face.

"Oh, no, Father dear!" she pleaded. "I— she—I would much *much* rather be alone. I can hurry faster. Please don't worry about me. I shall be quite all right. I'll telephone the police station," she added forcing a laugh, "if I get scared."

"Well, of course there is really nothing to be afraid of, and we'll soon be back."

She saw them depart with sinking heart, but kept up a good show of courage till they were gone. Then she hurried to the kitchen, pulled down all the shades so that nobody could look in on her, and flew at the work. Her small experience did not make the task easy, but she managed to get the dishes washed and the things put away, and then with a quick glance around she fled upstairs.

Her intention was to go straight to Charmian's room and fold those clothes as fast as she could and get them in piles, ready to pack away or send away somehow.

She paused at the front hall window for a moment trying to still the wild beating of her heart before she opened the door to Charmian's apartment, for it somehow seemed to her that she would meet again the dead face of Charmian when she went in there alone, and the thought was not pleasant. There was nothing to be afraid of, of course, but she could not get away from the feeling.

As she stood there looking out into the streets she saw a disreputable looking man walking up and down the opposite side of the street looking furtively toward the house, then turning and looking again; and while she stood there watching the door bell rang.

She could hear the sound all through the big empty house, and her heart went up into her throat.

She drew back out of sight of the man who had now stopped and was looking across to the door.

And then the telephone rang in her father's room.

6

CHRISTOBEL stood there with her hand on her heart, shrunk back into the corner of the hall and wondered for an instant what she ought to do.

Death seemed to hover like a pall in the room across the hall, some unknown horror was perhaps down at the front door, and the telephone offered another possibility from which she shrank.

Suddenly it seemed as if she must drop down in a heap on the floor and cry. In one frenzied thought came the dull monotony of the past few years of her dreary boarding-school life. How she had chafed under the alienation from father and home, how she had longed to be out in the world and living a normal girl's life. And now here she was suddenly plunged into all kinds of tragedy, and her frightened unaccustomed soul quivered in indecision.

But Christobel was made of sterner stuff than just a silly child. She had unusually good common sense, and she commanded her trembling limbs to obey her and forced herself to go into her father's room and answer that telephone. For it had occurred to her that it might even be her father calling and if so she would tell him about that tramp across the street and ask if she should answer the door bell.

But when she took down the receiver and forced her shaking voice to speak it was a woman's honeyed voice that answered her. Yet though it was not any threatening servant, nor strange frightening voice of a possible burglar—the voice she heard filled her with a far more subtle horror than any of her other fears made tangible would have done.

"Is that you, Christobel, darling?" the voice asked, and Christobel darling knew it for the voice of her caller of the evening before.

"This is Miss Kershaw!" she said coolly, and had to take a deep breath to keep her voice from shaking. It seemed to her that her heart was turning to ice. It was all the worse that her father had suggested that this woman come and stay with her. It seemed so inevitable that somehow, somewhere, eventually, this woman was going to get her—to get her father away from her—and come into her life like another terrible cloud.

"Oh, you darling! How cunning that sounds!" gurgled the woman on the telephone, and somehow Christobel fancied she could almost smell the lazy sweet perfume that she wore, even across the wire. Christobel waited in silence.

"I guess you know who this is don't you darling Christobel?" came the obnoxious voice.

The girl could manage nothing but a frigid little "I beg your pardon?"

"I said I guess you know who I am," said the sweet voice. "I'm Mrs. Romayne, dear. I thought you would recognize my voice."

"Oh!" said Christobel, trying desperately to think how to answer in a way that would get rid of the woman before her father came, and yet not be so impolite that her father would be angry with her. "Oh, Mrs. Romayne! You are the lady who called last evening when Father was away?"

"There! Of course I knew you would know me!" gurgled the lady sweetly. "And I called again last evening and talked with your father. Didn't he tell you?"

Christobel did not want to answer this, so she hurried into something else.

"Oh, you are the lady who was kind enough to take a message for me last night." She tried to make her voice gracious without too much intimacy.

There was a second of dead silence while the lady recalled something she had all too evidently forgotten.

"Why, yes, dear child. Was I so careless as not to mention that last evening when I talked to your father? You see your old servant was not at home. We waited some time and I tried to find some one to leave a message with, but the people who lived near seemed all to be out. I hope it didn't cause you any inconvenience. Could I take you there to-day dear? This morning perhaps, and then you could all lunch with me later."

"No thank you!" said Christobel hurriedly. "I have other things I have to do. You are kind, but it won't be necessary. My brother will attend to it."

"Well, then, dear, how about coming to lunch? Haven't you got it arranged? I hope your dear father will come too, and your little brother too, if he would care to. I haven't seen him since he was a chubby baby. He must be quite a little boy by this time."

"My brother is seventeen," said Christobel coldly.

"Oh you don't mean it! My dear! I had supposed he was only about ten. How fast time does fly!"

But Christobel was wondering. Did Mrs. Romayne's friendship with her father date back as far as when Rannie was a chubby baby? Was she perhaps an acquaintance of her mother's? Oh, was she being very wicked not to like this woman?

And then came the sound of the front door bell again. Christobel was fairly frantic. It would not do to tell the woman on the wire that the bell was ringing and she must answer it, for then she would have to explain all about the servants and Father would not want his personal affairs talked about she was sure. And besides this woman would immediately offer to come and run the house for them. She was quite sure of that. She might even suggest coming to cook for them if she knew how to cook, or at least getting new servants for them. Christobel was sure she would do that. And then she would somehow succeed in spiriting them all to her house for an indefinite time.

Meantime the smooth voice was going on and on, saying pleasant things, and Christobel in her own thoughts lost track of just what was coming into her ears over the wire. Pleasant nothings about how fast children grew and how pathetic it was that they had to be left without mothers; and how nice it would be if some of the lonely mothers who had always wanted young things about them and hadn't any could just step in and take their places.

Suddenly a great sob rose in Christobel's throat. Oh, she didn't want this woman to take the place of mother to her! Oh, what should she do, what say? If she could only round out the conversation to a polite close, say it was so kind of her to call and good-by, or something like that. But somehow she could not bring her voice to say the words in just the right way. So she kept utterly still and let the woman talk on except when she asked a direct question and then answered in a low monosyllable, so low that she had to be asked over again because it was scarcely audible. All at once there came a large thump in her ear, a clashing sound, and then silence. She had been cut off. She waited an instant to make sure and then quickly hung up. Mrs. Romayne would doubtless get the connection again, but if the bell rang she just wouldn't hear it. She went out of the room, stopped just long enough to look out of the front window to see that the tramp had disappeared, and then hurried back into her own room and shut the door. As a further precaution she opened the bathroom door and turned on the water full tilt. She did not want to hear that telephone bell. Yet even above the water she seemed to hear the faint jingle of the far-off bell. And finally her conscience troubled her, and she turned off the water and opened the door. At least the bell was not ringing now. And what was that? A key in the front door? Half fearfully she listened, and then she heard her father's voice calling her and she bounded downstairs eagerly wondering if she ought to tell him about Mrs. Romayne telephoning.

But he gave her no time.

"Come on, Chrissie," he called eagerly, using her childhood name by which her mother had called her most often, "get your hat and coat and come with us. We've finished up the disagreeable things and are going for a ride."

Christobel dashed into her room for her

wraps and came rushing down with great relief in her heart. To get away from this terrible house. How good it would be!

"What have you got on?" asked her father, turning to look her over as she came out the door. "That's not warm enough. It's a cold winter day. Run back and get a good warm coat. You'll need your fur coat this morning."

She paused in dismay and looked down at herself. She was wearing a fall costume of dark green cloth elaborately trimmed with baby lamb fur. It did not fit her and was altogether too old and sophisticated for her. She never had liked it. She hated these cast-offs of Charmian's which were all she had for several years past. Sometimes they were utterly impossible and then she had either folded them away in her trunk or sold them to one of the seniors who admired stylish sophisticated things.

But now as she stood there in the doorway of the marble mansion with her father's eyes upon her, her cheeks suddenly reddened as if the objectionable garment had somehow been her fault.

"I didn't bring anything else with me," she confessed. "I thought this was the most suitable thing I had for—a—funeral."

"But that's not a winter coat," protested her father frowning at the suit which somehow looked very inadequate and ungainly upon Christobel who was tall and slim, while Charmian had been quite petite. The sleeves were too short, and the skirt was most abbreviated and very tight.

"Well, my winter coat is a bright sort of yellow," said Christobel fearful lest her father would be troubled. "It's very gay you know, with a big reddish yellow fur collar of bear or fox or something. It really is quite conspicuous."

"But my dear, why didn't you bring your fur coat? Surely gray squirrel is as quiet as anything you could wear. It is quite suitable for a young girl I'm sure for I see many girls wearing them."

Christobel opened her eyes wide and then laughed.

"Why, I haven't any fur coat," she said. "I never had one."

"You *never* had one? But I sent you one for a Christmas present this very Christmas! What do you mean?"

"No," said Christobel with a look of loving pain in her eyes, "you sent me a little squirrel neck piece. Don't you remember? I thanked you for the dear little squirrel. I didn't bring it with me because I couldn't wear it with this fur collar, and I had no other coat to wear. But it was dear. I loved it because you sent it to me."

"Do you mean to say that you did not receive a long squirrel coat with a big high collar? Why, I helped to select it myself!"

A sorrowful comprehension filled the girl's eyes as she slowly shook her head. And a dawning comprehension came into her father's eyes, and his jaw set in a firm line.

"I think—" he commented slowly, "that there have been a good many different kinds of things going on that I did not realize," and his face set sternly. Then he suddenly asked: "Did you buy that suit you have on, Chrissie?"

"Oh, no!" said Christobel quickly, and with distaste in her voice. "It was one that my—at least Charmian—sent me." It had been Charmian's wish that the children should call her by her first name. She had not wished to be called Mother. It made her seem too old she said, but Christobel had never been able to say the name glibly. Her own mother had brought her up with a habit of respect for her elders, and though Charmian was not very much of an elder, still she occupied the position of a mother, and Christobel always felt she was doing it, despite her sense of the fitness of things when she called her Charmian. Of course if she had been at all loving and friendly, more of a pal, perhaps it would not have seemed so.

"I think it was one of hers she had got done with," added the girl, feeling that more of an explanation was due her father.

Suddenly he turned to his daughter and looked at her with a searching, yearning glance.

"She was really very young you know, daughter," he offered by way of apology.

"I know," said Christobel quickly, eager to relieve her father from his worry. "She didn't realize it wouldn't quite fit me."

Still he stood in the doorway thoughtfully.

"I am very much to blame for some things," he said slowly. "I didn't realize or I would not have permitted them."

"Oh, that's all right, Father," the girl hastened to say. "I didn't mind." And then thinking perhaps that was not strictly true she added, "At least, not very much."

The father gave his child another keen look and read in her honest troubled eyes some reflection of the bitterness and disappointment that had been in her young life.

The chagrin perhaps, and even humiliation. While at home her young stepmother was rolling in wealth, satisfying her every whim.

"I can never forgive myself!" he said severely, and then, after an instant of thought, "Just go on out to the car, Chrissie, I'll be there in a minute."

Christobel got into the back seat and in a minute or two her father came out bearing two big boxes and put them into the car.

"I thought we'd just stop at the store and return those fur coats," he said casually as he got in beside Rannie who was at the wheel.

"Oh, I say, Dad, it's good to get at this wheel again!" said the boy. "My, this engine is slick! Say, Dad why c'n't I have a car at school this spring? A lotta the fella have cars. I'm old enough now ta be trusted, I should think."

"I'm sorry," said his father, "but I'm afraid you're not."

"Aw Dad! What's the little old idea? You let me drive this car. You said if I had good marks all right you'd consider it this spring."

"Yes," said the father thoughtfully, "but some things have happened since. In fact I found a letter down at the office just now from the dean of your school. You see, Rand,

I took it for granted that those marks were to be well and honestly earned."

Rannie cast a startled glance at his father and waited, but the father closed his lips and gave his attention to looking out for the number he wanted.

The traffic was heavy and Rannie had to give entire attention to guiding his car. Moreover he did not know just what to say. How much did his father know of his doings? What did he mean by that word "honest"?

"Stop right here, Rand," commanded his father. "Let us out and drive around to the parking place in the street at the rear. Wait there till Chrissie and I come back. Yes, Chris, hop out. I shall need you perhaps."

Christobel followed her father into the great beautiful exclusive store. It was like fairyland to her unused eyes. The school where she had been for the past few years was in a little country town, not near to any large city, and the wildest most exciting shopping tour possible was in a five and ten cent store that had recently raised a pert little head among the country stores of the community near the school.

They took an elevator up to the fur department and her father disposed of the two boxes he was carrying, explaining in a low tone to a salesperson who seemed to know him, and showed him utmost deference. The two fur coats were turned over to another salesperson, and the first one led them over to another corner of the great quiet room, where were glass cases of fur coats.

"Now, what kind did you want? Squirrel did you say?" he said turning to Mr. Kershaw.

"There you are, Chrissie, pick out your fur coat. What do you want? Squirrel, or some other kind?"

"Oh, squirrel!" said Christobel, her cheeks glowing and her eyes shining, and then turning to her father as the salesman swung open a glass door.

"Oh, Daddy! Am I really to have a fur coat? A new coat?"

"You certainly are," said her father grimly, "and I want you to pick out the one you want, understand. Never mind what it costs. I want you to look like other girls."

Christobel was soon arrayed in a lovely squirrel coat. Her father surveyed her critically as she tried on several of them. He found he had to be critic after all, for the girl was so ecstatic over each one that a decision would never have been reached. She was like a little child in her pleasure, and a wave of almost shame mantled her father's face as he realized what his own little girl must have had to suffer of mortification and disappointment in wearing an older woman's freakish garments instead of those suitable for her age.

He studied the hat she was wearing. Did he recognize that too as one that had belonged to his wife? Yes, he remembered expressing disapproval of the queer outlandish ornament on the side. What had Charmian done anyway? Taken the money he had given her to buy things for Christobel and spent it on herself, and then sent Christobel her old things of which she had grown tired? Strange he could have been so blind as not to suspect that his little girl was not having the right things. He had wondered sometimes that she never wrote to thank him when he had thought he had sent her some especially nice thing. But Charmian had explained that all young things nowadays were merely little animals who had no such virtue as gratitude in their make-up, that he expected too much from a child. Ah! What a fool he had been!

When the coat had been selected, the thin little jacket sent up to the house and Christobel in her new fur coat stood ready to thank him enthusiastically, he put his attention on the hat again.

"That hat is awful!" he said. "Come, we'll get a new one right away. Where is the millinery department?" he asked the salesman.

"Right through the arch on this same floor" was the direction.

"Oh Father! You're wonderful!" breathed Christobel, and then showed herself quite capable of picking out the right hat, a jaunty little dark blue felt with a streak of a white and green quill cockily stuck in at exactly the right angle.

"Oh, I've wanted one of these cute hats all winter!" she sighed joyously as she came with the hat on for her father's approval.

"Well, you certainly have good taste," he said, noticing how pretty she was in the new coat and hat. "And now," he looked at his watch, "one thing more. You need a new dress right away. I don't like what you've been wearing. You'll need a lot of them I guess, but we'll only stop for one this morning or Rannie will get impatient."

Christobel tried on two to see which her father liked best, a dark blue wool beautifully tailored with a touch of white and green in the brilliant scarf that adorned the neck;

125

and a dark blue silk with white crepe vest and deep cuffs in lovely young lines.

"Take them both!" said her father briefly with a satisfied tone to his voice. "And there! That garnet velvet thing on the model there," he said pointing to a lovely dinner dress in transparent velvet with a deep scalloped cape collar. "I like that. Is that her size? Well, send that up too. No, we can't stop now to try it on. We're in a hurry. If she doesn't like it we'll return it. Just keep on that dress you have on Chris, and let them send up your old things."

"Oh Father!" said Christobel when she was arrayed once more in her fur coat and new hat and they were hurrying away, "you've fixed me up like a princess."

"Well, you are, aren't you? My princess!" he said with a look of wonder at the transformation a few garments had wrought. What would Mary, the child's mother, have thought if she could have known that he had neglected her little girl so long? Oh, what a fool he had been to marry that spoiled, selfish Charmian just because she had a pretty face and had seemed fond of him! How the fondness had disappeared when she had him hard and fast! How he had had to pour out the money upon her until there was nothing left for his business! That great mountain of a house that she would have!

He sighed and hurried Christobel down to the car.

"Now," he said, "we're going anywhere you want to go for an hour and then we'll bring up at a restaurant and have lunch. Where do you want to go?"

"Oh Father! Anywhere," said Christobel blissfully. "Or—could we? Would that be too far? I guess it would. Suppose instead we just drive to where Maggie lives and let me say good morning to her? Would that be out of your way?"

"Maggie? Oh, Maggie! Your old nurse? Why, where does she live now?"

Christobel told him.

"That's all right," he said, looking at his watch again. "It won't take long to get there, and if you don't stay too long we'll still have time left to go somewhere. Where else was it you wanted to go?"

"Oh, I would so love to see the old house where we used to live. I'd like at least to drive past there sometime. I do want to see if it looks the way I remember it."

"Yes, that's some distance," said the father, "I guess we'll have to let that go till this afternoon or some other time, but I'm afraid you'll be disappointed in it. It's not in a very exclusive neighborhood."

"I don't care," said Christobel, "I'd love to see it."

"All right!" promised her father. "We'll go and see it before you go back to school."

The conversation was cut short by Randall's exclamation as he saw his sister.

"Good night! Some baby doll! No wonder you were gone so long! I thought you'd got lost. I was just getting ready to have you paged. Say, Chrissie, you're a looker in that outfit. Never knew you were so good looking. Say, Dad, how about staking me to a couppla suits of clo'es? I ain't so flush with garments as I'd liketa be either."

"We'll see!" said his father briefly, and Randall couldn't tell for the life of him whether there was a coldness in his father's voice or not. He had had a most uneasy half-hour while he waited thinking over what his father had said, and wondering which of his misdeeds at school had been recounted to his parent in the letter from the dean. He had thought everything had been pretty well covered from that functionary's knowledge, but perhaps somebody had squealed about something. He wished he knew what it was. It would be well to be prepared with excuses. However, he fixed up one or two that would do for any of them, and then began to work on each separate sin providing ameliorations or alibis for all of them. By the time his father appeared he had felt pretty well prepared for almost anything, only it was a bit disconcerting not to have his father more affable. It must be one of his more serious offenses, that act for instance of burning the principal in effigy—only he wasn't the only one involved in that affair. Practically the whole class had been in that, as a protest against sending Hi Spencer home without a chance of returning just because he sneaked some liquor into the dorm.

Rand was rather quiet as they drove through traffic, threading their way to the little back street where lived the old nurse. Even when Christobel went in to see Maggie and he was left alone with his father the subject was not opened up, and Rannie didn't dare say anything lest he would give too much away on the wrong offense. No, he must wait for his father to speak first. Maybe he would forget about it and say no more. But it wouldn't be wise, Rannie reflected, to say anything about having a car till this was all cleared up.

But the elder Kershaw seemed abstracted,

absorbed in thought. As Rannie cast sidewise furtive glances at him he was startled to see that his face looked troubled, worried, and then right out of a wide silence he suddenly spoke.

"Why did you do it, Rannie?"

7

"Do what, Dad?" asked the astonished boy, wondering which of his various offenses could have produced such an expression on his father's face. Surely Chic Carter hadn't died or anything had he, the fellow he had a fist fight with over a crap game just the day he came away? Good night! What if he had? But what kid that had any stuff in him ever died from a mere bloody nose?"

Rannie drew a deep breath and tried to look innocent.

"Why did you steal the list of examination questions?" asked his father in a sad disappointed voice. "I knew you were full of monkey-shines but I never supposed you would be dishonest."

"Aw, that!" said the boy, a kind of careless relief in his voice. "Why Dad, that wasn't dishonest. That was merely a point of honor. You don't understand."

"No, I don't understand," said his father in a tired voice, "Tell me son. How could breaking into a safe and stealing the paper containing your examination questions for the next day be a point of honor? Your importance midyear examinations?"

"Well, ya see, it's this way!" said the son settling down affably to explain the customs of his school to an ignorant parent. "It's a thing that's always been done fer that particular exam. The mids mean sa much ta the class an' ta sports an' all ya know, an' sometimes there's fellas that aren't sa bright an' we see to it that they have a fair chance, see? It's always been the custom for years, Dad. Each class hands it down ta the next ta see that it's done. It's tradition, ya know. An' I was elected ta do the deed this year. It wasn't my own doings ya understand. I was *'lected.*"

"You mean that you were elected to do the stealing and you couldn't decline the honor?"

"That's right!" said the boy cheerfully. "It is an honor in a way. They wouldn't 'lect ya ef they didn't think ya c'ud get away with it. They know me. And I've monkeyed round combinations a lot. They knew I could do the deed. Ef I'd ben clumsy an' one that would be likely ta get caught, dontcha see, they wouldn'ta picked me out."

"But you did get caught. You didn't get away with it my son."

The boy's face clouded over. He had forgotten for the moment that this was the case. "Aw, Dad!" said the boy, and then with the resilience of youth, "Gee! I don't see how they found out! I had the window catch fixed, and the whole thing worked out. I didn't even carry a flash. I knew the combination, see?"

But his father's face was graver than he had ever seen it before.

"So I have a son who is in training to be a crook?" he said, and there was a quality in his voice of anguish that made Rannie writhe. He had never thought his father would take a thing like that to heart.

"Aw, Gee! Dad! It wasn't anything serious. It was just old 'xam'nation papers. You oughtn'ta take it so seriously. Nobody else does. They don't think anything of it at school. It's done every year. Last year—"

"I assure you you are mistaken, my son. They think it a most serious matter. In fact they have written me that they cannot receive you back into the school because of it."

"Dad!"

Rannie slumped down into his seat like a tire suddenly punctured.

"But Dad! They can't do that? I—I— I'm—Why I'm *cheerleader* in all the games!"

"They have done it son. Being cheerleader won't get you anywhere with a faculty when you have committed a dishonorable act."

"I don't see how they ever found it out," said Rannie. "Somebody musta squealed."

"That has nothing to do with the matter, my son. You committed a crime, and you will have to suffer the consequences."

"Oh, but Dad, if you write ta them they'll take me back. They think an awful lotta you!"

"I shall not write," said the father sorrowfully. "You deserve what you are getting and it is not right that you should get out of it."

"But—*Dad!* Just fer pinchin' the exams?"

"Randall, for whose benefit were those tests, those examinations? For the faculty, or for you?"

The boy mused sulkily.

"It's so the faculty can tell who ta promote," he answered at last reluctantly.

"No, you're wrong," said his father. "They are given so that you and your fellow students may find out wherein you are lacking.

You are in school to prepare for life. You have to stand certain tests that you may know and your family may know whether or not you are ready to pass into your manhood and stand the further tests of life. The faculty are pledged to give you these fair tests. But when you stole the questions they had prepared for this test and handed them out to others you not only failed in your own examination—"

"But I didn't fail, Dad. I passed a hundred percent."

"You certainly did not pass, my son. An examination taken under those conditions was not an examination. You failed it utterly. Your mark should have been zero. And you not only failed in your own test but you failed in other ways. You failed in honesty and decency and loyalty to your school. You failed in fineness of character, in uprightness, in loyalty to the traditions and standards of your family. And you also became a party to making all your class fail in every one of those things. There was only one out of the whole number of twenty-seven in your class who will be permitted to graduate at the time their class naturally should have graduated. They are all put back one year in the grading. All except one—"

"Oh, yeah, I know! That old stick-in-the-mud! He wears goggles, an' wouldn't accept the questions. The fellas rag him something fierce," murmured Rannie wrathfully. "I'll bet he squealed."

"No," said Rannie's father. "You were seen by a member of the faculty as you came out of the window. You were followed and watched. The faculty know exactly what every member of the class did from the time you climbed into the window until after the examination was completed."

"The dirty skunks!" ejaculated the dismayed boy. "An' they let us go ahead an' take the exam just the same!"

"My son, you have lost your sense of values! Your ideas of right and wrong are badly mixed. Now, get this. There was just one dirty little skunk and that was you! It wasn't the faculty, it was you, and—yes—there were others. They were your fellow classmates, who accepted the stolen questions and profited by them, or thought they were doing so. It's pretty tough, Rannie, to have one's only son expelled from school for a thing like that, a dirty low trick—!"

"But, Dad," protested Rannie, "I was elected—"

"Not everybody that is elected to a thing has to serve. When you were nominated for the office of goat for the class, couldn't you have declined?"

"Why no, of course not," said the boy with spirit. "That woulda been yella. Somebody hadta do the unpleasant things. It was a custom I tell ya."

"I fancy it won't be the custom any more in that school," said Rannie's father dryly. "They are taking the most drastic measures with all the delinquents. It is a little bit hard on me that it should have been my son who was the goat and had to be made the example most public of all, not allowed to go back to your school. Of course that queers you in all schools that have right standards."

"Aw, gee! Dad! They'll take me back!" swaggered Rannie knowingly. "Just you hand 'em over a neat little fifty thousand fer their old building fund an' you'll see how quick they'll do it. O' course I know you think you gotta rub it in a little and all that, but you don't needta worry. Sam Henty got fired last term fer getting drunk an' a lotta other things, and his Dad came across with the dough an' it was all smoothed over. I tell ya, Dad. You just make out a check fer fifty thousand an' I'll take it back with me. They'll keep me. You'd a hadta do something big anyhow,

Dad, cause all the other fellas' dads are do-ing it."

Rannie heaved a sigh of content and sat back feeling that he had made everything quite all right. But Rannie's father showed no signs of falling in with his plans, as he eyed him furtively with rapidly decreasing spirits.

"No, son, I'm not going to write you any check," he said sadly. "You see you deserve the punishment and I don't believe in offer-ing bribes to get my son free from a punish-ment he has let himself in for. But—Rannie—if I did believe in bribes and in letting you grow up with a ruined character and a false standard of living, there is another reason why I could not give fifty thousand to that building fund. I am not in a position to give any large sums anywhere at present. In fact, you may as well know that my business is in a very precarious position. I suppose you may have vaguely heard of a thing called the depression. Well, you may find it necessary to do more than hear about it in the next few weeks. Even if you were going back to your school it would be impossible for me to get you the car you have talked about so much. It is better that you should understand the situation. I may of course be able to weather the storm and not go under, but I have no fifty thousand dollar checks to fling about anywhere, not even to save my only son from a well-deserved disgrace."

Randall Kershaw sat stunned and looked at his father.

"Why, Dad!" he said and his voice sounded sympathetic and full of tears. "Why, Dad! I allus supposed you're *wealthy!*"

"Yes," said Dad bitterly, "so did I, but it begins to look as if I was mistaken."

Then suddenly the door of the drab little house opened and Christobel came smiling out followed by a little apple-cheeked Scotch woman with a gingham apron wrapped about her shoulders to keep her warm.

"But Dad! You bought Christobel a new coat and hat," murmured Rannie under his breath.

"Yes," muttered Christobel's father, "that was one of the things I owed. Rand, your sister hasn't been having proper garments. I wasn't looking after her as I should. You were a man child. I could look after that myself."

"*I* see!" said Rannie understandingly, as man to man, and settled into a deep gloom.

Maggie came smiling up to the car and greeted her former master deferentially.

"Yer lookin' weel," she told him embarrassedly. "It's fine Miss Chrissie is lookin'. I'm that proud ta see her come, thinkin' of her puir auld nurse, an' she a fine young laidy."

"It's good to see you again, Maggie," said Kershaw with a ring of genuineness to his voice. "Yes, the children have grown a good bit since you carried them around and fed them, haven't they? Randall is almost as tall as I am."

"Sure I'd never know him for my wee bit mannie that I cuddled an' rocked."

Randall Kershaw frowned and grew red from forehead to collar.

"My but his poor dear mamma would be that pleased ta see him the noo!" went on the nurse looking at him with her heart in her eyes.

And suddenly Rannie felt that he should weep. What was that stirring the depths of his heart and creeping with smart and sting into his eyes? He frowned more deeply and tried to grin to hide his feelings, but made a sorry mess of it.

"Miss Chrissie tells me yer havin' bad luck wi' yer servants," went on the nurse, perhaps sensing the mess she had made of it for the boy, "I wonder, cud I he'p ye oot fer a bit ta-day and the morra? I'm off meself this after, an' the Sawbath is allus an off day. In fact I'm forebodin' I may be dropped from the job althegither. There's rumors our place is ta close next week."

"Well, now," said Kershaw heartily, "that's the first break in the darkness I've seen. Would you come and help us, Maggie, till we can look around and know what we are going to do? We'll not work you too hard, and I'll promise you shall lose nothing by it. We can go out to our meals you know. But I do hate to leave this little girl of mine all alone when her brother and I have to go out for a few minutes. If you'd just come and be company for her and kind of help her put things together."

"Sure I will!" said the woman heartily. "I'd luve to be with my bairns again. I've a bit washin' ta finish for a woman around the block as needs it ta-day, but I cud git ter yer house in time ta git dinner ta-night ef it wasn't a fancy dinner."

"Oh, you needn't worry about dinner," said Kershaw. "We'll pucker a meal somehow. But if you could come as soon as you're ready, suppose I send Rannie back for you about six o'clock. Would that be too soon? I've promised to take the children for a ride."

With her Scotch blue eyes beaming and her apple cheeks glowing she watched them drive away, and then turned proudly back to get her work done and be ready. She was going back to her dear babies. Her heart raced with wild joy.

"Aw! If just their puir dear sweet mammie could but see them now!" she crooned to herself as she closed the street door.

Rannie was silent as he drove away, turning the car at his father's direction toward one of the quieter parts of the city, and arriving soon at an exclusive restaurant noted for its wonderful cooking and service.

He parked the car and followed the others into the stately dining room with its distinguished looking guests. He looked around him with suddenly enlightened eyes. This was not the kind of place they went to eat when the students from his boarding school had a day off. He knew it took money to eat in a place like this. Was this another debt his father owed? He seemed suddenly to be looking at life from an entirely new angle, and there was something pathetic in the thought that perhaps some of his father's debts that were worrying him were debts to him too. He realized how little of anything like real luxury had ever been in his young life. And now Dad was spending money he didn't have to treat him and his sister as he thought they ought to be treated. And he, Rannie Kershaw, was in the unpleasant position of just having handed out to his father a rotten deal! Again those ridiculous tears stung into his eyes and throat, and he had to be a long time hanging up his hat and coat to conquer them. Gee! He wished he could do something about it!

He slumped into his chair, and looked unseeingly at the menu that was handed him.

"I do'want much," he growled huskily. "I'm not really hungry. Order me a ham sandridge ur something," he said at last, unable to put his mind on the decision.

His father cast a quick anxious glance at him, and studied the menu carefully, then gave an order in a low tone, and presently an abundant lunch was set before them. But Rannie, though he ate what was set before him, was silent during the whole of the meal.

While they were finishing the dessert their father went to telephone a man with whom he had an appointment. When he came back he told them that his appointment had been changed to late in the afternoon, and if they would like to visit their old home there would be time.

Christobel caught at the idea eagerly, but Rannie said nothing till his father asked, and then he only shrugged his shoulders and said, "S'all right!" Rannie was not enthusiastic about anything. His father eyed him furtively and sighed, wondering if the boy was really touched by his present position, and if the punishment would go deep enough to eradicate the wrong. Oh, he had been most neglectful of his duty as a father. He felt it more and more, now that he was aroused to what had really happened during the years of their estrangement.

But Christobel was eager enough for two. All the way, she was recalling little things about the old home she remembered; the time when the mad dog was in the street and little Rannie was out in the yard by the open gate calling out to the "pitty doggie," and how frightened Mother had been, dropping everything and rushing out to snatch him in her arms and cry over him, and how Nurse Maggie had cried too, and scolded about people who kept dogs and didn't know they were going mad. She made the picture of Mother with Rannie in her arms, rocking him back and forth and crying over him, very plain, till Rannie choked and almost wept again, and the father cleared his throat and looked away blinded by tears of his own.

And then the little birthday party on the side lawn when Christobel was four and Rannie was not quite a year and a half. Rannie almost seemed to remember it himself. She told how he suddenly plunged both hands into the ice cream and took them out dripping cream, screaming with delight and messing up the lovely pink ribbons on his shoulders, till Nurse Maggie had to carry him away screaming from the party and give him a good scrubbing.

But somehow it didn't seem funny to Rannie. It choked him all up again. Gee! Think of having a mother like that and living in a real home with birthday parties. But good night! Think of Dad not being wealthy any more!

Christobel talked enough for both of them. She was full of eagerness and when they turned into Maple Street she clapped her hands like a child.

"Oh, I remember this corner," she exclaimed. "I used to come down to put letters in that letter box. Don't you remember it Rannie? You used to be allowed to take hold of my hand and come along. And once I lifted you up and let you put the letter in yourself."

"You couldn't very well lift him up now," said the father trying to dispel a little of the gloom on the face of the boy. After all, he was his boy, if he had gone wrong. And maybe it had been as much his father's fault as his. He had been turned off to school when he was a mere child. Who could expect him to have fine standards when he had never had much home teaching?

But Rannie didn't smile. He was looking around, painfully trying to do his part at remembering a lost heaven.

8

"THERE! I remember that house with the Gothic roof and the funny wooden lace work in the peak," said Christobel. "I used to be able to see it across the road away down the street if I flattened my nose against the window when I was watching for you to come home from the office, Father."

"There's the tree!" said Rannie coming out of his gloom as he spied the old home before either of the others.

"Oh, it's there just as it used to be!" said

Christobel with shining eyes. "It doesn't look quite as big as I remember it, but it looks *dear!* Father, could we go in? Have you got a key?"

"Yes," answered her father with almost a ring of eagerness in his own voice. And he fished a key from his pocket. "I thought if we should happen to get over this way we might look around and see if everything is in good condition. I suppose it will look terribly dirty and dusty. I haven't sent anybody there to clean in some time."

Christobel could hardly wait for her father to unlock the door. She laid a hand lovingly on the railing of the old porch with its paint all checkered and ready to crumble. It was like a dream being here.

Rannie was standing half way up the walk looking around and trying to find himself back in the years that were past and he thought were forgotten. Now as he stood on the actual spot again vague pictures floated before his mind. He could see his young sweet mother standing there in that front door in a blue dress smiling at him as he came up the walk showing her an all-day-sucker he had just bought with a penny at the corner store. A mist floated before his eyes, and he turned away quickly and looked down the street to hide his emotion.

Mr. Kershaw threw the door wide open and Christobel stepped in almost reverently and looked around.

"Oh, Daddy! Isn't it dear?" she said as she looked from one well remembered chair to another. Even dusty as they were it all looked precious to her.

"You like it, child?" said her father in amazement. "I was afraid it would disillusion you."

"Oh, it's Home, Father!" said Christobel, her voice full of happy tears. "I've just longed for it sometimes at school when I was lonely."

Her father put a quick arm about her and threw her to him, kissing her tenderly.

"Poor dear little girlie," he breathed softly, and Christobel reached her arms about his neck and gave him a real kiss, such as she had been too shy for before.

"Oh, Father! I'd give anything if we could live here!" she said earnestly. "I'd just love it!"

"What, here? You mean live here all the time, child?"

"Yes, Father dear, it would be wonderful!"

Her father was silent a moment looking thoughtfully about.

"But this is no neighborhood, and no house from which to bring you out into society."

Christobel was silent a moment still leaning against her father's shoulder. Then she lifted her head and looked straight into his eyes speaking gravely:

"Would Mother, my own mother, have cared about that sort of thing?"

He did not answer for a moment then he said just as gravely,

"No, I suppose not."

"Did my mother ever come out?"

"No."

"Then I don't want to," she said firmly. "I'd much *much* rather not, if you don't mind Father. I would like to be like my mother."

He drew her quickly to him again, speaking earnestly:

"You couldn't be like anybody better," he said.

"Then may we live here?"

"I'll think about it," he promised. "We must be very sure before we make so drastic a change in environment. You know we have no idea what kind of people live about here now. It might be most unpleasant."

"I wouldn't care," said Christobel insistently. "We'd have each other."

"Well, we'll see," he said slowly, thoughtfully. "It—might—be a good thing—in more ways than one," he mused.

Hand in hand they went through the rooms, speaking gently of her mother, of her little girlhood, and Christobel was very happy. It seemed to her that she had not been so happy since her own mother died.

"There used to be curtains!" mused the girl as she stood looking out one of the dusty windows.

"Yes, it seems to me I gave orders to have them washed and packed away."

"I would like to clean it all up and make it look as it used to look," said the girl. "And there is a fire place. It would be wonderful to have a fire and sit around it, the way we used to do. I remember hanging up my stocking on Christmas by that fire. And there were people who used to live across the road. Father, wasn't it in that house that those children lived? There was a boy, Phil Harper, and his little sister June. She was about Rannie's age. See. There is a little girl going in over there now. She might be a younger sister. Do you mind Father if I just run over and find out if they live there now? I won't be a minute."

"Oh, it's likely they've moved away by this time. Harper, yes that was the name. I remember he was a fine young man—when I was young." The father sighed. "Yes, run along if you want to, but don't stay. It's getting late and I've an appointment you know."

"I won't be a second." And Christobel ran ahead of her father down the stairs and out the walk toward the house across the way.

But Rannie was standing in one of the upper rooms looking in hungrily at a little crib drawn close to a great wide bed, and there were tears dropping down his face.

Christobel met the little girl coming out of the house again as she went up the steps across the way. It was an old red brick house and the paint on the brown front door was badly caked and peeled. The porch floor looked as if it had seen wear, and everything outside had a dejected look, but there were crisp muslin curtains at the windows just as there used to be when Christobel was a little girl and played jacks with little Phil Harper on the stone doorstep.

"Do people by the name of Harper live here?" questioned Christobel of the little girl.

"Oh, yes," said the child smiling. "I'm Hazel Harper."

Christobel caught her breath happily.

"Oh, I'm glad," she said involuntarily. "Are they at home? Is your mother at home?"

"Oh, yes, Mother's here," said Hazel, "and Father's here. He's always here now you know since he hurt his back and can't work any more. And Phil has just come in. But my sister June is at the office where she works. She's the only one of the family that has a job. Won't you come in?" and she drew back and held the door open politely.

Christobel stepped in.

"Just wait here a minute," said Hazel, "I'll call Mother. We keep that parlor door locked on the other side because it makes a banging sound and bothers Father all the way upstairs. He suffers a great deal and we like to spare him."

Christobel stood waiting in the dim little hallway and suddenly became aware of a voice speaking earnestly. It was a woman's voice and there was a note in it that she remembered, a sweet motherly croon; but it was pleading now, and there were tears in the voice:

"Oh, our Father!" the woman was saying, "You care for the sparrows. We know you

151

are going to care for us. We're down to the last dollar, Heavenly Father, and the mortgage interest is due next week. Take over our burdens and undertake for us. The man said we'd have to give up the house if we couldn't pay this time, and my poor John is lying there worrying. Help him to trust Thee, Father. Give us all more faith. And, if it be Thy dear will, give my Philip a job. He's been a good boy to us all, and he loves Thee, dear Lord. And now we are going to thank and praise Thee for what Thou art going to do for us. Lord give us faith to praise Thee even though we cannot see the way ahead, and now listen to my boy too as he claims Thy promise that where two of Thine own shall ask, it shall be done for them."

Then a young strong earnest voice took up the petition.

"Oh, God our Father, if there is any thing in me to hinder giving what I ask, show me what it is. Cleanse me and give me more faith. You know that I want Your will to be done in me at any cost, Lord, but oh, my Father, God, if it be possible don't let my dear family have to suffer. We know that You hear when Your children cry to You. Hear now Lord according to Your promise, for we ask in the name of Your Son, our Saviour, Jesus Christ."

The voice trailed off into silence, and then something like a sob seemed to be suppressed, and there was a soft stirring of rising garments, and suddenly Christobel realized that she had been listening to private prayer, and she must not be found there where they would know she had been listening. Oh, she ought to have gone before!

Swiftly, firmly she grasped the door knob, turned it silently, stepped outside, closing it behind her and fled on the tips of her toes so that she would not be heard.

Rannie was at the wheel already and her father standing by the car door. She slid in breathlessly into the back seat, her father stepping in beside her, and Rannie started up the car. Peering back through the window she saw the door across the way open, and some one come out and look down the street, and then as Rannie wheeled into the next street she sat back with a deep breath and realized that her eyes were full of tears.

"Well," said her father looking at her curiously, "you didn't find any one you knew, did you? I thought all the old families would have moved away."

"Yes, I found them," said Christobel

softly. "That is, they are there. But Father, I didn't wait to speak to them. They were praying. Father, they were praying for a job for Phil! I came away quickly so they wouldn't know I heard."

Mr. Kershaw questioned and she told him the whole story, the quiver in her voice and the tears coming to her eyes again at thought of the two earnest voices.

"So, John Harper is disabled," said his old neighbor. "That's hard luck. I used to think he was a rising man. I never expected to find him still in the same old house. No money, no job! Well, say, now, we might answer that prayer, anyway, mightn't we? I've been on the point of firing my office boy for a week. He's simply worthless. If this young Harper is any good at all he would be better than the fellow I have now. Rand, suppose you drive past that house again and let's get the number. I suppose to be any good as an answer to that prayer it ought to arrive mighty soon. I'll send a note from the firm by special messenger."

"Oh, Father! That will be wonderful!" said Christobel with shining eyes. "But— won't they know I listened?"

"Oh, no. I'll fix that. I'll write the note on firm paper impersonally, just say we've heard he's unemployed and if he is interested in working for us will he call and see me at the office Monday. And by the way, I wonder who holds that mortgage. I'll have our lawyer look that up, and see what we can do about easing that up for them."

"Oh, how splendid!" said Christobel. "You're just the most wonderful father in the world."

Christobel shrank back out of sight as they turned back into Seneca Street, but she need not have troubled. There was no one on the Harper porch. Mrs. Harper had shut the door and gone back to her duties and her cares, concluding that the visitor had only been a passing stranger, enquiring the way somewhere.

"Now, Rand," said his father as they drew near their home, "you can just let Chrissie and me out at the house and drive right on for Maggie. I'll have to be ready for that man who is coming, and I want to take time to call up my office secretary and let him know I have sent for this Harper boy and that he is to hire him if he comes and not let him know I have personally anything to do with it. That will settle the boy's mind about a job and start him in at something even if I don't have time to see him myself on Monday. Be careful when you cross the intersection by that second traffic light, boy. There is such a congestion at this hour."

"There's that man again!" said Christobel suddenly as they drew up at the house.

"What man?" asked her father eyeing the shabby-looking individual who stood leaning against a letter box across on the corner.

"Why that man. I've seen him several times over there!" said Christobel.

"Oh, I guess he's just waiting for somebody," said her father reassuringly. "Come son, hurry up and get Maggie."

So Rannie drove off, and Christobel went in with her father, entering the big marble mansion for the first time without an inward shudder. Somehow the sight of the dear old home in its dusty simplicity with its lingering sweet memories had exorcised the shadow of pall that hung over Charmian's house. As she took off her pretty new hat and coat she smiled at herself in the long silk-draped mirror of her dressing table. What a lot of lovely things had happened that afternoon. New clothes, lovely ones, dear old Maggie coming, the visit to home, the possibility that they might go there to live. Oh, if Father could only be persuaded! And now this lovely thing that he was going to do to answer those pitiful trusting prayers. Perhaps there was a real God, and He had fixed it so she would hear that prayer and send help. Who knew? The teachers at school, and all the girls said they didn't believe in a God. Christobel had never thought much about God. Only, in the secret of her own chamber at night when the light was out, and her room-mate asleep, she had often slipped out upon the cold floor and knelt beside her bed to whisper that old prayer her mother had taught her and her little brother. It had become to her a kind of charm, nothing more, to keep her soul from an inward unrest and longing.

Now I lay me down to sleep,
I pray the Lord my soul to keep.

She suddenly wondered if it had ever been answered, and if there was some One who had kept her soul, else—where would she have been?

The man came to see Mr. Kershaw very soon after Christobel came downstairs again, but she had the satisfaction of reading the exceedingly businesslike note that was written on the firm paper, and seeing it dispatched by special messenger in uniform to

Seneca Street, and she stood at the window looking out and thinking what would happen when it reached the little old brick house and was read.

And then suddenly she knew that they would go into the shabby little parlor again and kneel down and tell God how glad they were. Wasn't that just wonderful. The idea of thanking God for what He was going to do! She never heard of anything like that before.

She was still thinking about it when the car came back and Randall helped Maggie out and brought in her suit case.

"Don't carry that up," he said pleasantly to the nurse who had already won his heart over again. "I'll take care of it after I put the car in the garage. I won't be a minute."

Then he was gone, driving around to the entrance at the rear.

"I'll just run into the kitchen and see if there's plenty for dinner there before I take off me hat," said Maggie hastening through the hall to the back of the house. "We might havta send out fer something, ye ken. It's gettin' that late!"

Christobel went eagerly with her turning on the lights ahead for it was growing dark.

"There's plenty of meat for a meat pie,"

said Maggie, opening the electric refrigerator and looking over the contents with a practiced eye. "Aw, these hired bodies, how they do gouge their employers," she scoffed virtuously. "There's half a beefsteak an' a good bit of roast left, and just see how they've hacked it away. And the fine big ice box! It needs a good cleanin'. I'll be up early the morn an' get at it. Now, let me see, I wonder where they keep their vegetables. Would they be doon the cellar, or is there a store closet? Juist let me get into me house dress an' apern, an' I'll soon get me bearings. Where's me suit case? I'll take it up the stair."

"But Rannie wants to carry it for you, Maggie," said Christobel. "He'll be here in just a minute. I just heard the car drive into the garage. There. He's turned the light on, see! It's shining into the back window. He can't be long now."

"Well, show me which dishes ye use. Now, I know where to begin. No, I can't be bothered waitin' fer the laddie. I want to get me dress changed, and get at me dinner."

So Christobel let her have her way, and led her upstairs.

Rannie meantime had driven around to the garage which was entered from an alley or lane that went through the block behind the houses. He stopped his car, got out and unlocked the garage, turning on the light which snapped on close to the door.

He moved slowly, for his heart was heavy with a new kind of trouble. Rannie had never taken anything in life very seriously before. He was trying to face the fact that he wasn't going back to school, that he couldn't go back to school.

He slammed the door of his car shut, and turned to go back and shut the garage door behind him and lock it, but suddenly and most unreasoningly the light suddenly went out, and then before he could realize it something big and dull struck him on the head, a great black cloth fell over his face and the world blinked completely out around him. He did not hear the furtive rubbered footsteps about him, nor know when he was put back into the car. He did not even hear the engine start, nor feel the motion of the car as it jerked back into the alley driven by unskilled hands, hurried, frightened hands, and made its wild way out into the traffic of the city streets. Rannie was a long way off in a dark smothered place where nothing mattered any more.

9

THE man had gone and dinner was on the table and still Rannie had not come in.

"It's very strange," said the father coming into the dining room. "I told him to put the car right away, but perhaps he has gone on some errand for himself. He'll likely be here in a few minutes. Don't wait for him. He must learn to be on time."

They sat down and Maggie waited upon them, bearing the dishes with beaming face, and much ceremony. She had been deeply impressed by the grandeur of the house. She waited upon them as if they were royalty.

But when they had finished the delicious meal Rannie was still absent and his father looked deeply troubled.

"He has no business to do this way!" he declared.

"Oh, he'll have found some of his friends and be talking to them and not knowing how the time passes," excused the old nurse. "I'll just put by some nice hot dinner for him and keep it warm till he comes."

"He doesn't deserve that," said the father. "He knows better than to be so late."

Christobel went into the kitchen with Maggie to help about clearing away the dishes, and Mr. Kershaw went back to the library and his papers, being presently deeply absorbed in a mass of figures to the obliteration of all else.

The dishes were all assembled on their shelves at last amid many comments from Maggie about the slovenly way the kitchen had been kept, and Christobel was just about to go upstairs and show Maggie her lovely green room, for Maggie was greatly curious about this grand house. But suddenly Mr. Kershaw appeared in the kitchen doorway a look of deep anxiety on his face.

"Hasn't Rannie been back yet?" he asked looking at his watch. "I declare he deserves a severe punishment for this. It is nearly ten o'clock. I wonder what he is thinking of. Haven't you heard the car at all, Chrissie?"

"Why, yes, Father," said Christobel, thinking back. "I was sure he drove into the garage right after he brought Maggie. I heard the car when we first came out into the kitchen, and then I'm sure he turned on the light in the garage. I saw it beam up on the back window. But then it went out again and I forgot all about it. I supposed he would come in in a minute."

"That is strange!" said Rannie's father now thoroughly alarmed. "I wish you had told me at once. I had better go out and look. There are so many cases of gas poisoning in garages now. No, never mind my coat, Maggie. I won't be a minute. I just want to make sure he's all right. He just might have been overcome perhaps after he had closed the doors and turned out the light. He probably didn't remember the garage lights could be turned out from the kitchen."

Mr. Kershaw snapped the lights at the doorway, and went out in a flood of brightness to find a most amazing thing. The garage door into the back yard was still closed and locked, but the light inside the garage showed that the back door into the alleyway was wide open and swinging in the wind.

Wildly the father gripped the door and tried to shake it open, wildly he searched for the former chauffeur's keys, for he had given Rannie his own bunch, but no keys could be found. And then he called for a hatchet, but there seemed to be no hatchet nor any other tool available. Everything about the place seemed cleared up and guiltless of anything that could be possibly used to smash in a door, or break a lock, till the canny Maggie finally produced a hammer from the kitchen. Even then it was some minutes before the strong lock on the door finally yielded to the frantic blows of the excited father. Mr. Kershaw as he pounded away on that door, blow after blow, wasn't sure whether he was most anxious or angry. A great apprehension was over him. He couldn't help but remember the sullen, gloomy expression on his son's face ever since he had told him that he was not to be allowed to go back to school. Was Rannie trying to get it back on him by frightening him? Had he taken the car and gone off somewhere? Perhaps he would come back very late, drunk. Such things did happen. Perhaps he would become defiant.

Still of course it was within the possible that some terrible thing had happened to him. Yet of course that wasn't so. This was a sane world, a commonplace world after all. Tragedies did not happen to modern families. Oh, such stories got into the paper, but were doubtless exaggerated, or were mere fake cases. Rannie was likely running around right now having a good time, and would come in late and be sullen again, and what was he going to do with him? Oh, he was reaping now what he had sown in neglect of his precious children. What would Mary have said to him if she could have known he would have allowed his own children, her babies, to get so far separated from him that he knew practically nothing of their heart life? How crazy he had been to let a featherheaded little thing like Charmian order their precious lives.

He fairly growned aloud as the door at last gave way under his continued blows, and he staggered into the brightly lighted garage.

Maggie and Christobel were close behind him, with white anxious faces, and saw what the father was too excited to see, Rannie's soft felt hat lying on the floor crushed flat as if a heavy foot had stepped upon it. Indeed, Maggie, stooping close, could see the foot print of a shoe in a greasy outline, from a foot that had evidently stepped into a puddle of black grease on the floor of the garage.

"Here's the laddie's hat," she said in an awed tone. "I mind the dark blue ribbon. I noticed it when ye were stopping at me door. He can't have meant ta go far missin' it. That's some big body's fut mark there on the brim. See the mark of the rubber heel.

Handle it with a care! That fut mark may tell something."

Kershaw remembered Rannie's caution about the revolver, and cursed his own stupidity. Even Maggie was cannier than he was. He stepped closer to look at the hat without touching it and something crunched beneath his feet. He stepped back sharply and saw it was a fountain pen big and fat and arrogantly gay in a bright handle, jazzy like Rannie. Yes, that was Rannie's fountain pen, lying crushed there. He must have dropped it. And just a few inches away was his bunch of keys. What had happened?

Rannie wouldn't have dropped his keys and pen out of his pocket intentionally. He wouldn't have dropped them out if he had been in a car. He must have gotten out— Could there have been a scuffle, a struggle? The crushed hat, the pen, the keys all pointed that way. Had some one tried to steal the car and Rannie defended it? If so why hadn't he made an outcry? But perhaps he did and no one heard him.

And then he saw something lying off at one side that made his blood run cold and stopped his breath for a moment with a dreadful thought. It was a sand bag, lying as if it had been cast aside. He strode to it and lifted it. Yes, that was heavy enough to knock any one out. Suddenly he spoke:

"Go in and telephone for the police to come at once, Christobel. I don't want to close these doors nor change anything until they see how things are here. I'm afraid this is some work of that bunch of crooks."

Christobel rushed in to the telephone, and Maggie, distressed in her mind whether to go or stay by the master and protect him, finished up by hovering between the two till Christobel returned with a coat for her father and sweaters for herself and Maggie.

Kershaw meantime had been out in the alley looking up and down but found no further evidences, and almost immediately an officer in a police headquarters car came riding up.

Christobel and Maggie stood back in the yard listening, watching, while the two policemen went about with flash lights poking into every corner of the garage, even going up into the chauffeur's rooms. They lifted the sand bag and looked significantly at one another. They picked up the crushed hat and made Rannie's father identify the maker's name. Yes, it was Rannie's new hat all right that had been bought for the funeral.

Finally the officers carefully closed and locked the garage.

"Well, sir, we'll send out word in every direction," they said. "Of course they've got two hours start on us, but your car ought not to be hard to find. Of course, too, they might change the license, if they had time. But don't you worry, Mr. Kershaw, we'll likely find your boy. We'll have it broadcast to-night, too. And *if* he should turn up you'll let us know at once please."

Mr. Kershaw brightened at the thought.

"Oh, certainly," he said.

"Meanwhile," went on the officer, "you all better keep pretty close to home to-night. They seem to have it in for you. I guess they're aiming ta clean you out. We'll have the house guarded at once, and you let us know if anything develops."

They went into the house and looked at one another. Mr. Kershaw sat suddenly down in a big library chair.

It seemed to this father that he no longer had power to stand upon his feet. A great weakness had suddenly come to him. He sat looking at them for a moment, Maggie with her bare arms from dishwashing wrapped neatly in her gingham apron, Christobel standing by a big chair gripping its arms as if

168

her life depended on holding on, and then he dropped his face into his hands and gave one groan.

The tears were raining down the girl's face now, as she stood holding tight to the chair, her head drooped like a delicate flower.

Maggie turned herself about with her back to them, her blue Scotch eyes all drenched in tears like an April shower.

"The puir wee mannie!" she ejaculated suddenly as if they all were to blame, and then scuttled away to the kitchen to stare out the window into the dark back yard.

Meantime, down on Seneca Street, the messenger boy had reached the Harper house, discharged his duty and gone on his way, weaving a gay little pattern with his bicycle in and out between traffic, unaware of the importance of the note he had just carried.

It was Hazel who had answered the door. This was an exciting day in her little life, two knocks on the door in one afternoon, and now it was getting dark. She was just the least bit afraid of what might be coming. She had heard echoes of the talk that went on between Phil and Mother. She had come to dread something about a mortgage, though she wasn't just sure what a mortgage was nor what harm it could do one.

But when she saw a real live messenger boy with a bicycle carelessly thrown down on the step behind him, she drew in her breath in great excitement. People on Seneca Street did not usually get letters delivered by real messenger boys in livery with brass buttons on their caps. The importance of this happening choked her throat all up, and her fingers trembled. Of course, though, it might even be that mortgages came by special messengers.

She signed her name in the boy's book, closed the door carefully, stood an instant studying the envelope to see who it was for, then she hurried into the sitting room where her mother was darning a pair of Phil's trousers and Phil sat over by the window using the last streak of daylight to study the want advertisements.

"It's a letter for you Phil," she said quite quietly, managing to keep her voice steady, though she couldn't keep the lilt of hope and excitement out of it entirely.

"A letter for *me!*" said Phil bringing his paper down from the daylight so suddenly that it fairly crackled at his little sister.

"A letter?" said Mother, her hand going

with a swift motion to her heart, and a look of wonder on her face.

The two flashed one look at each other and the son looked back at his letter, took in the name of the firm on the envelope, tore open the end swiftly, and began to read. Then a great light came into his face, a kind of bewilderment too, and he looked at his mother. "Listen, Mother! Isn't this wonderful?"

Mr. Philip Harper, Jr.
871 Seneca Street
N——— ———
Dear Sir:

Your name has come before us as a young man unemployed. If you are interested in accepting a beginner's position with prospect of rise as you show your ability, please call at our office on Monday morning at 10:30 that we may talk the matter over.
Very Sincerely,
Carollton, Carew and Kershaw

"Blessed be His name!" said the mother softly.

"Yes!" said Philip fervently. "Mother, I'm

afraid I didn't have much faith when I prayed, I've tried so long without success."

"Yes, but you prayed for more faith, dear," said his mother. "Come let us thank Him at once."

"But—we don't know what it is yet, Mother. Perhaps—"

"Whatever it is it's from the Lord," said the mother. "Surely you're not going to pick and choose, Philip."

"Not I!" said Philip with a ring to his voice. "I'll take whatever He sends, no matter how humble it is, and be glad," and he went down on his knees beside his mother, his own thanksgiving was fervent as hers.

As they rose from the brief prayer they heard June coming in the door and Hazel rushed out to tell her sister the good news.

"Philip's got a job!" she cried softly, not to disturb the father who had had a bad day and was asleep just then.

"A job? Oh, joy!" said June. "I've been praying about it all the way home. What is it?"

"He doesn't know yet," said the little girl. "Come and see. There's a wonderful letter all about it. He's to go Monday morning to see about it."

June read the letter and looked up at her

brother. "How did that happen, Phil," she asked wonderingly. "That's a big house. Who do you suppose put your name in there?"

"God," said the mother reverently with a tender smile.

"Well," said June, "that's a famous bonding company. Everybody speaks of them with respect. I'm sure it would take nobody short of God to get an unknown name before them."

"Well, I'm glad we thanked Him before it came," said the mother happily as she went about setting the supper table for the very meager supper that was already on the stove, a savory soup that only hands long skilled could have made out of the cheap ingredients to be had. The soup and bread would make up the meal. All the few luxuries that they could muster must go to the dear invalid who had little suspicion of the real state of things, so bravely had the family carried on when he was stricken down.

But it might have been a turkey dinner with all the accessories that night, so eager and happy were they all as they sat down, so good everything tasted when eaten with bright faces.

"I notice there's a Kershaw in that firm," said Mother as she passed Phil his second plate of soup. "You don't suppose it could be a relative of those people who used to live across the street, do you, Phil?"

"Not a chance," said Phil. "Anyhow, Mother, that's ages ago. They wouldn't remember me. I was only a kid at the time."

"Well, I didn't know," said Mother. "I heard those Kershaws got quite wealthy, but it might not have been true. They did move away a long time ago of course. I didn't realize. I was just thinking that if it was the same man you might just say we remembered him or something like that. It would be a kind of recommendation."

"I'd rather let God work it out for me, Mother," said the young man cheerily. "I think that'll be good enough."

"Yes, perhaps that's better," said the Mother and beamed about upon her children.

"Shall we tell Father?" asked Hazel with round eyes of eagerness. She did love to tell good news.

"Not until we know all about it dear," said Mother. "He gets so excited over the least thing, and if he knew he might not eat nor sleep until it was all settled."

"Will he get a big, big salary, Mother?"

asked the little girl, "enough to get the 'spensive new doctor for Father?"

"Probably not a big salary," said Mother with a wise smile. "He's to begin at the beginning. But Hazel, dearie, suppose we don't think about that part now. Let's just be glad over Sunday at least that there is a hope of *something* and trust the Lord who sent this to send all the rest that we need in His own good time. Don't let's count our chickens before they are hatched. Let's just praise God for letting us know He is thinking about us."

Hazel laughed.

"That's funny, counting chickens before they are hatched," she said. "But I'm glad, glad anyway."

"That's right. Now pass your dish and I'll give you some more soup. There's plenty of soup to-night and that's all we need just now."

Hazel handed her dish with a smile and a deep content settled down on the little old shabby brick house.

The three young people had a happy time washing the dishes all together as they often did, while their mother was upstairs giving the invalid his supper and fixing him comfortably for the night. Philip went around putting away dishes that Hazel had just wiped, and whistling softly a hymn they all loved:

Fear not, little flock, He goeth ahead,
Your shepherd selecteth the path you must
*   tread;*
The waters of Marah He'll sweeten for thee,
He drank all the bitter in Gethsemane.
*   Only believe, only believe;*
All things are possible, only believe.

It was weeks since Philip had done any whistling. It made them all glad to hear him. In a minute more the girls were tuning in with him, singing a sweet low accompaniment. The good cheer reached upstairs to the invalid and he smiled.

"The children must be happy to-night," he said with a wan smile. "It sounds good!"

When the dishes were done Phil sauntered over to the home-made radio and tuned in. He knew his father enjoyed any good music, especially the Saturday night symphony orchestra concerts, so he turned the dials, and presently the shabby little house was filled with as good music as any mansion on Fifth Avenue could boast.

They all sat listening, thinking pleasant

thoughts, rejoicing at what had come to Phil. When, suddenly, just as Mother came tiptoeing down the stairs, the music stopped, right in the prettiest part of the New World Symphony, and a voice snapped out into the silence:

"This program is interrupted to make an announcement of the disappearance of Randall Robinson Kershaw, Jr. Son of Mr. R. C. Kershaw of Carollton, Carew and Kershaw, Wall Street.

"Young Mr. Kershaw was five feet ten and a half inches tall, seventeen years old, dark hair, blue eyes, weight 145 pounds, dressed in dark blue serge suit, tan overcoat, tan shoes, blue-striped silk socks. He wore no hat. The circumstances point to his having been kidnapped about six thirty this evening just as he was about to shut his father's car in the garage behind their Fifth Avenue residence. His hat was found on the floor of the garage."

There were more details, and an address given where information should be sent if any one knew of his whereabouts.

The Harper family sat in tense silence listening, looking at one another in horror.

"Phil, that is the same Kershaw that used to live across the road!" Mrs. Harper said when the voice had died away and the soft strains of the symphony soothed in upon the interruption. "The baby's name was Randall. He was named after his father. He would be about seventeen now. Philip, I think you ought to go and see if there is anything you can do to help."

"I'm going of course," said the young man rising alertly. "Don't worry, Mother, if I'm gone all night. Nobody will kidnap me you know," he said with a quick little laugh. "There are no bonding houses connected with us."

The mother smiled through sudden tears.

"There are worse things than being poor," she said gently. "Oh, Phil, how would I feel if it had been you! He had such a sweet little mother! But she's where it can't worry her any. But the poor father! And there was a sister I remember."

"Yes, a sister," put in June, "Christobel. I remember her. She was a nice girl. She used to divide her candy with me, and she needn't have. I was younger than she was. She wasn't selfish one little bit. I wish there was something I could do. If I was only a boy now—"

"You and Mother can pray," said Phil facing about from the doorway where he was putting on his coat. "They brought an answer to my prayer, Mother, we ought to give them a little service that way now."

"Yes," said the mother tenderly. "Our God knows where the boy is! He can help when others fail. Oh, I wonder if the poor family know our God!"

So Philip hurried off down the street, while the mother and June, and even little Hazel, knelt down beside the decrepit old couch and asked God to bring back Rannie Kershaw.

It was Christobel who opened the front door when Philip Harper rang at the Kershaw residence. For the last half hour police had been coming and going. A detective had just gone. She thought he had perhaps forgotten something and hurried to the door, with Maggie calling out to her anxiously:

"Bide a wee minit dearie, I'll go."

But she was not afraid any more with Maggie here, and all the police about. In fact her mind was so taken up with worry about her brother that she was no longer afraid of anything for herself.

She looked very frail and sweet as she stood there holding the door open, her hair blown about by the wind that swept in, her eyes showing signs of recent tears, which were even now held in abeyance.

At once the young man knew who she must be, realizing a resemblance to the little girl he used to know so long ago. But suddenly he doubted whether he should have come here at this time even with offer of assistance.

"I'm afraid I shouldn't have come to the house," he said. "I'm rather a stranger of course, though I used to be an old neighbor of the family when I was a boy. I've just come to say that I heard the announcement over the radio, and if there's anything at all I could do, I'd be so glad. I'd go to the ends of the earth to help find the young man."

But Christobel knew his voice instantly, even though she had not got a very good view of his face with the shadow of the dark street behind him. That was the voice she had heard in prayer only a few hours before. And she wondered if he had somehow found out that she listened to that prayer. Conscious of having listened to what was not intended for her ears, and also, conscious of her red eyes and distraught appearance, she spoke shyly:

"Thank you," she said. "Won't you—come in?" She did not know whether that was what she should do or not. Her father was out in the garage for the moment with one of the detectives from an agency.

"No," said Phil Harper quickly. "I don't want to intrude. Won't you just tell your father—you are Miss Christobel, aren't you? I'm Phil Harper. You won't remember me of course, but Mother thought a lot of your mother, and I'd be awfully glad if there was anything I could do. I thought there might be just a chance that there was some clue a young fellow could follow out or something. I'd like to be of use in any way."

It was just as he was saying this that Christobel heard her father come in. She turned and looked back at him quickly, her mind suddenly leaping back to their trouble, scanning his face anxiously to read if he had any news yet. Already, though only a trifle over a couple of hours had passed since Rannie had disappeared, her heart was acquiring that alert apprehensiveness, that burden as of a long-borne fear that cried out to be relieved and would keep hoping for good news that would lift the painful tension.

Christobel saw her father was looking keenly at the young man, and she spoke quickly, eagerly:

"This is Phil Harper, Father, who lives

181

across the road from our old home. He came to offer help."

Mr. Kershaw put out his hand gravely, still looking keenly at the young man.

"I appreciate that offer," he said, "and it comes just when I needed some one. I can't get away from here very well and I want to send a note over to a friend by some one I can trust, and get an answer back again. If you can do that for me I shall be grateful indeed."

"I am honored that you can trust me," said Philip earnestly.

"I would have no choice in the matter," answered the older man with a quick appreciative look at the younger one. "You look so much like your father that one would know you were trustworthy."

"You couldn't say anything that would please me better," said the young man.

A look of mutual warmth and liking passed between the two men and Christobel found a little passing gladness in it. She stood a moment talking to Philip while her father went to write his note, recalling the last day she remembered seeing him, riding away to school on his bicycle the day they moved from Seneca Street. Then suddenly the memory of Rannie's disappearance came over her in a great wave of anxiety and the tears welled up in her eyes and brimmed over.

"Excuse me," she said in a little quavering voice, "I'm so worried about my brother."

"I know," said the young man quickly. "I wish I could do something. How long is it since—you missed him?"

Christobel told him briefly the experiences of the last two hours, and then went back and told him about the miscreant servants and the tramp on the other side of the street. It relieved her to have some one to speak about it. Then her father returned with the note and gave directions, and there was something comforting to them both to feel that this young man was interested, helping, a real friend who was connected with the old dear life of home and Mother, and Rannie's little boyhood.

After Philip was gone her father was called to the telephone, and then had to go out to the garage with some officers once more, and Christobel was left alone in the big alien house.

She turned on the lights in the great reception room, looked about her to get rid of the feeling that some one, something was lurking there in hiding, turned on the lights in the small reception room and gave that a survey, and then sat herself down on the stairs with her chin in her hands and stared down at the thick rug from which strange menacing faces seemed to be grimacing at her. Somehow she didn't seem to belong anywhere in this huge house.

Out in the kitchen Maggie was cleaning up. She said the place wasn't fit for pigs. There were tears on her cheeks. She was too nervous to sit down. She was thinking of the tall nice boy with traces of the baby in his face, the baby she had cared for years ago. Christobel didn't want to go out with Maggie. She sensed that Maggie was anxious too. She wanted to stay near her father and see if anything developed from the telephone message. Perhaps they would have found Rannie. Perhaps he hadn't been kidnapped after all. Just gone off on some crazy errand. Maybe he had gone out to pawn his watch as he said he was going to do. That would be Rannie if he got some queer idea in his head. Dear blusterous Rannie! Oh, if that would only be it, and he would come back pretty soon whistling, angry with them for imagining that he was lost, furious when he found he had been mentioned on the radio. But oh, what a relief it would be if he came!

It was just then she heard a car stop in

front of the door, and a moment later the bell pealed annoyingly through the house, giving Christobel a shiver of apprehension as she rose from her seat on the stairs and hurried to the door.

10

BUT Maggie had heard the bell and came hurrying to open the door. She did not intend to have her other blessed lamb kidnapped. Christobel had retreated when she saw Maggie, and was standing on the stair landing wide-eyed, her hand upon her heart.

It was a lady at the door this time, and suddenly Christobel knew, even before she saw her, who it must be. She was not surprised when she saw the slight altercation at the door end by Maggie being swept aside peremptorily.

"I am an intimate friend of the family, my good woman!" said a hard imperious voice that yet resembled a fawning voice that Christobel knew. And Maggie, still holding the door open because she did not want to admit that she was conquered and shut the unwelcome guest inside, gave one protesting glance upward toward where her nursling stood, just in the act of flight. Maggie was not quite sure but she might be overstepping her new privileges as servant in the house. Of course this might be an intimate friend, but she didn't look like what Maggie would choose as an intimate for her master's family. Her lips were too red, and her perfume too subtle.

For just an instant Christobel remained poised on the landing for flight; then she heard her father return from the garage and enter the telephone booth in the back hall. At any moment he might come out and be the prey of this interloper. Christobel thought she could not bear to have this added to the burden of the evening. Very likely this persistent woman would somehow persuade her father that he must either allow her to stay here and share in their anxiety and distress, or else that she, Christobel, must go home with the woman and be protected. The thought of either was horrible to the girl. It must not be. She did not know how she was going to prevent it, but in some way she must.

So she turned quietly, adjusting an untried dignity, and went swiftly downstairs, a queer thought flitting through her mind. Afterward she wondered why it had come. The thought was a wish that Phil Harper would come back. A feeling that somehow he would sense the need and find a way to get this woman courteously out of the house. But she put it swiftly by, knowing that this was an emergency she must meet herself if it was to be met.

It was Maggie who spoke, raising an angry frustrated face and flashing blue eyes.

"This wumman was wantin' ta see yer fayther, Miss Chrissie, an' I was tellin' her that he was very much occupied, an' that ye was wore out with the thrubble and excitement."

Christobel smiled indulgently.

"It's all right, Maggie. Mrs. Romayne didn't understand. Never mind, I will speak to her for just a moment. Good evening Mrs. Romayne. Will you just step in here where we shall be free from interruption?"

Christobel swept the light on in the small reception room, drew Mrs. Romayne within, and pulled the curtains after her. Now, if her father came back he would not see who was there.

"I'm sorry, Mrs. Romayne," said the girl, suddenly feeling quite grown up and able to deal with this person, knowing that the situation was a desperate one, and she must somehow conquer it or she might have it to deal with the rest of her life. "You have been very kind to call of course, and we appreciate all your solicitation. But I'm sure you will understand that to-night my father is too deeply engaged to see you or any one. In fact we both are too much worried and disturbed to talk."

"Oh, but my dear, I certainly do understand all that!" cooed the lady. "I've not come here to talk or to ask questions, that is any more than are necessary. I've come here to save you from others. I've made arrangements just to stay indefinitely and look after the house and the servants for you, and answer all callers and questions. I'd even be willing to see reporters and detectives for you. Poor dear Rannie!" She got out her delicately bordered handkerchief and dabbed at her eyes with an effective gesture.

"That is kind," said Christobel trying not to have her voice sound like an icicle, "but it is not necessary. The household is running perfectly smoothly and needs no help. As for reporters and detectives, those will be looked after by the police. We do not intend to admit any reporters or detectives either. I do hope you will understand when I tell you that the very best way you can help us now is by staying away. I'm sorry if that sounds rude, Mrs. Romayne, but it really is the truth. In fact I heard the officer tell my father it would be best for us not to admit any one just now, even very close friends, until he has the case a little better in hand. You know it may be quite possible that my brother just took it into his head to go somewhere for the evening. He may come home pretty soon—" She said it with a confidence she was far from feeling, and tried to summon a brave smile.

"Oh," said the lady eagerly, with ill-veiled curiosity in her tones, "have you any reason to expect any such thing? Was there any reason for his having gone off like that? He hadn't had a quarrel with either of you, had he?"

Christobel laughed a nervous little ripple that scarcely hid her indignation and weariness.

"Oh, no indeed!" she answered. "Of course not. What would we quarrel about? Rannie never quarreled. We were so happy together." And suddenly her lip quivered and her eyes brimmed over to her great dismay and annoyance. Then she drew her head up and smiled bravely into the lady's face again saying with dignity:

"We are quite sure this will all clear up very soon, Mrs. Romayne, and Rannie be back again safely, but Father thought it wise in these days when so many queer things are happening to have him paged on the radio. Now, would you mind going? The officers may be back at any time and Father prefers that there be no one present even of the family when they come in to consult with him."

"Oh, but my dear," protested the lady wafting the sickish perfume on her frail handkerchief fairly into the girl's reluctant nostrils, "I couldn't think of going away and leaving you. I'll just go upstairs and stay with you till news comes and I'm sure you are all right. Or, if you should prefer, suppose you come with me. A young girl should not stay around alone where there are policemen—"

"I am not alone," said Christobel. "I have a trusted servant with me, and I certainly do not want any one with me, and will not be willing to go away from here at present. If I should need your help I will call you up and let you know." She was still struggling to be courteous.

"Well, then let us sit down a little while and talk," said the visitor with a subtle cunning in her voice, yielding for the time being to the inevitable. "I want to know all about it. What time did your brother go? When did you last see him? What were the circumstances? Have you the least idea where he may be? Does your father think he may have gone back to school? Who were his young friends in the city? He might be off at a dance you know."

The smooth voice rattled off the questions and they fell like sharp pebbles against the sister's consciousness as she stood watching this impertinent, beautiful woman and wondering what other way she might try to get rid of her. Then she became aware that Mrs. Romayne had paused for a reply and she turned bright determined eyes upon her guest.

"I'm sorry, Mrs. Romayne, I can't answer your questions at present. The officer in charge has asked us to say nothing to anybody."

"Not even a friend of the family?" said the purring voice with a velvet scratch to its tones.

"Not to any one."

"But that is ridiculous!" said the lady indignantly. "My dear I shall have to insist on seeing your father!" and she made as if to pass the girl and go in search of him.

Christobel had been aware of soft noises in the hall, feet stirring on the thick rug and hushed voices. She was frantic to get rid of this woman, yet she must not send her out if something was going on in the hall. Perhaps her father was there! What should she do?

Then, just as she had opened her lips to protest, some one pushed the heavy curtain back and there stood Phil Harper, tall, grave, courteous, peremptory.

"I beg your pardon, Miss Christobel," he spoke like one vested with authority, "you're wanted in the other room at once please, and if you will kindly introduce me to this lady I will escort her to her car. I presume that is hers outside?" He lifted questioning eyes to the lady's and summoned a grave smile. "Sorry to interrupt," he added apologetically as Christobel murmured an introduction. "Mr. Harper, Mrs. Romayne." "But you see we are all under orders just now." He motioned the girl to go, and held out his arm to escort the lady with all the grace a man of the world might have shown.

Mrs. Romayne, never quite impervious to the charms of a good looking young man submitted herself to be led away quite willingly, tossing back a sweet caressing farewell to Christobel calculated to impress the young man.

Christobel slipped quickly away to the library, tears of swift relief filling her eyes. It seemed too good to be true that Mrs. Romayne was really gone before her father appeared on the scene. It was wonderful that the young man had seemed to understand and had managed it all so courteously without offending the lady. How much had he heard her say, she wondered?

There were two officers in the library waiting for her father. They arose as she came in. The chief asked her if she was Miss Kershaw.

"We want to ask you a few questions about the tramp your father says you saw lurking around the street and watching the house."

Christobel sat down with wildly beating heart and forgot everything but the tragedy that had befallen the home, as she searched her mind for exact data, just what time it was when she had seen the man, whether he might have been lurking in the shadow of the street when her brother drove away to put the car in the garage, and then, almost casually with nevertheless a keen searching look, the chief asked her if there had been any unpleasantness in the family, any reason to suppose her brother might have gone away of his own accord, or had he mentioned any errand which might have taken him away?

"Oh no," said Christobel earnestly. "He was intending to come right in to dinner. He said he was hungry. And—why, we never quarreled!" There was indignation in her tone. How terrible it was to have outsiders, strangers, prying into their family affairs, having a right to think all sorts of terrible things against any of them. A sudden and oppressive sense of what this thing was going to mean to them all in the way of publicity came over her.

"Why, we were all looking forward to the evening with Father. You know we have been away at school and have had little opportunity to see him. And besides, there was Rannie's hat in the garage, all crushed as if somebody had stepped on it."

The officer relaxed in his narrow watch of her face, evidently convinced, and just then to her relief she heard footsteps coming to the door. But after her father and Phil Harper had come into the room she remembered how Rannie had spoken of pawning his watch to pay his school debts. Could it be possible that Rannie had changed his mind and gone to pawn his watch? But then how would his hat be on the floor of the garage? Of course he might have driven in, somehow dropped his hat, perhaps got out of the car, and then remembering his watch he might have backed out of the garage again, not waiting to pick up his hat. Rannie was like that. He wouldn't mind whether he had his hat on or not.

But, if that was what he had done why didn't he come back home again for supper? He surely wouldn't have driven back to school without Father's permission.

Christobel decided that she must tell her father about Rannie's debt and the possibility that he might have gone somewhere to pawn his watch.

The men were talking about a car that had been seen backing out of the driveway behind the house. An officer on his beat had thought he recognized it as the Kershaw car. He had not noticed the license number. Word had gone out to watch for such a car on all highways. Several cars of the same make had been stopped and investigated, but they all had wrong license numbers. By this time of course there had been ample time for license plates to be changed.

Even while they were talking the telephone rang and there came reports of cars found here and there, but no trace of identification with the Kershaw car.

As the midnight hour drew on Christobel suddenly felt as if the load on her heart was almost too heavy to bear. Her father happened to look at her white anxious face just then and noted the strained tenseness of her slender body, the whiteness of her lips and cheeks, the feverish anxiety, and his heart smote him. He drew her aside gently.

"Chrissie dear," he said, "you should go to bed at once. You will be sick. There is no need for you to sit up longer. You can't do anything now. Get Maggie to go up with you and get some sleep. Don't worry about your brother. Doubtless there is some explanation to this strange disappearance. We shall likely discover it by morning. I've just been telephoning to his school. I thought somehow he might have got it into his head to go back there. They are to let us know at once if he arrives."

"Well, there is something perhaps you ought to know, Father," said Christobel anxiously, "but I didn't want to tell it before everybody."

Her father drew her out into the hall and she told him about Rannie's idea of pawning his watch to pay his debts. She saw a startled flash of intense sorrow pass over his face.

"I'm glad you told me," he said after a minute. "There may be something in it. Perhaps you ought to know that Rannie had not been doing as he ought at school. In fact he was seriously involved in a matter of stealing the examination questions from the safe, and he had practically been expelled."

"Oh, Father," said Christobel with distress in her voice. "Did Rannie know that? I'm sure he didn't know it when he talked to me. He was so eager to get back."

"No, he didn't know it until this afternoon. I just received the notice from the school before we went out to ride and I told him while you were in calling on Maggie. I am greatly troubled lest your brother has taken the matter to heart and gone away of his own accord."

The father sighed heavily, and Christobel's heart was wrung for him.

"Then he wouldn't have gone back to the school, would he? If he knew he was expelled?"

"I don't know," said the father with another troubled look. "You can't tell just what he had in mind. Rannie took an altogether cheerful view of the case. He seemed to think the action wouldn't hold. He may have got it into his head that he could persuade them to take him back and waive the disgrace. He said something to that effect. He seemed to think it wasn't serious at all. In fact he suggested that if I subscribed a good fat sum to the endowment fund it would all speedily be forgotten. I've just been thinking that perhaps he may have thought if he went back and ate humble pie and got around some members of the faculty, that he could avert further trouble."

"Have you told the police that?"

"No, not yet. I'm waiting till I hear from the school. If in a reasonable length of time he hasn't arrived, or by to-morrow morning at the latest, why I'll be sure it wasn't that. Anyway, child, it isn't essential that they know more than they do already. They are watching cars in every direction. Chris, go to bed at once. You are white as a sheet. There is no virtue in getting sick."

"Oh, Father, please let me just lie down on the couch near you somewhere!" she pleaded.

Just then the telephone rang furiously, and the anxious father hurried away, leaving Christobel like a little lost shadow hovering about the hall.

It was an hour before the father was at liberty. The telephone kept ringing just as soon as the receiver was hung up again. Business acquaintances calling up, asking questions, strangers with supposed clues to the missing son. One was sure he had seen him in a night club, another had seen a young man being driven furiously through a neighboring street, crying out and struggling. There were mysterious offers to restore him to his home for a consideration varying from fifty dollars to a hundred thousand and Christobel, shivering near the telephone booth to try and listen in felt her head grown dizzy and her heart sink. Her only hope was that there would presently come a message from the school, that after all crazy-headed Rannie had driven there in the hope of reinstating himself in favor and relieving his father from embarrassment and mortification over his only son.

Christobel knew enough of her brother's temperament to be sure his pride must be terribly hurt, and that he would not want to rest under humiliation. He adored his father.

The night wore on.

Maggie, who ordinarily would have been on the alert for Christobel, was absorbed in an orgy of scrubbing the kitchen, feeling that the quicker it was in immaculate order the sooner she would be able to rightly serve her master's family. Also her mind was much distraught at the disappearance of Rannie, and for Maggie to be anxious meant that she must plunge into her work hard and fast. She worked with wild Scotch prayers on her tongue, and tears flowing down her face, and she did not want the family to discover what she was doing and send her to bed, therefore she did not come out of the kitchen to discover that Christobel had not gone to bed.

It was Phil Harper who finally discovered her shivering behind the heavy curtains in the small reception room in the dark, crying her heart out all alone. It had seemed to her that death held sway upstairs where the vanished Charmian's room seemed to dominate the whole house; and that out of doors lay the menace of the great unknown underworld that might have spirited away her brother. Oh, why was life anyway? What an awful grilling thing was uncertainty. Perhaps even now Rannie was suffering somewhere, in peril of death, and they could not go to him because they did not know where to go.

"Now, little girl," said Philip, putting a firm brotherly hand upon her arm, "you are going to lie down. Wouldn't it be better for you to go up to your own bed? You could rest so much better there."

"Oh, no!" shivered Christobel, "I—I'm— quite all-r-rright!" Her teeth were fairly chattering.

"Oh no, you're not all right at all," he said gently, "your hands are like ice. Come over here then and lie on this couch." He led her over to the soft divan where she and Mrs. Romayne had sat that first night and piled pillows about her.

"Now, lie down there! Wait! You must have something over you."

He pushed her gently down among the pillows and vanished. She could hear him opening the door of the coat closet in the hall and then swinging back the door of the butler's pantry that led into the kitchen. In a moment he was back with a great soft robe that belonged to the car, wrapping it carefully about her with hands that were gentle as a woman's.

"You make a splendid nurse," she smiled up at him shyly in the dimly lighted room. The warmth and rest beginning to sooth her excited nerves and stop her trembling.

"I ought to," he answered pleasantly. "I've served my time waiting on Father."

"Oh, has he been sick a long time?" she asked sympathetically.

"Three years," he said grimly. "Now, you're going to drink some hot milk and go to sleep awhile. I'll promise to wake you if there's any news."

And there was Maggie, parting the curtains, and carrying a cup of hot milk. Oh, it was good to be taken care of. Christobel felt the tears coming to her eyes again. But she drank the milk and nestled down again among her pillows with just a little of the burden lifted. She was not going to sleep of course. She couldn't while the anxiety lasted. But it was good to lie down and relax.

The next thing she knew it was broad daylight, and there was a sound of confusion in the hall. A man was being brought in surrounded by several policemen. To her bewildered senses it seemed as if the hall were full of policemen, and then Maggie appeared cautiously, her cheeks redder than ever with excitement, tiptoeing toward her.

Christobel threw back her warm covers and sprang up in a hurry.

"I'm awake!" she said sharply. "What is it, Maggie, what has happened?"

"It's just that they want you to coom an' identify a dirty old tramp mon they've brought. You've only to take a luik at him, my bairnie. I tried to mak them wait till ye waked, but they was that hurried ye must cum the noo. He's just a wicked old filthy lookin' mon, but they would hev ye at oncet!"

So Christobel went to the library faithfully attended by Maggie, to face the man with the furtive eyes and stealthy step who had walked the pavement across the street the day before. A colorless creature with an indefinite face belied by the smoldering gaze he could cast. A thin, shadlike figure with the slump of one who had no shame. Just a drab scrap of fallen humanity who made a little link in a chain of vice and crime that might reach to the world's end. Who knew?

That smoldering gaze rested an instant on Christobel as she came into the room, and then flitted past her and faded into drabness again, and she shivered as she turned away and followed her father from the room attended by the faithful Maggie.

She was glad when they took the man away from the house. Was there no end to this procession of criminals? Were they all linked together for the ruin of her father's house? The cook, the maids, the chauffeur, the butler, and now this man? What a terrible world it was. Death and crime! And

Rannie had not been heard from. Father had talked with the president of Rannie's school and no one there knew anything of his whereabouts. Rannie was *gone!*

As the day passed on the house was besieged by visitors, friends and strangers, reporters and detectives and people who thought they had a clue that was worth following out.

And it was Philip Harper who found himself established in the house, standing between the master and this throng.

Hour and hour passed and each new report brought new hope, that faded into blankness again, and still Rannie was missing and no real clue to his whereabouts even faintly established.

11

AT last a mysterious typewritten letter arrived purporting to be from the kidnappers, demanding an appalling sum of money for Rannie's release. It bore a postmark in the far far west and even sent enclosed a bit of the blue silk necktie that Rannie had worn the night he disappeared. It stated that later arrangements would be made for placing the money under conditions of great secrecy and safety for the criminals, but that the money must be ready for instant demand in certain numbers of bills of small denomination, and that if the money were not forthcoming when the demand was made the young man would be killed.

Mr. Kershaw endeavored to keep knowledge of this from Christobel, but his agitation was so great, and his haggard appearance so aroused her anxiety that she finally got it out of him.

"It is better for me to know the truth, Father," she said. "I'll maybe think it is even worse than it is."

"How could it be?" said the father with a groan.

"I guess things can always be worse, can't they?" she answered with a wan smile.

"Perhaps you're right," he said and let her read the note.

"Are you going to give them all that money?" she said appalled at the sum demanded. "Can you, Father? Are you as rich as that?"

"Unfortunately not," said Mr. Kershaw with a wry twist of a bitter smile. "I used to be, but things have been going hard with me. I couldn't muster half that sum now.

Not even on credit. You see I've lost a lot lately. My stocks have gone away down so that they are not worth half their former value as collateral, and some of them wouldn't even be accepted at all. And there have been two big bank failures which have put me in a terrible situation financially. I have been afraid that I would not be able to weather the storm in my business. We have been holding our own, but I knew it was going to be pretty stiff sailing. And now this comes when I just do not know where to turn for money or credit. I shall have to go out and see what I can do. I have friends of course but some of them are in a worse situation than I am. I suppose I ought not to be telling you these things, but you will have to know sooner or later if I go under."

He sat slumped in a big leather chair in the library, a thin white hand up to his face, partly shading his eyes, his whole attitude that of a man who felt himself down and out. Christobel's heart went out to him and she found the tears slowly dropping down her cheeks.

"Oh, Father dear!" she said, "and you knew all that yet you bought me that lovely coat and hat and those new dresses."

"That was only a tiny drop in the bucket,"

206

sighed her father trying to smile indulgently at her. "Besides, they were things you needed, things that were your right and due. You have been too long cheated out of your birthright, Chris, dear. I hope if things ever straighten out I shall be able to make it up to you somehow, but as it stands I cannot forgive myself."

"Oh, don't talk that way, Father dear!" begged the girl. "It has been good for me, I know it has. I would have been proud and snobbish if I had had things the way I wanted them. I'm glad I learned first to do without them. And I'm glad they don't matter to me now."

"Well, you are a dear child. I don't want to say anything about your stepmother. She is dead. It is too late to undo the past. But sometimes I think I shall never forgive myself for having married such a woman, who spent my money on worthless friends and let my own children go without. However, she was young and ignorant and selfish. I was the most to blame. I should have known better than to marry her."

"Oh, don't feel so badly, Father!" begged Christobel, putting her arms about her father's neck and drawing his face close to her breast. "You are a dear, dear father, and you shall not talk about yourself that way—!"

The telephone bell suddenly ended the conversation, as it did so many of their talks. But when there was another opportunity Christobel said:

"Father, wouldn't it help you some if you were to sell this house and let us go and live in the old home?"

He lifted his sad eyes thoughtfully, then after a troubled silence he spoke.

"I suppose it might, if we could find a buyer, which is doubtful in these times, without absolutely throwing it away. But I can't bear the thought of going back into poverty with my children when I have been living in a palace with a selfish woman who did not care what became of me or mine."

"Listen, Father dear, please don't think of that. I would just love to get back in the dear old home with you and—and Rannie, wouldn't you? Wouldn't that be better than any palace?"

"Oh, it would!" groaned the father. "If only Rannie were back safe and well I'd gladly live in a tent the rest of my life."

"Well, he's coming back," said Christobel with an assurance she was far from feeling.

"I'm sure he is, and we'll be happy yet. Don't you believe so, Father?"

There was a pitiful pleading in her voice and her lip was trembling. Her father tried to smile, failed utterly and burying his face in his hands groaned instead. Then he lifted his head and spoke more steadily.

"Poor little girl. I oughtn't to give way. Yes, I feel almost sure we'll get Rannie back. We've got to believe it! The police are very sure. They think since this demand for ransom has been received there is a lot of hope. Now, good-by little girl, I've got to go out and see what can be done toward getting some ransom money ready. If I can get credit or loans—if we could just get Rannie back— why I'm sure I could pay it all back. Cheer up little girl. We'll keep hoping. We ought to be thankful you found young Harper. He's being a great help just now. I don't know what I'd do without him."

"Oh, I'm glad," said Christobel, "I've wondered whether you'd forgotten all about them. I don't suppose he's said anything about their house to you has he? I hope they won't lose it. He says his father has been sick several years."

"Their house? Oh, I told McCann to get in touch with their agent and arrange to take it over if the owners would sell, and re-finance it giving them more time. I'm sure he did it. McCann always does things at once and he would have let me know if there was any hitch. I talked to McCann just a little while before we found Rannie was missing. However I'm glad you reminded me. I'll check up on that and see if it was done."

Three minutes after her father left Philip Harper came in. There was something brisk and hopeful about him and Christobel felt cheered just by the very sight of him. He asked one or two questions about what had been happening since he was at the house last and then lingered watching her intently. Suddenly he said:

"I've been wanting to tell you—I don't know whether you believe in prayer or not, but my mother and I have been praying very earnestly that your brother will come safely back to you; and something happened to-day that has given me more faith than ever that our prayer is to be answered. Do you mind if I tell you a little thing that has happened in our own home? It seems very wonderful to me."

"Oh, I'd love to know," said Christobel hungrily, eager for anything that gave a shadow of hope for her brother.

"Well, you see we've been pretty hard hit during this depression," said the young man speaking in a low rapid tone, "and we got behind in the payments on our house. You see since Father was hurt there has been only June and myself to earn anything and sometimes one or the other of us didn't have work. But we managed to keep up the payments until about four months ago when we began to get behind again. The firm I was with had to close out their business and that left me stranded. I just couldn't seem to find a job anywhere. And the very day your father's firm wrote to me about coming to his office I had about given up. Mother and I had gone into the sitting room and shut everybody else out and knelt down to pray about it. It just seemed as though nobody but God could help, and after hunting a job so long without results it was hard to have faith that even God could do anything, with the state this country is in now—only of course we knew He could."

Christobel listened with rising color, feeling almost guilty that she should hear this intimate story of the prayer to which she had been an unintentional listener, but he was hurrying rapidly on.

"You see, I was pretty well all in, and my

faith was at a low ebb. In fact I had staked my faith on an answer to that prayer, and if it didn't come pretty soon I couldn't see anything ahead of us all but utter ruin. But that was what made it so very wonderful. Just that night, within a few hours from the time Mother and I had prayed and put it up to the Lord how desperate we were, the letter came offering me a job! *Offering* me a job, mind you, not my having to go out hunting and find one at last, but it came of itself. And then, this afternoon while I was praying in the few minutes I always take at noon, it came to me that I ought to be doing something about our house, and I couldn't take the time because I was really needed here while your father was away. And so I just put it up to God again; asked Him to look after the house for me while I helped you find your brother. And what do you think? Before I left the house the former agent called and gave us new papers, and told us the house had been taken over by a new owner and refinanced, and the payments made much easier. Why, it was just a miracle! Nothing less. And he said it would be all right if we waited another month before beginning the new payments. I can't get over the wonder of it. I never heard anything like it in business ways before. It was just God's doing, that was all!"

Christobel beamed a smile at him.

"I'm glad!" she said, and then with a sad wistfulness, "I wish I knew God. I would like to ask Him about Rannie."

She turned away with a quivering lip and her eyes brimming over with tears.

"Let's go and ask Him now," said Phil earnestly, "He knows you even if you don't know Him."

"But I would have no right," she said, "I haven't prayed to Him since, oh, a long time ago. A little while after my mother died. Things all went wrong and I prayed and prayed they would come right but they didn't and Rannie and I had to go away to school, and when I got there I stopped praying. My roommate didn't pray and she laughed at me for doing it, and I soon stopped. I thought it didn't do any good. I thought God didn't care anything about me any more. I wasn't even sure there was a God. Most of the people at school said there wasn't, only just a Force."

"Well, there is a God," said Phil convincingly. "He loves you and longs to have you trust Him."

"How do you know that? He answered you but He might not love me."

"I know because He says He does. Listen. 'For God so loved *the world*,' doesn't that include you? 'that He gave his only begotten Son, that whosoever believeth in Him should not perish but have everlasting life.' Doesn't that sound as if God loved you?"

"I suppose it does. But—what would I have to do?"

"Just believe," answered Phil gently. "Believe that His Son took your sins on Himself, when He died on the cross. The moment you accept Him as your Saviour you become a child of God, and have a right to come to Him and ask for the things you need."

"I've always sort of believed there was a God," mused Christobel with faraway gaze. "Mother of course used to tell Rannie and me about Jesus dying on the cross for our sins, but I never paid much attention."

"Well, this is an active belief. It is deliberately choosing to accept the gift of salvation that He bought for you with His life. Are you willing to believe that way?"

"Why, anybody would be willing to accept a gift of course," said Christobel, puzzled.

"No. Some people want to live their lives

without God. They will not believe. They want to trust in themselves, or in riches, or in people,—anything but to take the great gift God has given them."

"Oh, I would take it, and be so glad," said the girl lifting sweet earnest eyes to his face. "Just how do you do it? I would like to do it now."

A great light came into the boy's face.

"Come," he said placing a hand on her arm, "let's go into that little room and tell Him so. We shall not be interrupted there."

He drew the silvery curtains behind them and they walked the length of the great modern room and into Charmian's smaller white velvet shrine, sheathed in white frost of lace.

Christobel tossed the pagan silken doll from her cushion and there they knelt together, hand in hand, though they were not perhaps aware of that, and talked quite simply with the Heavenly Father.

"Heavenly Father," spoke the youth, "Christobel wants to accept Jesus Christ as her own personal Saviour. Thou hast said that the only way to be saved is to believe that He died in our place for the death we deserved. Now hear her according to Thy promise."

Phil hesitated, feeling the quickened pressure of the girl's hand in his, then he heard her voice, clear and sweet as a child's, "O God, I know I'm a sinner, but I do believe, and I want to be Thy child." It was all as quiet and simple as that, but when they rose to their feet there was a depth of gladness in Phil's eyes.

"Do you suppose He really heard us? Am I His child now? I don't feel any different, Phil," said Christobel wonderingly.

"We aren't saved by feeling, Christobel, and I'm mighty glad of it because sometimes I don't *feel* anything about it. We are saved because He says we are if we believe. That's the test of whether we really believe, if we are willing to take Him at His word without any feeling." He reached his hand into his pocket and thumbed through the worn pages of a little book.

"Read that, Chris," and he pointed to a verse.

" 'But as many as received him to them gave He the power to become the sons of God, even to them that believe on His name.' "

"All right," said Christobel trustingly, "I believe that. So I'm really a child of God!" Her eyes shone. "Now I want to ask Him about Rannie!"

Then down went the two heads again, and

Christobel's petition was like that of a little trusting child that left the precious brother in the safe keeping of a true and trusted Friend.

Maggie came trotting on her faithful old feet to hunt for her nursling, wanting to cheer the sad sweet face. Her own was red with anxiety, and her blue Scotch eyes bluer than ever and blurred with tears.

She heard low voices and pulled up a bit of the big silver drapery. Peering in across the great dim room she saw the two heads against the white frost of the window, bowed side by side in prayer. She noted the two hands clasped together, she heard the bairn praying for her brother, and dropping the silver curtain suddenly and turning her back she ducked her face into her gingham apron and sobbed noiselessly, her faithful shoulders shaking for a moment. Then she raised her head, and whispered under her breath: "Bless the bairnies!" and trotted away to her kitchen again to try to get up something to tempt the numbed appetites.

When Philip had gone Christobel sought Maggie in the kitchen. There was a peace upon her brow that had not been there an hour before, and the heavy burden seemed gone.

"Yer luikin' better, my bairnie," said the servant.

Christobel looked up with an unexpected smile.

"I've just found Jesus, Maggie, and He's taken the trembling away. I'm sure He's going to take care of Rannie, and maybe bring him back to us."

"I'm sure He will," spluttered Maggie, quite choked up with tears and brushing her hand quickly over her eyes. "Yer mommie believed, Miss Christie. Her last words was 'I'm trustin' Jesus!' Just like that! An' then she smiled and closed her eyes and was gone!"

"Oh, Maggie! Did she say that? I'm so glad you told me. If I had known that I would have tried praying before. I didn't know she believed."

"Oh, sure, she was a fine Christian, just an angel lady she was. Why, don't ye remember how she taught ye to say yer prayers? I mind oncet when Rannie, just a wee mannie, wouldn't say his 'nowIlayme,' an' yer mommie she looked sair grieved, an' she tuk him in her arms an' talked sweet like to him. Oh, yer mommie was one in a thousand!"

"I'm glad to know," said Christobel taking a deep breath. "I feel as though it is going to help."

She stood for a moment looking out the kitchen window thoughtfully and then turned back to Maggie.

"But Maggie, I came out to ask you if you would mind going up with me while I put away Charmian's things. I think Father would be glad to have that done and over."

"Sure, my bairnie," said Maggie giving a final polish to her flaming face with her drenched apron. "Sure I'll help ye if ye think yer equal to it to-day?" She gave the girl a scrutinizing look.

"Yes, Maggie, I've been kind of dreading it. I would rather feel that they were gone."

So together they went up to the locked room and began to set it in order.

It was Maggie who spread a sheet on the silk coverlet of the bed and began to fold garments and put them into piles upon it.

Christobel forced herself to go among the dresses picking out things she thought perhaps Charmian's mother could use. There were several suits, and smart silk frocks in dark colors. One could scarcely fancy the frumpy little mother of Charmian in anything so sophisticated, but perhaps they would give her pleasure.

Maggie folded everything neatly, advising and suggesting with wise elderly hints.

"I'm sure I don't know what we'll do with these evening dresses," said Christobel looking at the armful of tulle and taffeta.

"You'll not be wantin' to use thae yersel' sometime?" asked the nurse speculatively.

"Oh, no!" said Christobel with a little shiver. "I—would rather not. Besides, I'm not going into society. Father said I needn't. Mother didn't."

"Right you are, lambie!" said the nurse. "There's many dangers out in the world taday. Yer safer in than out. This world's gangin' all aglae! Well, why not sell thae claes then? I know a lady sells in one o' these second-hand shops. They pay wonderful prices fer dresses that's only ben wore a few times. Some o' thae dresses look like they'd scurcely ben wore at all. We'll look out some suit boxes an' fold them fine. Then I'll send fer my friend, an' yer poppie'll be surprised ta see how mooch they'll bring. Good money. I mind once I went with her to the shop an' I see nice ladies buyin' at big prices."

So they worked, sorting and folding and packing, until Charmian's wardrobe was in neat piles ready for immediate disposal. Plenty for Charmian's mother, a lot to be sold, and a goodly assortment to be given away, Maggie affirming that she knew a few people where they would do good.

"And the jewels we'll ask yer poppie aboot," said Maggie, as she finished with quick hand and discerning eye, separating the common strings of beads and costume jewelry from the real stones and jewels.

"He may like to sind a jeweler here ta look 'em over an' appraise 'em. They'll bring a-plenty if I'm not mistaken."

"I'm glad!" said Christobel simply. "Father may need a lot of money to ransom Rannie."

"Belike he will!" said Maggie heaving a quick sigh.

Then Maggie brought paper and string and boxes which she had somehow managed to locate in spite of her brief stay in the house, and presently Charmian's personal property was all under cover, and the room put in exquisite order again.

Christobel drew a long breath of relief when they had finished. Somehow the spirit of Charmian and of death seemed to be exorcised at last, and she no longer dreaded to look around the room. It was just a room now, no longer a reminder of the tomb. Or, was it possible that during that afternoon even a tomb had lost some of its horror? Christobel went downstairs wondering.

No one ate any dinner that night, though Maggie had prepared a tempting meal. There was an influx of officers into the house, a hurried consultation in the library, officers telephoning in different rooms where extra instruments had been installed, and a definite statement that a car answering to the description of the Kershaw car, had been found in the river several miles below the city. It had evidently gone over the embankment and been submerged for some days. There was a body in the car, but they had not yet been able to lift the machine enough to be sure whether the man was young or old. There was a rumor that there were several young people in the car. And the late afternoon papers came out with wild headlines and suggestions of possibilities. One might have thought to read them that Rannie Kershaw was a man of the world with a wild record behind him.

Mr. Kershaw and Philip went out with the officers very soon after the message arrived, the father with a white drawn face, and Christobel, after dutifully drinking the glass of milk upon which Maggie with tears insisted, stole into the darkness of the little white room beyond the great velvet parlor and knelt down beside the white velvet cushions to pray.

There was only the light that sparkled through the lovely crystal blossoms from the street arc lights, and sifted through the room like silver splinters. One fell across the pagan doll sprawled upon the floor near the kneeling girl, and lighted a curious dim picture, perhaps for the angels to look upon.

So Christobel prayed while her father went to the river to wait and watch for what should come, and presently she began to pray for her father.

"Oh, Father in heaven, let my precious father on earth come to believe, and to trust you!"

Over in the library the telephones rang, the officers tramped in and out, and the dim empty rooms echoed words back occasionally across the great black and silver and scarlet room in the dark, but they could not hurt Christobel any longer because whatever came she was hid in the "secret place of the Most High."

And then there was a sound of a car outside, of footsteps coming with measured tread, and with one final cry to her new Father in heaven Christobel sprang to her feet, with her hand upon her heart, and waited, saying over to herself that whatever came was all right because God was doing it.

12

BUT the man drowned in the river was not Rannie. So much was established beyond a doubt. He was short and thickset, and dressed in coarse garments. The car was not the Kershaw car, and this clue too had failed.

Christobel felt a great joy when she heard them talking about it in the hall, but when she caught a glimpse of her father's face after that long cold wait by the river, the wait that ended in the morgue, she knew that the heavy burden of her brother's disappearance bore down heavier than before upon his shoulders. After all, death was better than some things, and the agony of suspense was perhaps the most terrible thing that one could bear, especially when hope flickered and seemed about to pass out.

So Christobel stole back to the white velvet room and knelt alone again and prayed far into the night.

The next day a grim silent dogged determination seemed to settle down over the house. Desperate, that was the word that described Mr. Kershaw, and desperate Christobel would have been also if it had not been for her experience the afternoon before. She recognized that and longed that her father might find the Source of help that had been shown to her.

Quite late in the afternoon Mr. Kershaw came home with a stranger, a loud-mouthed, flashily dressed, illiterate person. Christobel looked at him half fearfully wondering if he could be connected with the kidnappers, if kidnappers they were who had taken Rannie away. But presently as she hovered in the offing and saw her father taking the man from room to room, heard his loud exclamations of delight, noted her father's grim silence, she began to surmise that this man was a possible purchaser for the house, and in spite of her anxiety, her heart gave a little spring of relief. Oh, if they could get out of this house which was connected with nothing but loneliness and death and horror! If there could be a real place called home for Rannie to come back to, how wonderful it would be!

The man came back just before dark and brought a woman and two girls about her own age with him. They were showily dressed and went about evidently gloating over the splendor of the rooms.

This time Philip was present and went around with Mr. Kershaw. Christobel kept out of sight but not quite out of hearing. She could catch some of the exclamations and comments upon the different articles of furniture, and especially the lofty condescending tone of the daughters as they essayed to instruct their mother in modern fashions and customs.

Christobel could see the weariness in her father's white, lined face, the utter disgust at their remarks, and his quiet reserve unless a direct question was asked him. She could see too that Philip was taking the heaviest burden of the matter from him, answering the questions of the mother and daughters, explaining the furnishings that were not understood. Christobel found herself wondering how he knew some of the things he told them, Philip Harper coming from the shabby old brick house on Seneca Street? For there was an ease and grace about Philip that made him a good salesman now, and the feminine strangers were evidently filled with deep admiration for him.

But oh, it was terrible that in the midst of their frantic trouble they had to stop to dicker with people like this. Christobel felt it deeply for her father.

Then there came the question if they could have the house, furnishings and all, just as it stood, and when they could have possession? They were evidently eager to bind the bargain and move in as soon as possible.

"He'll likely be a bootlegger got sudden rich!" whispered Maggie coming out of the pantry for a peep at the strangers and stealing up behind Christobel.

Philip came seeking her presently, and she heard her father saying:

"I think we can get out by the end of the week. I shall have to consult my daughter. And I'll ask her if there is anything she wants to reserve. If not it is as I stated, everything but the furniture in the master-bedroom, second floor front, and a few books and pictures and personal belongings."

So Christobel came out of her seclusion for a moment and stood with her father at the back of the hall while Philip took the strangers upstairs to look once more at the reserved furnishings of Mr. Kershaw's room.

They all came noisily down again in a moment, at least as noisily as any one could on the thick Turkish rugs that covered the stairs.

"It's all right," said the man loudly, "the wife says there ain't a thing in that room worth having. We'll have to get new things for that room but I guess that won't bother us any."

Christobel retreated once more from the prying eyes that would have studied her coldly and curiously, and the bargain was bound, to be consummated in the presence of a lawyer the next day.

Christobel and Maggie went down to Seneca Street the next morning and began to clean the old house.

There was a certain relief and pleasure in having something really necessary to do.

But Maggie would not let her nursling put her hands in water. She said it would roughen them. And though Christobel protested and wanted to do whatever Maggie was doing, she saw that it gave the faithful old nurse such pain that she finally consented to confine her labor to looking out clean sheets and table linen and getting out blankets and airing them on a line in the old back yard where she used to play as a little child.

Maggie had a regular system for housecleaning. The kitchen had to be cleaned first, and she lost no time in getting all the dishes out and piling them on the tables in dining room and kitchen while she washed all the shelves in the china closets and cupboards.

Then she let Christobel help with drying the dishes and putting them back. The girl did it almost reverently, for she remembered helping her mother put away the clean dishes when she was a little girl.

The gas and water had been turned on before they came so there was plenty of hot water, and when they went back to the big house that night they left behind them a clean kitchen and cupboards, with shining rows of dishes. Even the kitchen curtains of starched cheesecloth, yellow with age, but crisp as the day Maggie had packed them away in the big sideboard drawer, were hanging at the windows. The kitchen at least was ready to live in.

When Christobel went back in the late afternoon she began to hope and pray that there might have been news, wonderful news of Rannie while she was gone, but her father's face was as white and drawn as ever, and the three policemen who sat at the library desk with three telephones beside them seemed as busy and anxious and aloof as they had been the night before. There was nothing definite to tell, though the evening papers again flaunted rumors wild and tragic and unfounded, and people still kept coming to bring what they thought were new clues to the lost boy.

After dinner Christobel took refuge again in the little white room, for since the prayer yesterday it seemed to have lost its alien air and have become a sanctuary. The doll, too, had disappeared, for Maggie, in her scrupulous rounds, had told herself it was an outlandish, heathenish huzzy, and had tucked it away behind some books in the queer angular box-like case of inlaid wood that Charmian had called a bookcase. Then she stood a priceless sofa pillow up in front of it for safe keeping.

So Christobel sat beside the crystal light, and looked out on the street with eyes that unconsciously scanned every passer hoping to see Rannie, and constantly she prayed her little untaught prayers.

Philip found her there late in the evening and came and sat beside her.

"Are you all right?" he asked anxiously, studying her face in the flickering light of the street that came in over the crystal flowers.

"Yes, I'm all right," said Christobel softly. "I've just kept trusting all day or I couldn't have stood it."

"Bless you, child," he breathed, and it seemed like a benediction. "Keep on praying. I'm praying for you all the time. Don't forget that. I may have to go away to-morrow on an errand for your father, but I shall be praying all the time I am gone."

"You are such a comfort to Father," she said. "He told me."

"Thank you for telling me. I want to help all I can. Is it going to be hard for you to leave this magnificent home?"

"Oh, no, I'm so glad to go," said the girl quickly, with a little involuntary shudder. "I never felt at home here. In fact neither Rannie nor I were ever here more than a day or two at a time. This house was bought for my stepmother. I don't believe even Father ever was fond of it. I have been longing all these years to get back to our dear home on Seneca Street and now I'm so glad we can go. If Rannie were only here I would be happier than I have been since my own mother died. Maggie and I were down there nearly all day getting the house cleaned. We finished the kitchen and to-morrow we do the dining room, and then the bedrooms. If I wasn't so sorrowful about Rannie it would be lovely fun. It is so wonderful to touch the things my mother owned."

"It is wonderful of you to feel that way about leaving a palace like this. I am so glad you are that kind of girl. One would have expected you to be spoiled by wealth and the world. I am glad you are real," said the young man with deep admiration in his eyes, "and so glad," he added in a low tone, "so glad you know my Lord."

"I shall always owe that to you," breathed Christobel earnestly.

"It's a great joy for me to know you feel that way," said Philip, watching the lovely outline of her head against the brightness of the windows. "There is no joy on earth like being allowed to help some one find the way to Him."

Then suddenly a call came distantly from the hall.

"Mr. Harper? Is a Mr. Philip Harper in the house? Mr. Kershaw wants him on the phone."

Maggie came bustling down the hall to find him.

"Coming!" said Phil, hurrying across the big room and meeting Maggie at the threshold.

He came back from the telephone booth in a moment, his overcoat on, his hat in his hand, and smiled at her gravely as she stood in the doorway waiting to see if there were any new developments.

"I'm off," he said in a low tone. "It's a good lead. It may mean something real. I may be gone several days. But pray! Pray hard! With God all things are possible!"

Then he was gone, and Christobel crept back to the white sanctum to pray. It was all so new and strange to her to feel that God was really watching over the affairs of the earth and caring for individuals. She had anew to reassert her faith whenever she prayed on her own account. But somehow she felt when she prayed for Philip that it was more sure for he had known God for a long time, whereas she was only a beginner in faith.

The next day Maggie and Christobel worked on the dining room. It was to them both a great boon to have something legitimate in which to absorb themselves. Otherwise the long strain would have been terrible. For even the old nurse was suffering intensely from the anxiety about the missing boy.

They washed the paint, they took out the rug and hung it on a line, and gave a passing boy a quarter to come in and beat it and sweep it clean. They scrubbed the floor and washed the windows, at least Maggie did, and she set Christobel to ironing out the creases from the sweet old tamboured muslin curtains that belonged at the windows.

"It is so precious," said Christobel as she worked away running the rods into the smooth curtains, "to think that these are the very same curtains that Mother had. It makes the home so much more dear."

"Yes, it's fine," said Maggie, blinking back the tears that would come whenever they talked of the old days. "I mind when yer mommie bought thae curtains. She was that proud o' them, an' she had a red geranium on the winder shelf, an' a hangin' basket wi' wanderin' Jew an' ivy. Oh, it was a pretty room. I mind when we got thae curtains hung first. I helped her hemmin' them. They was that pretty—! That was only six months afore she died. I laundered thae curtains meself an' put 'em away but I never dared hope I'd be here to see 'em put up again in this same hoose. Oh, yer mommie'd be that glad ta see ye comin' back again!"

One good thing about working hard was that Christobel would be so tired out when she got back to the big house she would fall asleep in spite of her anxiety and the excitement that seemed to be in the very air the minute they opened the door.

For there were always strangers there, people of all classes come to bring word of having seen a mysterious car, or an unaccountable airplane, or an unidentified coat hanging over their back fence; anything that might possibly be connected with any kind of mystery, just so that they might come to the notice of a possible reward. It was pitiable how many poor creatures there were who had come miles to give some trifling bit of information that could have no possible connection with Rannie's disappearance, and who professed not to have money enough left to get back home again.

At first Rannie's father insisted on giving each one something but gradually the number increased so alarmingly that it became impossible to reward them all, or to judge rightly which deserved to be rewarded, for each bit of information that was run down proved to be worthless. The informants were carrion crows each hunting for gain, and using the slightest thread of a story to get entrance into the great house.

The third day Christobel and Maggie started in with the bedrooms, one at a time, cleaning paint and rugs and curtains, and oiling furniture. Christobel had never known before how much work there was to a house, just to put it in order for living, but she loved doing it all. It seemed as if for the first time since her mother died there was really some interest in living. If only Rannie were back! That thought put a blight upon everything she did. Yet she continually bolstered her hope by the thought that she was helping to get ready the house for Rannie's homecoming.

Mrs. Harper came over that third afternoon. She said she had meant to come sooner, but Mr. Harper had been suffering a great deal and she could not leave him.

Christobel loved her at first sight. She seemed to remember those sweet brown eyes out of her past, though they were tired and somewhat faded looking. She said to herself that Philip's mother was dear.

Maggie asked questions about "yer gude mon" as she called Mr. Harper, and told how kind she remembered he always was to "the childer." And Mrs. Harper seemed relieved to have some one to speak to about him. She said the doctor had been there that day and mentioned a great nerve specialist who was to visit the city in the spring, and said he wished his patient could see him, that he was a man who almost wrought miracles, and it might be that he could find a way to cure Mr. Harper.

"But we never could afford a great specialist, of course," sighed Mrs. Harper, "and I suppose I mustn't even think about it. But when I remember what he used to be before he was hurt—" her kind brown eyes filled with tears.

"Oh, but," said Maggie, wiping her ever-ready tears with the corner of her apron, "when Mister Phil hears of it he'll find a way to manage it I'm thinkin'. Mister Phil is a fine young mon. He's one ta be prood of."

"Yes," beamed the mother, "he is. But Phil is already carrying a heavy burden. Even with his new wonderful position I don't see how he can manage any more than he is carrying."

"Oh, there'll be a way!" insisted Maggie. "If only our Mister Rannie would come home I'm sure there'd be a way. Don't you get down-hearted."

Before Mrs. Harper left she spoke of June and how she was longing to renew her childhood acquaintance with Christobel. The lonely sorrowful girl's heart warmed with pleasure at the thought of having a girl friend who was brought up by a mother like this one.

Christobel had girl friends at school of course, but not intimates. She had been a shy child when she first went away from home, and had acquired a habit of reserve. Moreover she had not liked many of the ways of the modern girls who were in her classes, and so, though she had mingled with them of necessity, and taken part in all of the social activities and festivities of the school, she had kept much to herself, and as far as one could do so she had gone her own ways, shy, grave, wistful, and not at all a real part of the wild eager tempestuous youth that swarmed around her. For the truth was that her stepmother's act of sending her away from her home and her father had so utterly made her feel like an alien everywhere that at times her aloofness acted as a protection against the evil influences of the world.

But now, with the old home life again in view, suddenly that inferiority complex that Charmian had imposed upon her, was being torn away, and the sweetness of her nature was being revealed. It seemed too, that since she had found the Lord Jesus and begun to pray, her outlook on life had changed, and what had been blank and uninteresting before, had suddenly become vivid with interest. So that if only Rannie had been at home she would have felt that her cup of joy was overflowing.

But when they went back to the house that night they found excitement at the top heat. Two men had been arrested driving a car that bore the serial number of the Kershaw car. They were even now in custody and going through a grilling questioning. Mr. Kershaw was closeted with the detectives, and when he appeared for a moment he looked so worn and sick that Christobel was frightened.

Christobel and Maggie worked late that night, for Mr. Kershaw had come out long enough to drink a cup of coffee and tell them that the house was sold and the new owners must have private possession in five days. Christobel must go through the big house that evening and take anything that she wanted to keep and either pack it with her own personal baggage or put it in her father's bedroom, which would be locked, for to-morrow the new owners were to go through the house again and it was understood that everything that was left out was to go with the house. He mentioned a few articles, most of them trifles that he had himself purchased, one or two more rare paintings that he had brought home from a recent trip to Europe, that he wished to put away in his room for safe keeping.

If the daughter of the house had had her way, almost nothing would have been carried with them into the new life, but Maggie quite sensibly pointed out a few things in the kitchen, and here and there that would save new purchases for the other house, electrical contrivances that would greatly facilitate work, and would save much expense in many ways. So Maggie had her way, and several boxes and crates came up from the cellar and were neatly packed ready for moving.

Charmian's things had already been sent their various ways, and her room was ready in outlandish modern extravagance for its next crazy occupant, black bath tub, taffeta hangings, velvet carpeted dais and all.

It was a strange house, so little in it that any of the present occupants seemed to care in the least about. It was not until they went up in the great attic, floored for dancing, and arranged with game tables about, that they found in some of the closets a few old trunks and boxes containing possessions that were distinctly Mr. Kershaw's and had nothing to do with his second wife. A good many of the things in the trunks held wornout clothing, but down beneath it there were rolls of flannel containing silver, Christobel's mother's wedding silver, marked with her maiden name. Not a great deal of it, but lovely and heavy, and worth a great deal to the girl, who unwrapped some of the teaspoons and cried over them and thanked God for saving them for her.

Mr. Kershaw had scarcely time now to eat. A letter had arrived bearing another scrap of blue silk purporting to be another bit of Rannie's necktie, the only trouble being that it did not match the first sample sent. The pity of it was that neither Christobel nor her father were familiar enough with Rannie's ties to know whether either of the bits of silk was a part of the tie that he had worn the day he disappeared. His sister had cried over the silk and spent time going over the blue ties that were left in his room, but neither she nor her father nor Maggie, who professed to have noticed every thread the lad had on when she first laid her eyes on him, could be sure about it.

The letter however had demanded a still larger ransom than the first one, and went further into details as to how it should be delivered, and Rannie's father was in a feverish haste to gather enough money together to have in readiness. Oh, the weary waiting hours! Oh, if Rannie would only come back! Oh, if Philip Harper would come back. It was so much easier, when he was around, to pray and to believe that God was hearing.

Quite early the next morning a large moving van arrived and took all that was to go to the other house except a few clothes and toilet articles, and when the new owner of the house arrived the place was ready for inspection and approval, and the bargain was completed. Mr. Kershaw had the check in his possession, and Rannie's ransom was materially increased.

There were still some possessions in various parts of the world that might possibly be disposed of. There were Charmian's jewels to be appraised, and a substantial amount might be raised from many of Charmian's other possessions. There was a riding horse expensively housed at a riding club. There were two cars, practically new, that she had bought and tossed aside like toys. There was Mr. Kershaw's own life insurance. He would lose heavily of course if he cashed it in now, but every penny had to count now, for the ransom must be ready.

And meantime the newspapers and radio

were broadcasting enormous suppositions of the amount of the rumored ransom demanded.

13

OUT of the darkness of a strange new kind of night crept Rannie, back into a queer numb unconsciousness.

There were strange memories of wheels going around, the humming of a motor, the screeching of brakes, the jarring of his body being bumped up and down, a ringing in his ears, an unpleasant taste in his mouth. His head seemed to belong to somebody else and his eyes were weighted down. At least they would not open. Gradually it became clear to him that there was a bandage bound about his eyes, and when he essayed to lift his hand and pull it away he found his hands were so heavy that they would not move. In fact they seemed to be made of lead. After what appeared to be eons of thought he decided that he must be dead, and perhaps buried, which accounted for the thing over his eyes, only he could not understand the strange disturbance under him, like wheels under a car, and ruts under the wheels; there was a bumping and tossing of himself about. Perhaps it was some strange disturbance under the earth.

He felt a chilly draft down his back. His neck felt like ice. He wished he could pull his collar up. If his arms would only work! But people were cold when they were dead of course. That was natural.

After an unmeasurable interval of blankness again he began to remember unexplained stoppings of the motion under him, and being lifted somewhere in haste, and roughly, only he couldn't cry out because of an ill-smelling rag in his mouth. Now what could that have to do with the scheme of things? And why did they have to move him so often? Could it be that they were just having the funeral? After all this time? Where were they burying him anyway? Away off up in New England where his grandmother and grandfather were buried? Gee! Would he have a stone like theirs, all moss covered and tippy, with Randall Robinson Kershaw, born—He began to feel all choked up thinking about it. Good night! He didn't know people could think and feel this way after they were dead!

A little while later it occurred to him to wonder how it was that he had died? He hadn't been sick. Why, the last thing he could remember was bringing Maggie home and carrying in her suitcase. Then what did he do? Oh, drove around to the garage to put the car away. Had there been an accident on the way, some other car run into him and smashed everything up? Say, that was awful, for Dad to have to go through a thing like that, lose his car maybe, but of course he would have it insured. No, he distinctly remembered now having turned into the drive behind the house, and no other car ahead of him. He could see the long streaks of brightness in the lane from the car lights. He remembered driving into the garage and stopping the car. He was sure he could. He could even remember getting out of the car, and then a sudden remembrance of that dull thud on his head and everything ended. Blinked out! Black obliteration!

What had he done? Stooped over and hit his head against something? It began to hurt his head to think about it, and another blackness came blessedly over him again.

But the next time he came out of it he knew. Sandbagged, that was the word. It figured in lots of mystery stories. Some thug had hit him over the head! But what for? He hadn't a thing about him to steal except his watch. Would just a watch be worth running a risk like that?

And then he heard voices, low and rough. Gee! Could you hear people talk when you were dead? That was going to make it interesting. He hadn't expected that.

" 'Bout time for the kid ta wake up," one voice said. "Guess it'll be safe ta take that stuffin' outta his mouth sometime soon. We don't want 'im ta croke, not just yet anyhow, an' he's ben a long time that way. We're two good hours inta the woods now. No chance of any spies around here this time o' year."

"He ain't a-goin'ta croke that easy," said a harder voice firmly. "Wait till we're over the ridge of the mountain an' can carry him inta shelter. We don't want no hollerins till we get him outta sight. You never can tell what's around in the woods, even deep woods like these, an' we ain't takin' no chances, see?"

Silence succeeded this ultimatum and Rannie lay like a log and thought it over.

Then he wasn't dead after all, unless he was just hearing things about somebody else. His mind seemed very hazy. Perhaps he was only dreaming. Perhaps he wasn't really here at all. He might be at home in his bed having a nightmare. Or even at school and everything that had happened since that telegram about Charmian's dying was only just a dream. He tried wiggling his toes, and found they worked. He surely wasn't dead if he could move his toes. Even in a nightmare one couldn't move anything.

Just then beneath him there came a tremendous thump like bumping over a rough road.

"Say, what're ya trying ta do? Wreck us?" said the hard voice in command. "What's the idea runnin' over a log like that?"

The other voice murmured something incoherent about not being able to run a car around every twig in unknown darkness.

Then the hard older voice spoke with a quiet terrible edge.

"Try it again and I'll put you on the spot!" it said, and Rannie heard a click as of a ready weapon.

"I was only havin' a little joke," pleaded the other.

"This ain't a jokin' matter, see? This here is serious business. You ain't the only one who can run a car. An' I c'n carry that kid ta the cabin an' think nothin' of it. Not so many ta divvy up with either when the ransom comes in. Dead men can't tell no tales either."

There was silence again, awful silence, and

the car rode more steadily, just grazing branches sometimes for Rannie could hear their sweep against the sides of the car, but he did not stir; just lay there and listened, and thought over what he had just heard. And then, while he was trying to piece it all together with his muddled brain and make out just what it all meant, the older man spoke again. And this time the things he said were beyond all that Rannie's wildest school-boy imaginings, gleaned from highly wrought detective stories, had ever conceived. It was bloodcurdling, cruel, inhuman. The boy shuddered and turned sick with the horror of it all, and suddenly knew clearly and normally what he was up against. It was like a dash of cold water in his face that brought him entirely to his senses. He knew that he was in the power of men who would stop at nothing. He was utterly helpless. He had been kidnapped for a price, and these men would hold out for a large ransom or kill him as easily as they would have killed a rat.

Rannie was glad that it was dark. He did not have to study to control his face nor worry lest there might be sudden tears in his eyes. He had time to think it out and see what he was up against. Lying there like an inert thing, with his senses all alive again, and all his bright hopes of life in the power of these two ruthless men in the front seat, he had time to look his situation in the face.

It is true that he wasted the first few minutes in helpless wrath and fury against his fate, in wishing for weapons that he might return upon the heads of his kidnappers some of the evil they seemed so ready to deal out to everybody.

Then his healthy young mind began to see the futility of such thoughts and came back to calm, cool reason. He began to wonder why his hands and arms seemed so numb and useless, and testing them he found that they were not only shackled but bound firmly to his sides, and the attempt to lift one foot made it evident that his ankles were shackled together.

Quickly he relaxed, fearful lest the shackles would make a noise and attract the attention of his captors. He must think this thing through and plan out a line of action before they reached whatever destination was meant by the cabin they had spoken of.

Should he try to remain asleep indefinitely? Well, that would have to end sometime or other of course, or he would die. There would likely be an attempt to bring him to his senses if he simulated unconsciousness too long. No, he had got to have a line of action ready. It was his only weapon.

So Rannie lay and thought.

And between thoughts and plans there came waves of mortification over him. He could feel the hotness even in his cold cheeks, and rushing up the back of his neck where the draught was creeping down so intimately. And the mortification was that he, the cheerleader of the basketball team, should be lying here helpless, unable even to think of anything he could do to frustrate this outrage.

Gradually his anger died down and he was able to face his immediate situation. The word ransom came home keenly. That meant that his father would have to pay a large sum of money if he ever was to be free. Indeed, from the words of the cruel-tongued man, he judged that he was by no means sure of freedom even then. If there was any danger at all of exposure for the captors they were planning in cool blood to kill him and stow him away where never through the ages would his body even be found. They talked about that, too, in low tones, arranging the details in case of sudden raid.

Well, there he was, facing a situation like that, and nothing between him and torturing death but money, great sums of money! And his father was about to fail in business!

Clearly it came across his memory now, all that his father had said to him about his financial condition, while Chris was in talking to Maggie. Queer he should have got to know that just before this happened! If he hadn't known how Dad was situated it would have seemed a trifling matter! Dad would fix it up, hand over the money any way they said, and he would be out and away, a hero with a great experience to look back upon.

But as it was, how could he let his father pay money for his ransom? He hadn't the money to pay. And the appalling sum these thugs were going to demand was out of the question of course for any but a multi-millionaire, such as he had always supposed his father was.

After thrashing the matter over and over with his poor aching head Rannie came to just one decided decision. Somehow he must manage that Dad wouldn't have to pay a cent. Some kind of scheme he must concoct that would prevent any demand upon his father. Perhaps they would insist upon his writing a letter asking his father for the money, and how could he write it knowing what straits his father was in? No, he certainly wouldn't. Let them kill him or torture him with red hot pokers if they wanted to, the way they did in the Dead-eye Dick stories. What difference did it make if he was dead? He was no good any way. Fired from school. What was there left for him in life? Nothing except to die manfully.

There were intervals when his mind lapsed into a haze again and couldn't quite piece things together any more, intervals in which perhaps he slept, he wasn't quite sure. It was humiliating to have slept with such momentous things to settle, but his captors must have given him some knock-out drops or dope, he felt so dizzy and sick at times, and the pain in his head kept coming back again.

But after what seemed like hours and hours of bumping over an uneven road, the car at last came to a halt, and Rannie had made up a general line of action to which he meant to stick like grim death in spite of all obstacles.

One thing he had decided as a basic principle. He would not let these thugs see that he was afraid of them. That was to be his main reliance.

Acting on this principle he decided that to remain unconscious as long as possible would be a good way. He would be apt to overhear more of their plans, and might get a line on something that would help.

So when he was finally lifted out of the car by the united efforts of the two men he made himself a dead weight, and let his head roll as if it had no volition of its own. Of course he couldn't have moved very far if he had tried, but he felt it better to keep out of the picture as long as he could, seeing there was nothing to be gained by appearing conscious.

He lay inert on the ground; it seemed rough stony ground where he lay, and he was sure his head was on a piece of flat rock. But he could smell pine needles, and when they laid him down the men's feet had slipped.

And now by the sound the men were unloading boxes. They spoke little, except warnings about hiding the stuff among the thick laurel bushes. He could hear the car driven away down the mountain in the opposite direction from which they had approached, and the remaining man sat down near by and smoked. A little later Rannie could hear him puffing and panting, working with something about his feet. Sometimes he got up and shook his feet and stamped a little, and Rannie finally decided he must be tying bags about his shoes to hide his tracks.

The boy decided it must be morning for something warm and comforting like sunshine was on his face, and one spot on his shoulder, and his hand. He wanted to shiver with the pleasure of the warmth, but he held himself rigid, trying to breathe but very little, and after what seemed a long, long time the other man came back on foot, mulling along heavily as if his feet were padded.

"Tie them things on tighter, Bud," said the older man whom Rannie now perceived was the boss. "If they come off on the way it'll be just too bad."

"Kid moved yet?" asked Bud.

"Still dead ta the world," said the boss.

"How fur is this?" asked Bud clumping near to Rannie's feet. "I'm about wore out now, drivin' all night an' half yes't'day."

"I thought you were a *man!*" sneered the boss in a meaningful tone. "Ef you say the word I'll put a bullet through ya yet an' take the whole ransom myself."

"Cut that out!" said Bud angrily. "I'se only kiddin' an' you know it."

Only grim silence was the answer.

A moment later Rannie felt himself lifted and carried forward much as if he had been a dead body, one man at his head, the other at his feet.

For an hour or more they went forward thus. Rannie could not be sure how long for his body grew sore and weary, and the strain seemed desperately unending. From time to time they would put him down, and each time he hoped it was the end of the journey, for it was beginning to seem impossible to endure, but suddenly with a lurch the men stumbled inside a shelter. He knew because even through the bandage that swathed his eyes he felt the light grow dimmer.

They dropped him down on the floor and he heard a door shut, a heavy wooden door that did not fit its frame and had to be jammed into place. He heard a great bolt drawn, and then to his utter relief the horrible gag was removed from his mouth, and his jaws which were aching desperately might slowly relax.

He heard the breathing of the boss as he stooped over him to listen, felt a great hand pawing around over his heart.

"He's okay!" said the hard voice as the boss straightened up. "Let's put him in the end room and take off his bandage. He'll come to all right. Lift up yer end there, ready now!"

Again Rannie was lifted and moved; this time much to his surprise he found himself on a hard little army cot.

"Now, take off that binder!" commanded the boss, "and then we can leave him be for a bit. We gotta get some grub. He'll come to in plenty o' time."

Bud somewhat roughly removed the bandage from his eyes, and dropped his head back ungently upon the pillowless cot, but Rannie kept his eyes closed and his face motionless, and only drew a small short breath like a sigh.

The men stood still near him for a moment, then slowly clumped out fastening the door shut behind them. It sounded as if there must be a bolt on the wrong side of his door.

Rannie lay still and knew he was a prisoner.

Cautiously he opened his eyes and looked about him. It was a small log room in which he was incarcerated, with only one small high window far above his head, through which a thickly shadowed daylight crept dimly, and wafted leaves of trees made faint flicker on the opposite wall. The window was high over his head and back of him and the side of the cot was against the log wall.

A movement outside his door sent his eyelids shut again till he heard the men talking in low tones. Bud was being sent back for some of the baggage which had been cached in the bushes. He was protesting, but the boss was inexorable, and always the ransom money was held over him like a forfeit.

Bud's footsteps had hardly died away when Rannie heard the gurgle of a bottle, the clink of a glass, the gulping of a drink, and his soul began to thirst for water. Oh, if he might just have a taste of cool water on his tongue. His swollen, dry tongue! How he longed to cry out. How his soul loathed the taste of the old rag that had been so long in his mouth! But the silence settled down about him, with a soft faint sound of branches scraping against the roof, a blessed reminder that there was still an out-of-doors not far away. Rannie must have fallen asleep for a little while, for afterwards he had no memory of any happening till he heard Bud's footsteps once more, and the hard voice berating him for being so long.

Then there were sounds in the outer room, footsteps, the clatter of something tin, a cup and a plate put down on a table, the delicious maddening odor of bacon cooking, the smell of coffee coming through the thin partition.

Rannie presently discovered that there were cracks in the rude partition where he could see through, and he watched the two figures moving about making streaks of darkness over the brighter cracks between the logs. Then he began to know that he was desperately hungry, hungrier than he ever was before, not even excepting the time of the training table of football season. He began to wonder when he had last eaten and if his captors were going to starve him to death.

He could hear them mouthing their food now in the next room, not stopping to talk till their hunger was satisfied. Then as they gradually were filled he could hear a word now and then.

"As soon as it's absolutely dark you eat again and then get a hustle down ta that car," the boss announced. "You gotta get that first note down acrost the state an' a good two hundred miles away ta mail by tamorra mornin'. It had oughtta be mailed afore daylight at some little country town around where we was last week. Then you streak it back around the other side of the mountain an' get back here around tamorra night ur at least afore daybreak, see? After that we'll havta depend on Spike fer signals afore we'll dast make the second strike."

Bud grumbled but the boss shoved back the box on which he had been sitting and gave another command.

"Bring that here plate of vittles an' some coffee an' we'll go an' feed the kid now. It's time he was comin' to. We gotta be able ta say he's safe an' well ya know."

Rannie drew a deep breath as he heard his bolt drawn back and waited. His time had come. Would his scheme work? He must make it.

14

THE door was thrown back and Rannie's closed eyes felt the daylight coming into the dim room where he lay. He waited until the two men had advanced and stood beside his cot looking down at him, and then he suddenly opened his eyes wide, blinked a moment to get used to the light, gazed around at his surroundings, and tried to lift a casual hand. He looked in well-feigned surprise down at his shackles, then focused an amazed scrutiny on his two captors and suddenly

and amazingly let his face break into an impish grin of pleased surprise.

"Oh, gee!" he said in his best school ver-
nacular, "I ain't been kidnapped have I? Not
really? Gee, isn't that great! I've always wondered how it would feel! Say, this is great! I
wonder what the fellas back in school 'll
think when they hear it. They'll be green
with envy."

The two captors stopped in astonishment
and scowled at their captive, disarmed for
the moment. The boss spoke, softening his
hard voice into a gruff growl intended for a
false pleasantry.

"Feelin' pretty good, ain't ya kid? One o'
them high-sperited modern kids ain't ya?
Well, I guess ya'll have plenty use fer high
sperits afore ya git through 'ith us. But ya
ain't got no need ta be scairt ef ya do jes' as
we say. We don't aim ta hurt ya ef ya do yer
part an' everythin' goes through okay. Here,
eat yer grub. Ya oughtta be plenty ready fer
it."

"Sure thing!" swaggered Rannie essaying
to rise and finding his head swimming diz-
zily. "Got any water there? Seem kinda dry
after that old rag you stuffed into my mouth.
I s'pose ya hadta do that, didn't ya? It's okay
with me of course, only I can't say it's the

tastiest mouthful I ever had. Say, after we get fixed here and ya have plenty a' time I'd liketa know just how you pulled this off from start ta finish. I've always wondered how they did it, but I don't seem somehow ta remember much that happened about the time you began on me."

The two men cast a second astonished glance at one another and lowered the plate of uninviting dinner to Rannie's knees.

Rannie tried to lift a shackled hand to steady the plate but his arms were still bound with cords to his sides as far down as his elbows.

"Say, ya couldn't just loosen up these bracelets an inch ur so, couldya?" he asked genially looking up at the boss. "I can't seem ta navigate so well. It's just that I ain't accustomed ya know. It takes practice ta eat with things like this on ya. Something like chop sticks I guess. Ever been ta China? There was a fella in our school whose dad was a sea captain and he went around the world with him when he was a little kid. He useta tell how they ate with chop sticks just as easy as we use forks."

They loosened up the cords leaving Rannie's arms freer, and arranged the chains on his wrist so he could move his hands more easily.

Now that food was before him, it looked so unappetizing even in the dim light, Rannie felt little inclination to eat. The bacon was reeking with grease, and was quite cold. The bread was stale, and the coffee had a queer taste. He decided against drinking it. He felt it might be doped. He drank the water eagerly, however, that Bud brought at the direction of the boss, and managed to make a show of eating. But when he looked up from the last bite he saw that the two men before him each held a revolver in his hand, and that the boss' gun was pointed straight at him.

Something seemed to happen to his heart just then, but he took a deep breath and broke into his impish grin again. Some one, some trainer perhaps, in his faraway football days had once said that if you were frightened the best way was to laugh, so Rannie grinned. It was the one thing he was sure he could do well, and lips couldn't very well tremble when they were stretched in a wide grin. So Rannie grinned.

"Oh gee!" he said when he had got control of his wits again. "Is that what you carry? What make are they? Are they the noiseless, smokeless kind? I've always wanted ta see one. Say, will ya teach me ta shoot ef I stay here long enough? I sure would liketa own one of those babies. I guess they make a pretty shot, don't they?"

Rannie was nothing if he was not impudent, and at school he was known as having a line of talk equal to any one on campus. The boys said he could kid the eye teeth out of a cop if he really wanted to, and they always sent Rannie on the difficult errands. So now Rannie summoned all his arts of speech, and grinned straight into the eye of that terrible instrument of death that he knew in the waft of a breath could blow him into the next world.

His two captors eyed him almost with admiration, though the boss narrowed his gaze as he watched the boy. He wasn't altogether sure he was as carefree and gay as he looked. He was pretty white around the gills though he sure was a game kid. The boss was old and experienced.

"You get a chance ta see what kind of a hole they make in yer own heart ef ya don't do as yer told," growled the boss. "See?"

"Oh, sure," swaggered Rannie, "I know yer a tough egg all right. That's why I admire ya sa much. Say, this is goin'ta be a great experience fer me all right ain't it?"

"I'll say!" said the boss dryly. "Now, Bud, ya can take him out fer a stroll just ta see how fur he is from any help, an' when ya come back it's time fer ya ta sleep, see?" He winked one eye in a professional way and sauntered out of the room, but Rannie had a feeling that he had eyes in the back of his head.

Bud helped Rannie to get to his feet, and though he felt exceedingly shaky, and was greatly hampered by the chains about his feet he managed to get himself out through the main room and across the threshold into the outer world.

It was thick woods where the cabin stood. The growth was so dense that it seemed just dusk instead of late afternoon as it really was.

Rannie had no idea how long he would be allowed out, so he scanned the place most carefully, while trying not to seem to do so. He remembered a party he had attended once where in one of the games a table filled with a number of objects was brought out for a ten-second inspection. Rannie had won first prize for remembering every one of them. He had always been good at observation. He prided himself on being able to remember everything he had seen. So now he cast a quick glance about and then looked up to the sky which must be overhead, but was entirely obscured by tall plumy pines.

"Say, it's great here, isn't it?" he declared drawing in a deep breath and grinning at his guard. "This would be wonderful in the summer time with the trees all out and birds singing." He had the jaunty air of a guest at a house party, though he was shivering in the keen mountain air, and for the first time really noticing the shoddy, ill-fitting, much worn garments he was wearing.

"Wish I'd remembered ta bring my over-coat along, ur my heavy sweater," he said with another grin pulling his inadequate coat collar up around his neck. "Great oversight. However, I s'pose one gets usedta bein' chilly."

Rannie tried not to wonder who had worn these clothes before he fell heir to them. He tried with all his dizzy frightened might to keep his grin and act as if he were enjoying himself. Bud looked at him curiously with a growing admiration.

"Well, this certainly is great fer a summer camp," said Rannie as Bud led him along around the tangled growth, and out into a semi-clearing where rocks jutted out from the side of the mountain and one could see a long way off.

There were mountains on every side, and more mountains stretching purply like clouds along the horizon. Rannie scanned them eagerly to see if there was a single familiar outline of the rugged peaks they could see from the school camp last summer. He had an idea that perhaps he was somewhere in the Adirondacks or Catskills, or perhaps even farther north and east up in the lonely stretches of Vermont and New Hampshire. He had nothing whatever to judge by for he had no idea how long he had been traveling before he began to come to consciousness. He felt sure by his own wretched feelings that it had been a long journey he had come. But his sense of direction had always been great, and now as he scanned the landscape quickly he took careful note of where the sun lay, and tried to get the points of the compass. But there was no sign along the skyline of the Presidential range or any of the mountain peaks he knew. Nothing but wild bare trees varied by great patches of dark plumy pines.

"Any water around here for fishing?" queried Rannie affably. "You 'n' I might go fishing if we had any line an' bait."

Bud whirled him around and led him to the other side of the cliff where was a startling precipice, sheer and steep, and below a rushing mountain torrent tearing and plunging and boiling into a deep green caldron far below where they were standing. Rannie instinctively drew back and closed his eyes a second to steady his dizzy head.

"Bad place ta fall!" suggested the attendant dryly, almost significantly, turning Rannie about and steering him back to the undergrowth to the cabin.

"It sure is," said Rannie politely, reflecting on how easily his body could be made away with in this lonely spot with such a watery tomb so close at hand.

Back to his small dark log cell went Rannie, glad to lie down on even the hard army cot because it seemed as if he had been on a long journey. How could one get so weary just taking a few steps?

Quiet settled down upon the wilderness save for the stirring of a branch now and then in the breeze, the crack of a twig here and there under some silent stealthy furry foot perhaps. And presently he could hear two separate kinds of snores from the other room.

He had heard the bolt slide sharply into place and knew that he was shut in hopelessly. He wanted to get up and move around his tiny box cell and explore a bit, see if he could possibly climb up to that little square of a window and measure his shoulders to its size, but a great inertia was upon him, and also he feared to wake his captors yet. So he lay still and must have been almost at once asleep.

When he woke up he sensed at once even before he opened his eyes that it must be night. The blackness about him seemed so dense that it could be felt. He reached out and touched the wall, and then a cover that had been spread over him. A rough ill-smelling blanket. He was grateful for the warmth, yet startled that it could have been spread over him without his knowledge. Then his captors must have been in to look at him! Had they doped him again that he slept so soundly, or was it just the effect of the first knockout that had not yet worn off?

He lay still and listened to the far sound of water rolling down over age-old rocks, and shuddered at the sinister pool that he knew might be so easily reached. Yet even so, the boy reflected, it might be a more welcome death than some, if it came to that.

He thought he heard a distant howl of an animal. Would that be a wolf? Were they far enough from civilization for wolves and coyotes?

He thought of his father and Christobel wondering where he was. Well, perhaps his absence might somehow make his father more forgiving toward his misdeeds. He had a passing sorrow that he had brought that gray look to his father's face, that tired look to his eyes. He thought of Charmian, lying dead in her coffin, a silly little empty painted face, painted even in death, and he felt a strange wonder at her, that the dignity of death should have been granted her apathy toward life. Then he knew that against his will he was falling asleep again. He wondered how long life would be like that, whether it would ever end? Would it end in that deep green pool after a shove from the precipice, a swift hurtling through space, and then oblivion? Would it be oblivion, or was there something else beyond? Where was his mother? Did she know where he was now? That little crib beside the big house on Seneca Street! How sweet it must have been to be a little boy and lie there cared for and guarded!

Morning came with a rough shake. The boss had brought him his breakfast. Dry bread and condensed milk. The boss was impatient. His breath smelled of sour liquor. Bud was not anywhere around. Rannie recognized suddenly that he liked Bud a great deal better than the boss. Why should one admire one crook above another? But he did. There was sometimes a gleam of something almost human about Bud.

Rannie managed a few bites, and wondered why he had complained so much about the table fare at school. The food was not appetizing and the surroundings were filthy. But Rannie tried to be gay.

"Say, Boss," he said as he handed back the tin plate that obviously had not been washed since yesterday's meal of bacon, "what about givin' me a job? I got fired from the school the other day an' I gotta get myself a job. I'm pretty good at gettin' away with most anythin'. What d'ya say? Got an opening for me?"

The boss looked at the boy quizzically a moment and narrowed his eyes.

"Yep," he responded. "I gotta job fer you right now, leastways as soon as Bud gets back. One you gotta do whether ye like it ur not. I want a letter writ an' you gotta say jus' wot I tell ya. Savvy?"

"Oh, sure, I can write letters," said Rannie with a sudden sinking of heart. It was coming now, and what was he going to do about it?

"Say," he said hoping to change the topic, "ever play basketball?"

"Whaddaya think I am?" growled the boss. "Somebody's darling? I was doing tough stuff when other fellas was the age ta play basketball. I reckon that's about your size, basketball! Basketball! Ugh!" he uttered a grunt of disgust. "An' you think you'd train fer a buddy of ours do ya! Ha! Been dancing round on a ten cent piece pattin' a ball an' trimmin' it inta a basket with a hole in the bottom! Hot stuff! You'd make one all right," said the boss with a sneer that was ugly to see.

"Aw, now, don't get funny," he grinned gayly. "I was just cheerleader for 'em, kinda help 'em out ya know. I wasn't givin' that as a reference. Say, how 'bout wrestlin'. You're up in that aren't ya? You gotta grand build fer wrestlin' I should think."

"What's the idea?" roared the boss now thoroughly mystified. "What ya gettin' at?"

"Oh, I was just thinkin' of a little exercise," said Rannie nonchalantly. "Feel a little stiff myself after that long trek yesterday, don't you? I thought ef you were a good wrestler we might have a round or two. Or boxing. Only of course we haven't any gloves."

The boss frowned deeply.

"You better get in yer box, young feller, an' stay there till I tell ya different, ur y'll have a kind a exercise ya ain't useta, and I'm tellin' ya."

With that the boss went out and locked the door, and Rannie was left to his own meditations.

He felt better than the night before. His spirits were better also. He had got away with kidding the boss, he might get away with more. At least he was sure the boss hadn't known how near the surface were tears while he was grinning. And what was more he hadn't had to write any letter home as yet. The next task was to discover a way to get out if there was such a way, though his reason told him that as long as those two bullies guarded his way with two smokeless, noiseless guns there was little chance.

He took the first opportunity when he heard the boss step out of the door to climb cautiously up as high as he could toward the window. There were only a few chinks where there was a foothold and it was a slow task because the chains about his ankles clinked noisily. He did not want to get caught in the act. He did not know what might be the consequences. Also, it would injure his attitude of indifference to be found looking out the window, or trying to. So presently he gave it up and dropped like a cat to the floor again.

An awful feeling of being trapped came over him. In prison, that was what he was. How long could he keep it up?

He began to feel around in the tattered pockets of his alien suit to find a stray pencil or scrap of paper, anything to occupy the time, but there was nothing. It was terrible to be shut into the contracted dimness when outside the sun must be shining. He knew that by the color of the yellow beam that struck down across the wall from the little high window.

He lay on his back with his shackled hands impatiently picking at the rough blanket, his eyes wandering along the lines of his log walls. If he only had something to do he felt he could stand it better. As it was he could only lie there and think of home and Dad. But this awful inaction was getting him. He was afraid he wasn't going to be able to keep up this brave front before his captors much longer, yet he knew he must.

Suddenly his eyes focused on a little place between the logs where the crack was filled with something, a little gray line it seemed. In the dim light he could scarcely tell. It was away up at the very edge of the roof where it joined to the side wall, and it was so in shadow that he thought his eyes were deceiving him. He lay for some time just watching it. He had reached the stage when he couldn't bear to find out that it wasn't anything. He wanted to keep up the delusion that it was something besides just wall and crack. Even if it was only a folded paper it would be interesting to get it and unfold it. If it was a bit of folded newspaper put there to keep the wind from a crack it might have something on it he could read. If only he had some of the magazines and mystery tales he had left on his closet shelf at school! He wouldn't mind reading them over again. Just anything to read would be so good.

He managed to get through the day at last, sleeping a good deal and climbing up to his window now and then when the boss was snoring or away from the place for a little. He tried applying his eye to a crack here and there, but it was so little he could see from any of them, a twig perhaps, or a tossing cone or a plume of pine. Once he worked for a long time trying to catch with a bent nail he found on the floor a needle of pine that rubbed the log wall. It was a game just to see if he could hook a brown pine needle and draw it inside between the logs. It would be a little touch with the outside world. But once when he thought he almost had it the nail slipped through and fell away from his grasp and the needle waved on outside. Then he fell back despairing on his cot and finally fell asleep. So passed another day in captivity.

Before the dawn next morning Bud returned. He heard them whispering in gruff grumbles outside his door. He could see a crack of light under the door. He could smell the coffee heating. And presently his door was unlocked and the two men came in. Bud bore a plate of food, and looked sleepy and discontented. But about them both was a determined look that made Rannie's heart sink.

15

THE men urged the food upon Rannie, and offered a second cup of the vile coffee, but Rannie refused. Then the boss spoke.

"Well, young feller," he said with a false softness in his voice, "we've come now ta get ya ta write that there letter I was speakin' about."

Rannie sat up and grinned affably, although his heart was beating wildly. He felt that yesterday's inaction had made him weak and flabby. He wondered if he had strength to carry on. But he grinned.

"Oh, sure!" he said nonchalantly. "Bring on yer stationery. Gotta good pen? I like stubs if you know what I mean."

Bud brought a piece of pine board, a much crumpled sheet of paper and a government envelope. He drew up a wooden box from the other room for a table, and set thereon a small bottle of ink and a cheap wooden handled pen.

"Okay," said Rannie scrutinizing the point of the pen. "Now, what do ya want said?"

"The letter's ta yer dad, see?" said the boss narrowing his gaze and watching Rannie's face for a quiver or flicker of eagerness. But Rannie's face was immovable.

"Aw, gee!" said Rannie regretfully. "I shouldn't like ta write ta him just now. He'd be coming right up here after me an' I wantta see this thing out."

"No fear o' that!" growled the boss. "The letter's goin' ta be mailed several hundred miles from this here mountain."

"Oh, I see," mused Rannie. "Great stuff! Still, I wouldn't wantta write anything that would worry him o' course."

"This here will make him glad," said the boss grimly, "because it'll give him hope you're soon comin' home. Now first set down that yer well an' bein' treated right."

Rannie frowned.

"This letter from you ur me?" he asked biting the pen handle meditatively.

"From you o' course," said the boss firmly.

"Okay 'ith me!"

Rannie wrote rapidly:

Dear Dad: Don't worry about me. I'm okay and having the time of my life!

His pen paused and the two men watched him and studied what he had written.

"Now tell 'im everything'll be all right if he'll just obey orders herein contained."

"Everything'll be all right—" Here Rannie paused again and looked up at the two men standing in the light of the flickering candle which Bud held high over Rannie's shoulder.

"What are those orders?" Rannie asked the question casually, his pen poised in air, a speculative look on his face.

"Why, just about the ransom, how much money, all in small bills, an' where it's ta be put."

"Aw, gee! That's too bad," said Rannie leaning back from his rude desk and looking engagingly up at his two scowling captors. "I can't ask Dad about money! I'm sorry but I really can't. He's awful generous when he's flush, but just now he's about broke an' 'twould only make him feel bad. He couldn't pay any ransom money."

"Here, what'r ya givin' us? Ya can't put anythin' like that over on us!" said the boss getting out his ugly gun threateningly. "You write what I tell ya ur I'll blow ya inta air, see?"

"Tha's awright," said Rannie quickly. "P'raps it's better that way anyhow. You see I'm kinda in bad everywhere just now. Got fired from school an' come home ta find my dad about ta be bankrupt an' the house ta be sold 'n' everything. Guess if I fade outa the picture it'll make it easier all around."

The two men looked at one another aghast for an instant, fear of frustration in that glance. Rannie saw it and drew a deep breath. Perhaps if they realized his father wasn't rich any more they might "lay off of him" he thought. But he had not long to hope. The boss fairly roared at him.

"You needn't think you can put that over on us. You're a game kid all righty. I'll hand ya that. But we got our eye teeth cut yestiday. Dontcha think we looked up your old man and found out what he was worth afore we started on all this? You little liar you! Take up that pen an' write what I say. Hear?"

Rannie looked steadily into the evil eyes for a moment, looked also into the eye of the gun that was leveled at him, then thoughtfully picked up the pen again and write:

Good-by Dad. Don't you feel too bad, and don't you pay a cent for ransom. I wasn't worth much anyway. Give Chrissie my love, I'm sorry, Dad.

Your bad boy, Rannie

"There!" said Rannie throwing down the pen. "I've written all I can. If you don't like it you can do what you want with me."

He threw himself down listlessly on the cot behind him, and his chains clacked dismally.

The two men picked up the paper and read, Bud peering over the boss' shoulder with a dour look in his eyes.

The boss frowned deeply, cursed as he read, and then stood reading it over again.

"That'll be all right," he said in an undertone. "I'll fix it. May be even better."

They went out and bolted the door carefully. Rannie lay still upon his cot and tried to think, but all he could think of was his father's face when he told him he couldn't send that fifty thousand dollar check to the college. All he could remember was the night he and Chrissie had sat on the big leather couch in Dad's room with his arms around them both. All he could see was a vision of his own little crib beside the big bed, and the big tree and the side yard with a mother standing there to protect him from a mad dog. Somebody to protect him and love him!

Undreamed of wonder! And what would she feel now for him if she could know?

Well, he was on his own. He must face it alone. He mustn't even let his dad know how to save him because his dad couldn't afford it and he'd think he had to.

How long he lay there he didn't know. There was talking in a low tone out in the other room, now and then an angry rumble with louder references to one they called Spike and what he would think. Spike was coming it appeared, some time soon. What would Spike be like? Could he work anything with him or wouldn't he see him at all? Rannie was fed up with crooks he decided. He was ready to pass out of the picture quick and be done with it, even down there deep in the green waters with a bullet through his brain, but to lie here and do nothing all day was deadly. To do nothing but think!

It was then that a beam of the afternoon sun struggled through and shot into the gloomy place for an instant, and flung a double reflection across to the place at which he had been looking so long and cherishing a thought of something sticking out between the logs. His eyes turned to it, and there surely was something gray, about six inches long and a quarter of an inch thick, lying neatly along the ledge under the roof, just a thin line of gray.

Well, if it was a hallucination he must get it out of his thoughts. He would disillusion himself.

So he got up cautiously. The men seemed to be outside in front of the cabin and could not hear him there so well. Moving carefully to keep his chains from clinking, he reached the wall and slowly, carefully, found footing, a step at a time, pausing each step as he climbed lest his captors should hear him. There were few holdings between these logs. It was not an easy place to climb and the beam of light was already shifting, but he made it at last, his hand touched the gray line, grasped it, and found it real. It was some sort of little book or pamphlet. He ran his hand over the ledge before he lifted it to see if there were anything else there and found a hard sharp instrument. Excitedly he drew it forth, almost dropped it, but recovered his grasp and looked at it, his breath coming hard.

It was a broken rusty bit of file. He was so excited that he almost forgot the book. But he managed to steady his nerve and satisfy himself that there was nothing else in the crack, or as far as he could reach along the ledge. Slipping the file into his pocket and holding the tiny booklet in his teeth, he descended slowly, cautiously.

And just in time. The men were coming back into the cabin. He could hear them talking now, almost deferentially. And there was another voice with them. It must be Spike!

Back on his cot with his booty he guiltily hid the file in the depth of a crack between the logs behind his cot. It would never be found there, and it might be wonderful to have in case there ever came a chance to use it.

Then without stopping to look at the book beyond deciphering the single word "John" he stuffed it smoothly in another crack just below the level of what would have been his pillow if he had one. It was too dark now to read the book even if he dared, and he might be interrupted at any moment, so he hid his treasures and lay trembling with excitement. At least, if he had to stay there another day he had something to look forward to besides interminable hours of just thinking and seeing what a rotten failure he had been.

Sometime after candlelight a supper was prepared. He heard them going about with bustle opening cans and a savory odor of frying ham greeted his hungry senses. Then to his surprise he was brought out to share in the meal, given a box to sit on and introduced to Spike who sat at the head of the crude table.

Spike was a gentleman with frank, kind, fearlessly ruthless eyes. He looked at Rannie pleasantly, greeted him as an equal and spoke to him as man to man. In spite of his natural intuition Rannie warmed to him. There was a charm about the man, distinction in a way. It was easy to see why men obeyed him. Was this one of the gang leaders of the underworld? Rannie's quick judgment aided by his ever-ready imagination made pretty good guesses, and kept his caution in control. His schoolboy code had been when in a doubtful situation to keep still and let the other fellow do the talking. Rannie kept to that now. He listened intently and drew several canny conclusions from the general talk going on at the table. He noticed the almost deference the boss and Bud paid to Spike. He stowed away several veiled allusions for careful thought afterwards, and rightly judged that he was out here eating with the rest that he might be sized up and worked upon.

So he grinned when they all laughed, answered wittily in his own peculiar schoolboy slang when spoken to, acted for all the world like a guest of a gentleman at his country home. And he could see that Spike liked it.

It was not until the tomato juice cocktail, the fresh bread, the fried ham and coffee, and the delicious grapes and pears that the guest had evidently brought with him, had all been consumed and Bud and the boss were silently tidying up in their crude way that Spike turned to Rannie with a keen friendly look and said:

"Now what's all this about your not being willing to ask your father for ransom?"

Rannie faced him bright eyed knowing that a crucial time had come, his young face hardening into dogged determination.

"I couldn't do it!" said Rannie firmly.

"Not if your life depended on it?"

"Not if my life depended on it." There was a ring to his voice that would have thrilled his father if he could have heard it, and made him forgive even all the childish outrages and scrapes he had been in at school; and if Rannie had lifted his eyes an instant sooner he would have caught a glint of admiration in the eyes of the gentleman crook who watched him. But all Rannie saw when he dared to study that strong face before him was a cruel look in the man's eye. Very well, if it was fight to the death Rannie had determined to fight. It was probably the one chance of his lifetime to retrieve the silly wasted past. That was his thought as he put steel into his own young frightened eyes.

"Tell me about it," ordered the crook in an impersonal tone.

"Well, you see this is the story," burst forth Rannie in his schoolboy tone. "My dad is about ta fail. He told me about it just a few minutes before your men got me. You see I'd been pretty rotten, got into all sorts of a mess at school, stole the exam questions and got fired for it, and my dad had just found it out and felt pretty bad about it. I tried ta tell him he c'd make it right an' he said he couldn't. He didn't even have a little trifle like fifty thousand ta put up, an' he said he wouldn't if he did have it. He said I deserved what I got an' he'd haveta suffer with me, and things like that. And then he told me how his business had about gone under, and he didn't know which way ta turn, an' how I'd disgraced him in school, an' how my mother'd feel if she was alive, an' all like that. An' then right after that I hadta be so simple as ta go an' get kidnapped. I ask ya, ef you was in my place could you ask yer bankrupt dad fer any kind of a ransom after all that?"

There was something about Rannie's earnest young face, white with excitement and strain, that held the three men silent as they watched him, and Spike after a moment answered him quietly:

"Perhaps not," and there was something about his face that was quite inscrutable.

Almost at once Bud led him away to his room and he lay on his bed in the dark and heard a low murmur of voices for a long, long time, though he could not catch a single word from the carefully guarded conversation.

He could not remember just when he drifted into an uneasy sleep filled with unhappy dreams of home and mother and the old house where they all lived together. The whirr of an airplane seemed to mingle with his dreams, and the bed was hard and the night cold.

He woke in the early morning with memory getting him quickly in hand, and listened, but heard only Bud's steps as he stumbled about the outer room, and later the boss grumbling at him. Spike seemed to have faded like a dream from the cabin. No one spoke of him nor referred to last night in any way.

As soon as there was enough light in the room, and Rannie was reasonably sure that no one would come in for some little time to interrupt, he pulled out the little packet he had hidden so carefully in the crack behind the cot, and examined it. It was in a little envelope with printing on the outside, and a line of script with a name signed. He half sat up and held the packet where the light would shine better on it.

"This little book will help you to win the game. Read it and find out how." And the name signed below was the name of one of the world's greatest athletes, known in college and athletic circles as "The Grand Old Man of Football."

Rannie fairly caught his breath and read the magic words over again. What prize was this that he had found hidden away in a dreary cabin in the wilds of a far mountain? That it would be well worth reading he had no doubt. Rannie had once had the great privilege of picking up a fallen program and returning it to the great hero on the bleachers at a national game which privilege and an unerring ability to worm himself to the front had blessed him with a position at the great man's feet. Oh, Rannie would read that book with his heart as well as his eyes. Already the thought of Spike had dropped back a pace or two in his mind, and Rannie was eager to read the little book. He pulled it reverently out of its paper case and turned it around in his hand. "THE GOSPEL OF JOHN" he read in clear black letters on a bright red cover. But it meant nothing to him. Who was John?

Rannie opened the book and began to read.

The first few verses puzzled him. It was strange language and he couldn't quite get at what it meant. He still had in his mind the words written on the sheathing envelope. This was some queer kind of introduction to the story of an athlete named John probably. Rannie skimmed it and came to the sixth verse. Ah! Here was John. "There was a man sent from God whose name was John." That was a queer way to put it. What did God have to do with athletics? Probably some new modern kind of praise, considered the highest one could give. He read on and gathered that here was a story of something that it was important everybody should believe. This John was a kind of trainer perhaps, or manager, or somebody who went out and arranged for the games, was that it?

Then gradually as the majestic figure of the God-man Christ Jesus emerged from the page in all His glory, as a "Lamb of God" Rannie stood in awe before the thought of Him. Why, it was talking about Jesus Christ, this book was, and trying to make everybody understand what He was. This person John had known Him and was His witness, that was it.

He went back a few verses and caught up a little more of the meaning. Why if this was true, and of course it was since his hero of the football field stood for it, then Jesus Christ was very different from what Rannie had ever supposed. This book made Him a real person, yet more than a mere human person. It tied Him up to God so closely that it actually stated that he was God.

Rannie went back to the beginning and caught up vaguely a trifle more of the meaning of the "WORD" that was in the beginning with God and was God. The Word that made all things that were made. That, too, was a new thought. He had never connected the traditional Christ of the Bible with the creation. Of course not. He knew almost nothing about the Bible except as he had sketchily read in text books about the Bible. He knew no real truth at all. He was a little pagan brought face to face with the Book of God for the first time in his life, and he was amazed.

But when he came to that astounding announcement "Behold the Lamb of God, which taketh away the sin of the world," he paused and read it again.

Sin of course was anything you did that was wrong, that is, one didn't recognize it by that name unless it got to some heinous stage like murder or kidnaping or theft, but it was sin in a general sense anyway. And—yes—his father had practically told him he had been a thief when he stole those exams, though he had always looked upon that as only following out an old custom, poetic license as it were, for the sake of the traditions of the school. But likely in God's eyes, if there was a God, and He took account of things individuals did, he was counted a sinner. At any rate he had been guilty of disloyalty to his father and family and the rules of the school, and he felt mean enough now in his present situation to count himself as the worst sinner in the world.

But—take away the sin of the world! How could that be true of a man long ago? Oh, of course he knew Christ's death on the cross was somehow connected with philanthropy toward mankind, but what had that to do with taking away guilt? Guilt. That was what he was feeling. That was why he couldn't ask his dad to help him out now. He felt guilty. And this book suggested a way for sin to be taken away! Well, he wished he knew how.

It was just this faint wish to find out how that kept him reading on through phrases that he did not understand, phrases that so far as his knowledge was concerned meant just nothing at all.

But he gathered through it all that this book was a plea, a witness to the sincerity and character and ability of Jesus Christ by one named John. And John seemed to be a bright guy who wasn't doing it just to make a good show for himself. He was all for the Christ. He wanted people to believe in Him. In fact that word "believe" figured more and more as Rannie turned the brief pages, absorbed in the Word of God. Belief? Why did belief seem so important? He wanted to find out. There, perhaps that was the reason: "And I saw, and bare record that this is the Son of God."

Well, if He really was the Son of God that was enough to talk about so earnestly of course.

Then Rannie found himself following with the two disciples, asking with them, "Rabbi, where dwellest Thou?" and he seemed almost to hear the Master's answering voice: "Come and see."

Could he find Him in those few pages of that book, Rannie wondered? Probably not, or all the world would have come to believe in Him by now, but at least it was interesting. He read on, gathering new data, new testimony of this man named John who at least evidently himself believed what he was telling. The power of Jesus' first miracle interested him. He paused to think out how that water might have been made into wine by sleight of hand or some such method, and concluded that one could prove nothing about it without having been there to watch the whole process. Then suddenly came the thought that if this was the Son of God, if God was what a God was supposed to be, all-powerful, why, neither He nor His Son would have to resort to trickery to bring about a thing like that. A God wouldn't be a God unless He could do things beyond man's power or thought. It occurred to him with a pang that if a God were here now He could probably get him out of this cabin and down across space to his home without any ransom being paid at all. How he wished that God were there.

Then he came to the verse: "But Jesus did not commit Himself to them, because He knew all men, and needed not that any should testify of man: for He knew what was in man."

Then a God wouldn't need to be here to know one's need. Perhaps God knew right now what was happening here in this cabin. Perhaps He knew a way out for him.

Rannie was plunged deep into the matchless third chapter of John, reading the testimony on miracles of one, Nicodemus, who came to talk with Jesus by night, when suddenly he felt that some one was in the room. With a sense of imminent peril he looked up over his little red book and there stood his two captors watching him with suspicion. The door stood open behind them, and he had not heard it!

16

RANNIE'S first alarm was lest they should take the book away from him before he had finished reading it. And next he remembered the file. If they should find that! If they should go to searching his room and take that away he would feel that there was no hope left.

But he summoned his wicked little grin and spoke:

"Good night!" he said, "I didn't hear ya come in. W'at ya been doin' ta that bolt? Oiled it? It didn't make a sound."

But the boss was up in the air. One could see that at a glance. He was eyeing the little red book with suspicion.

"Where'dya get that?" he demanded pointing to the book.

"Found it over there between the logs right in plain sight. Somebody stuffed it in ta keep out the wind I guess an' then went off 'nfergot it. It's real interesting. Listen, I'll read ya some. This is a story about a man named Nicodemus."

"But what kind of book is it?" insisted the boss coming over to the cot and looking over Rannie's shoulder.

"Oh, it's some kind of a record of witness in a court case as far as I can make out. The witness' name is John. Stand outta my light there Boss, I can't see ta read this fine print."

"Come on out in the other room," urged Bud, curiosity and interest in his ugly face.

"Well, come on then," said the boss

grudgingly, "but I ainta gointa listen long. I ain't got no time fer books."

"Well, just listen ta this," said Rannie, and sitting down on the first box he came to he began to read.

The story form of the narrative caught the interest of the men at the start and Rannie was a good reader. He had always taken prizes in declamation. From the first word he had his audience. Neither of them had perhaps ever heard any reading aloud before in their lives and they sat down spellbound. Even through the wonderful imagery which they did not understand they sat with strained expression listening to the old, old mystery story that a man must be born again before he could see the kingdom of God.

But when Rannie reached John three sixteen they sat forward on their wooden boxes, their elbows on their knees, Bud's mouth half open in wonder, the boss frowning heavily.

"'For God so loved the world,'" read Rannie.

The boss openly sniffed. Not much love had come his way. He didn't believe in love. His idea of love anyway was something vile and impure and uncertain. Real love was a thing about as far from the hitherto lives of these two men as the east is from the west. God loving the world simply couldn't be comprehended.

" 'that He gave His only begotten Son—' "

The boss edged his box a little nearer and stretched his neck to look over Rannie's shoulder.

" 'that whosoever believeth in Him should not perish—' "

Bud edged a little nearer, his chin in his hand and cleared his throat.

" 'but have everlasting life,' " finished Rannie, and Bud held up his hand.

"Read that there bit again, won't ya?" he asked huskily.

Rannie read the whole verse.

" 'For God so loved the world, that He gave His only begotten Son, that whosoever believeth in Him should not perish, but have everlasting life.' "

Rannie read it well, and without lifting his eyes went straight on to the next verse:

"'For God sent not His Son into the world to condemn the world.'"

Ah, those men could understand that language. More than one of their number had been condemned to die. They listened breath-

297

lessly, with heavy frowns and smoldering eyes.

" '—but that the world through Him might be saved.' "

The two listeners turned and looked at one another as if this were the most incredible thing they had ever heard.

"I never heard they made God out ta be that kind of guy, did you?" Bud said to the boss.

"He ain't," said the boss. "He's hell fire an' perdition. That book's all bunk! But g'wan, Kid. Le's see what else it says."

Rannie went on reading:

" 'He that believeth on Him is not condemned: but he that believeth not is condemned already, because he hath not believed in the name of the only begotten Son of God.' "

"There it is!" said the boss. "Wha'd I tell ya? Condemnation! That's allus the answer ta everything in this world. Condemnation."

"It says ya don't havta be condemned, don't it?" said Bud. "Read that there again, Kid."

Rannie read it again.

"There!" said Bud. "Ya don't *havta!* It's easy enough ta b'lieve, ain't it? Anybody c'd do that!"

"How c'n ya believe a thing ya don't b'lieve?" asked the boss angrily.

"Well, ya could," said Rannie interested and thoughtful. "Just like you'd believe in the radio. You might think it was impossible, but if you tuned in you'd find out it was true, wouldn't ya? And now, take flying. You gotta believe a lot you don't know is so when you get in an airplane."

"That's so, Boss," said Bud. "You mind the fust time you got in an airplane? You just couldn't figger how it was safe but you hadta get there in a hurry an' finally you said you'd just havta swing off an' trust ta luck an' let the old ship prove herself. Dontcha remember that time you went up to Chicago ta meet Spike an' get—"

"Shut up!" said the boss with an ugly look at Bud. "Can't ya ever learn ta keep yer mouth shet? Read on, Kid."

Rannie read on.

" 'And this is the condemnation, that light is come into the world, and men loved darkness rather than light, because their deeds were evil. For every one that doeth evil hateth the light, neither cometh to the light, lest his deeds should be reproved.' "

The men watched Rannie with frozen glances as if he had been the author of the book, then dropped their gaze down to the floor with a half-shamed look. They had never heard themselves described before except in language that was vengeful.

They listened on through the chapter to the last verse:

" 'He that believeth on the Son hath everlasting life: and he that believeth not the Son shall not see life; but the wrath of God abideth on him.' "

"Hell!" said the boss furiously, drawing his feet back noisily, "That's all bunk!" and got up and slammed out of the cabin. They could hear his feet stamping off down through the woods. They could hear his angry voice rumbling as he went.

"Any one could believe that wanted ta," said Bud. "Read on."

Rannie read on through the story of the woman at the well, and the healing of the nobleman's son, and the man at the pool who took up his bed and walked at the word of the Master. The boss came in again just as Rannie was reading the twenty-fourth verse of the fifth chapter:

" 'He that heareth my word, and believeth on Him that sent me, hath everlasting life, and shall not come into condemnation; but is passed from death unto life.' "

The boss stopped as though he had been arrested in spite of his best intention.

"Read that there again," said Bud, and Rannie read the verse once more, slowly, distinctly, and then went on:

"'Verily, verily, I say unto you, The hour is coming and now is, when the dead shall hear the voice of the Son of God: and they that hear shall live.'"

"Time ta eat!" roared the boss. "Get that kid back into his box."

Rannie went back to his cot in the darkness with his thoughts, the little book clasped tight in his hand.

What a book it was! How strange were the things it talked of. Being born again. Believing. Life. Those were the two words that stood out now, "believing" and "life." One believed and one had life. Everlasting life. That was a great verse about believing and having life. He must learn that if he got a chance. He didn't want to forget it. They might take the book away any time now, and maybe he never could find another copy. He wouldn't like to forget that. How did it begin? "For God so loved the world." That was it. He would memorize it in the morning as soon as it was light.

The next two days were times of strain.

There was no other opportunity to read the book to both men. The boss seemed furious when Bud suggested it. Rannie could hear them talking it over. The boss said the Book would make him a softy. Spoil his technique, and all sorts of things. Sometimes the boss's voice grew very loud as if he wanted Rannie to hear him. He even talked of how they would have to do away with Rannie in case the ransom was not paid pretty soon in answer to the demand. He described in detail to Bud just what he was to do in case there came a sudden warning to themselves.

It was easy enough, he said. Just plug him with a bullet and fling him over the rocks. Or easier still, take him out for a stroll and give him a push over the precipice.

Rannie came to contemplate this possibility and wonder what it would be like and what would be afterwards, and always that verse rang over and over in his mind: "God so loved the world"—and that other one "He that believeth on the Son *hath* everlasting life." And one evening lying in the dark it came to him.

"Why, I believe! I do believe! And He says 'he that believeth *has* everlasting life.' I must have it then, and if that's so, I shouldn't worry what they do to me!"

Then in a new gentle reverence he got himself down upon his knees by the rickety cot and began to pray.

"Oh, God, I believe, and you have said it so I guess it must be so, and that means it's up to you. If anything happens you'll look out fer me. Help me ta be a man, an' if I don't believe right, please show me how, and please look out fer Dad and Chrissie. Amen."

The next morning the boss went off down the wooded hill and was gone a long time, and as soon as he was out of hearing Bud came in and asked for some more reading.

Rannie because he had been reading much to himself, began at the scene in the garden where the soldiers came for Jesus, and read on through Christ's trial and crucifixion, and Bud sat with folded arms and eyes that were sometimes full of tears as the story went on through that resurrection morning down to the last two verses of the twentieth chapter:

" 'And many other signs truly did Jesus in the presence of his disciples, which are not written in this book: But these are written that ye might believe that Jesus is the Christ, the Son of God; and that believing ye might have life through his name.' "

"Would you figger that any one could

303

take that?" asked Bud suddenly, looking at Rannie earnestly.

"I don't see why not," said Rannie confidently, and wondered why he was glad that Bud felt that way.

Then, before any one could speak or think anything more there came a sound up in the air over their heads; faraway at first and dim, but growing louder every minute. The two looked at one another for an instant, hope in the eyes of one and fear in the eyes on the other.

"It doesn't take a second ta believe," said Rannie.

"No," said Bud, and sprang to the door.

Rannie could not hear the bolt slide, but he was pretty sure he was still a prisoner. He lay quietly on his cot and listened as the airplane came on. He knew better than to try the door. If the boss was around, and likely he was, he wouldn't miss that sound. Rannie knew that a bullet would end his career quickly enough if he tried to come out into view. So he lay still with the little bit of the Book of Life in his hands, and listened. Then he closed his eyes and began to pray.

"Oh, God, I don't know what to pray for, but won't ya please look out for me?"

The airplane came on low, slowly circled

once over the cabin and went on. The boss was out there in the other room. Rannie could hear him talking.

"That's Spike's plane. I see the number. Get onta that? He's sendin' a message down. It'll be in code. You read it out so I ken keep watch. There! See that! It's coming straight. Look out and see where it falls and slide out an' get it."

There were furtive steps, a sound of creeping outside the cabin and presently Bud returned and the door was shut again.

Bud spelled the message out slowly. The two seemed to have forgotten that Rannie could hear them.

"Police on trail. Big posse organized. Too late to save captive. Destroy all evidence. Lose no time. Meet you same field."

Rannie wondered why he felt so calm as he heard his fate discussed.

"I don't see why the kid couldn't go along," suggested Bud. "He's a game kid. He'd stick by."

The answer was the sound of a terrible oath.

"Yella, are ya?" asked the boss. "Softy?"

"Aw naw!" said Bud with a good imitation of his toughest tone. "But how ya goin' ta get rid of him?"

"Dead men tell no tales," said the boss. "Jest take him out fer a stroll as usual an' it's easy 'nough ta give 'im a shove. Accident ya know. Dead men's hole 'll take care o' the rest. Hustle up there. Get yer things together. I'll give ya five minutes ta collect everythin' an' take it down the back side o' the mountain. You know where we planned. Cache the things at the cave there an' come back an' keep watch while I take mine down. Now, get on a hustle."

There were sounds only of swift movements, articles hurled into a sack, and then Bud's footsteps out on the ground, descending a rocky way behind the cabin.

Rannie lay and listened. Would the boss come and execute the cruel sentence upon him? His sinking heart told him there would be nothing he could do. So he held the little red book tight in his hands, and closed his eyes again and prayed.

"Oh, God, help me. I believe you can. Save me if it's all right with you. If you do I'll be your witness too, like John."

He could hear Bud coming back now. He knew Bud would have to obey, even against his will. The boss was a dead shot, and that noiseless, smokeless gun would be right in his hand this minute. Humanly speaking there was no hope for Bud if he disobeyed orders. No hope for Rannie if he did not.

The boss gave quick sharp orders.

"There's a cloud over yander. I can't see through the glass for sure but it might be more planes. We gotta hustle. I'll get down the hill an' you do the deed. Don't have any sob stuff. Accidents are easy. You needn'ta look. Just push an' run, an' make tracks down tha hill. Spike knows his stuff an' he said not ta waste any time. Ef you don't do yer part we got plenty against ya, an' ya don't durst squeal on us, see? There's that Noonan case, remember! Now, all set? Meetcha down at the cave in three minutes."

The boss' footsteps hurried off down the hill and Bud approached Rannie's door cautiously.

Rannie, his heart quickened by his nearness to death perhaps, noticed that Bud did not have to unbolt the door. Then it was open all the time, and he might perhaps have escaped without their knowledge if he had only been clever enough! But no, what could he do with his feet hobbled with chains?

He tried to breathe quietly as if he were asleep as Bud stole across the floor. It was a task almost beyond his powers to keep up that steady breathing, but he kept crying to God in his soul for help.

He heard Bud steal softly across the floor, heard him stoop and lay something down, and then bend over his cot. Was Bud going to shoot him now and leave him here alone? Rannie took a gentle breath to stand the strain. And now he felt Bud's hand upon his own. What was he trying to do? Why, he was taking the little book out of his grasp!

Rannie relaxed his hand and let go of the book, greatly wondering, and then he was aware that Bud had moved noiselessly away from him—had most amazingly gone out of the room, had closed the door, probably bolted it again. What did it mean? A second later he heard his step outside the cabin hurrying down the mountain, slipping, sliding, gone. Was that a shot? What had happened?

A long time he lay perfectly still listening till it seemed his limbs ached with the strain of holding them tense. Then far away he heard a dim sound like humming. Was it another plane or the same one returned?

Suddenly he was all alive. The humming had increased to a buzz loud and clear. Were they enemies or friends?

And then he was upon his feet springing toward the door, forgetting the shackles on his ankles, forgetting everything but that several planes were coming and he must look out and see if he could find out what was going on.

But the chains were too short for rapid strides, and Rannie fell, his foot striking something hard and metallic on the floor. He recovered himself and looked around. Was that a gun on the floor by his foot? He reached for it. Bud's gun! Was that the thing he had heard him lay down when he took the book from his hand? Had he just laid it down to get the book and then forgotten it, or had he left it there on purpose?

Cautiously Rannie picked himself up and stared at the door. It was open! Bud had not bolted it after him! He had not even closed it. He had left the captive free, and he had not led him out for the stroll and pushed him off the cliff as he had been told to do!

Bud was white!

Rannie's heart suddenly went out to Bud with a great sweep of love and gratitude. Poor tough Bud, hard-boiled and wicked, but he had dared his boss to give Rannie a chance! And he had wanted the little book to take with him.

Then a new thought came reverently to Rannie. The book had saved his life perhaps. The little book stood to him in place of a ransom if he got free now.

But Rannie was cool again. He heard the planes tearing along the sky overhead now, going like mad. They were past the cabin now and sweeping round to the north. It was too late to signal them of course, even if he could have done it with his shackled hands. Besides, he must be wary. His captors could not be far off yet. When they saw the planes were gone they might return.

The first thing to do was to get rid of these shackles of course. He swung himself over the cot and felt around for his file. This was the moment he had faintly hoped would come some time. This was what he had been keeping the file for. Indeed he had gone so far as to select the very first link in his fetters that should be sundered first and marked it with surreptitious strokes of the file given now and then when his captors were outside the cabin and he was sure they could not hear the low grinding of the metal.

One link of the chain that held his feet had quite a deep nick in it where he had worked on it quietly. He had been afraid to do much on it lest it would be noticed by the boss who was keen for every little detail.

Now as he caught up the file from its

hiding place he was fairly out of breath with excitement. Eagerly he worked, impatient over the rough old instrument that would not bite the steel as deep as a sharp one would have done.

It seemed hours before the link finally dropped apart and he kicked one foot loose and felt a thrill of ecstasy. Now, whatever happened he was free to move. There was still a chain attached to one foot, but at least he could take long steps, and that was a lot in making a getaway.

The next thing was to set his hands free and for that he needed more light for the dimness of the inner room sorely hampered his efforts.

He picked up the gun, stowed it in the only whole pocket of his alien clothes, and strode into the other room, rejoicing that at last he could take a real step, even though a length of chain was still dangling and clattering from one foot. Of course he must get rid of that before he tried flight. It was too noisy.

It was not so easy to unshackle his hands. It was an awkward position in which he had to work. Now and then he would get up and peer cautiously out the window or door in the midst of his feverish work to make sure the enemy was not in sight, and perhaps with a faint hope that a friendly plane might return, though he was not sure whether he would more welcome or fear a plane if one should be heard.

At last one hand was free. Now he could at least steady himself and take hold of things without having to keep his arms in such a constrained position. He decided that he had better get out into the open somewhere to do the rest. No telling when the bloodthirsty fiends would return, and then it would all be up with him again. If the boss should discover that Bud had not pushed him over the cliff he would likely come back and finish the job.

Rannie rose and gave one quick glance about, saw the open cupboard door, the empty shelves. His kindly caretakers had left no food behind. Or say! Was that a can of tomatoes back in the corner? He strode over to the cupboard, reached back for it, felt around for anything else that might be there and found an end of a loaf of bread, an inch or so, hard as stone.

With these two he fled, pausing only at the doorway to give a hasty cautious glance about, and then an upward glance.

"Oh, God, help me please. Show me which

way to go," he said aloud in a guarded voice, and then dashed out into the woods down the mountain side.

17

THE Kershaw family had moved to Seneca Street. Not that it was much of a move. A single load of furniture was all they took. They left the big house immaculate and the new owner moved in that afternoon.

That was the day that a keen-eyed son of the law took Mr. Kershaw aside to tell him that there was definite news about a clue that he had followed up himself, secretly.

"I'd like to have young Harper in on this interview, if it's all right with you, Mr. Kershaw. That boy has a head on him and he can help us with this."

So it happened that Philip Harper was scheduled for an important part in the resultant plans that were to be carried out in utmost secrecy. Throughout the whole time of Rannie's absence, Phil had been the one who sheltered the poor father from the herd of reporters, the questions of well-wishers, and the prying of the curious. He had become the intimate friend of the family.

"He is like another son. I don't know what I should do without him," said Mr. Kershaw, sitting with his elbows on the desk and his head in his hands trying to rest his aching head and inflamed eyes. He had slept scarcely at all the preceding night. The whole amount of sleep he had had since Rannie's disappearance was negligible.

"I think God sent him," said Christobel softly. "Don't you, Father?"

"Perhaps—if God cares—" sighed Mr. Kershaw. "But if He cares why did He let it happen?"

"There might be a reason," said Christobel thoughtfully.

"Well, I can't see it, but at least I'm glad we have Philip now."

And so it was Philip who volunteered for the flight across the mountains, in search of Rannie. Philip had been to flying school, and had even hoped for a career in that line until his father's accident made it imperative that he get an immediate remunerative job.

So, with the best plane for the purpose that could be procured, and a trustworthy pilot Philip was sent out to hunt Rannie.

But the night before he left Philip and Christobel went into the little white velvet sanctum once more and knelt to pray.

Then in the dim crystal light Philip took Christobel's hands in his and held them close for a moment. Looking down at her as her eyes shone starry with wonder, and yet dread of the morrow, he said in a low earnest voice:

"You are very precious to me little girl. I wish I could do something to make this hard way easier for you."

"Oh, but you have," said Christobel, thrilling to his words, and returning his warm clasp with a clinging pressure. "It's been so wonderful to have a real friend. I've never had one before. And you've done the greatest thing you could ever do for me. You've shown me to Jesus Christ. I shall never cease to be thankful. I couldn't go through these days without Him."

For answer Philip stooped and pressed his lips tenderly on the slender fingers he held, and when he spoke his voice was like a holy caress:

"Dear!" he said, "I'm so glad you feel that way. Perhaps—perhaps some day I may win the right to show you something else. Now—God keep you!" and with a quick pressure of her hands he was gone.

So Christobel prayed for three after that; for Rannie in the unknown wide world, for her father in his grim sorrow, and for Philip on his uncharted dangerous flight.

Christobel was not sorry to say good-bye to the great house. She and Maggie walked away from it scarcely turning to look back. They were going on the street car to Seneca Street, for all the cars had been sold to eke out more ransom money, all except the little run-about her father was using this morning to go with one of the officers following up a clue.

But Christobel mounted the steps of the street car with content. What were trifles of convenience and station when trouble was upon them all?

Maggie wisely interested Christobel in making Rannie's room ready for him. She talked cheerily about when he would return and how much boys enjoyed having a nice room all of their own. She chattered away continually to Christobel about which bed had the best springs and whether the walnut bureau was the best for a boy's room or would the maple one be better?

Maggie fondly supposed she was keeping Christobel from thinking about her troubles by all this chatter, but Christobel's eyes were far away thinking of a flyer out about the mountains, and Christobel's heart was thrilling with the sound of a voice that had called her precious. There was a new wonder in her eyes, and in her soul was a trust in God that was reflected in the quiet smile she wore upon her lips and in the peace upon her brow.

So the plain old home on Seneca Street became a home once more, with rooms where rest and quietness and peace could be found even for the haunted soul of the father whose heart was continually wrung with a hopeless remorse for what might have been. There was always a fire laid upon the hearth, ready for the return of the wanderers, there were beds ready for the weary, and a store of good plain homemade things to eat. When things began to get into good shape Maggie started inventing things for Christobel to do to keep her busy, and so the days went by, till Philip had been gone a week on his mission and still no definite message as to progress made.

Of course there had to be utmost caution about any messages that passed, for the public would get hold of the least rumor, and make much of it, and it was most important that the enemy should not have an inkling that any one was in pursuit.

So Christobel had to content herself with prayer and trusting. Only the briefest messages came, a single word sometimes, never to her, nor to any one known to be connected with the family. And often her father would be so engaged she dare not trouble him to ask about any possible progress that might have been made in the search.

In these days Philip's mother was a tower of strength, and his sister June would run in evenings, and between the two girls there grew up at once a warm friendship, the cementing of the old memories of childhood days. Christobel thought constantly how happy she would be now if only Rannie were back and the cloud lifted from their home. She counted up her blessings, and first she put her new-found Saviour. How precious it was to have some One to whom to go at all times in Whom she could utterly trust. Oh, if she had only known Jesus Christ before what a different thing her lonely little childhood would have been. Sometimes she even looked back with a sigh and wondered if Charmian had ever known about the Lord. It was all too evident that she had never actively believed on Him. It was plain to be seen that her own self had occupied her utterly. If Charmian had known the Lord how different everything might have been for them all.

There was no question in her mind about her own mother. She could remember early teaching, Bible stories, prayers with herself and Rannie kneeling at her mother's knee. And it made her almost happy to think that her mother was with the Lord Jesus.

Of course Christobel had very little teaching. Just the few words that Philip had been able to give her now and then in the few contacts he had had with her. She was shy about asking even Philip's mother. Her Christian life was so very new. She just pondered over things by herself, and prayed. As yet she did not know her Bible at all. That was to come.

One day a great shining car drew up at the door and Maggie, always alert for any new sound in the street, came trotting to the front window to take a sly peep between the curtains.

"Belike that'll be that proud lady with the smooth voice that came to the big house one night," snapped Maggie in a warning tone to Christobel who was hemming a dish towel at the suggestion of the faithful old nurse who was doing all in her power to keep Christobel busy.

Christobel looked up with a sudden sinking of heart.

Could that be Mrs. Romayne? And her father was expected any minute now. He had gone out hoping to bring back some definite news from the searching party, and if he came in while there was a caller she would have to wait till she was gone to know the news. Oh, Mrs. Romayne,—why, why did they have to be pestered with her now on top of all the rest?

But it was too late to escape. Besides, the stairs in the Seneca Street house were in full view of the front door and the living room and of what use to escape when one would eventually have to appear?

So Christobel arose with her dish towel in her hand and stood with a youthful dignity while Maggie reluctantly admitted the haughty caller.

"Oh, you're that servant woman, aren't you?" remarked the lady as she stepped into the neat little hall and glanced around. "Is this your house? It seems to be a very comfortable place. You're nicely fixed, aren't you? Do I understand that Chrissie Kershaw is here staying with you? I was told I would find her here somewhere."

"This house belongs to Mr. Kershaw," said Maggie with a hauteur worthy of the house of Kershaw in its greatest glory. "This

320

is Mr. Kershaw's residence at present. Miss Kershaw is in the living room. Did you wish to see her?" Maggie could erase the burr from her tongue well enough when occasion required.

"Living here?" exclaimed the caller. "Oh, but not really, of course. Just staying here for the moment to get out of the eye of publicity I suppose. It must be quite inconvenient. I don't understand why they could not have let their friends look out for them. It really would have been a lot more comfortable at my house, and nobody need have known where they were. Did you say Chrissie was in?"

"Miss Kershaw is in the living room," said Maggie haughtily.

Mrs. Romayne entered dramatically.

"My darling Chrissie!" she exclaimed. "To think I should find you in a place like this! Why didn't you let me know? I thought I made it quite plain that my home was at your service. And who are the horrible people that are staying in your own house on the avenue? Caretakers I suppose, or do they have some connection with the police? They are simply impossible! They actually thought I had come to call upon them, and they appeared in the most gaudy array. I declare if the police have to be given your lovely home for a headquarters for awhile I should think you could at least control the people they have around them. They were almost insulting."

"Those are the people that own the house now, Mrs. Romayne," said Christobel sweetly.

"That own the house? Why, what can you possibly mean? Your father's house on the avenue? The house where I called upon you the night your brother disappeared?"

"Yes, Mrs. Romayne, the house was sold a few days after that."

"Not sold! Your lovely home! Why, what can your father be thinking of? He had no right to sell that beautiful home when you are just growing up and needing a place to entertain. Why, what could he be thinking of to do such a thing? He must be crazy."

"He's thinking of my brother, Mrs. Romayne," said Christobel coldly. "My father needed the money for ransoming my brother. We have sold everything we had that was salable." She was angry at this woman for prying into her affairs, but she was astonished to see the startled look on the caller's face as her words went home like a well-aimed shaft.

Then the caller rallied and laughed.

"How ridiculous!" she burbled. "Of course you don't mean that. Your father is rated as one of the richest men in the city! That is simply absurd."

"You are mistaken, Mrs. Romayne. My father has lost a great deal of money in the last three years. His business has been deeply involved for some months past, even before Rannie disappeared, and now he has had to take the money he needed for collateral for loans connected with his business as a nucleus for the ransom demanded by Rannie's captors. It will probably take all we have and all we can borrow and then there will not be enough to meet the demand they have made. We had to sell the house and the cars and everything that was salable. We have kept only this dear old house where we used to live, and we could not even afford to keep this I suppose, only we have got to live somewhere, and we can live more cheaply here than anywhere we know. Besides, this house would not be worth very much if we did sell it."

"I should say not," said the woman with a withering glance about the pretty room that Christobel had made so lovely and livable and old-fashioned cosy.

"Won't you take off your coat, Mrs. Romayne," asked Christobel, heartily hoping she wouldn't.

"Oh no," said Mrs. Romayne drawing up her sumptuous furs about her shoulders, "I have only a moment. I just thought it was my duty to hunt you up. You poor child. How terrible all this must be for you. How could you allow your father to do such a very impossible thing as to sell your lovely home? It was your birthright, Christobel. He had no right to sell it away from you. Didn't it nearly break your heart to come away from the luxury of that wonderful mansion?"

Christobel almost laughed.

"Why, no, Mrs. Romayne, truly, I never cared for that house. In fact, the day before Rannie was taken away I begged Father to come down here and live. This is the house where my own dear mother lived, you know. It is where I remember her when I was a little child. I love it here and so does Rannie. Father loves it too. We would be very, very happy here if Rannie were just back."

Mrs. Romayne stared at her incredulously.

"What a very strange child you must be!" she said coldly, and then added with a kind of I-wash-my-hands-of-you tone, "Poor Charmian! How she loved that beautiful mansion which she really created for all of you! And to think that you have let it go irreparably to people of that class. Just common people! It seems unbelievable! I did think your father had more sense. I had quite idealized him. But it seems that I am mistaken!"

She drew her furs about her shoulders closer and arose.

"Well, Christobel," she said severely, "I must hurry away. Of course if there is any little thing you find I can do for you I hope you will let me know."

She put out a limp gloved hand coldly, and Christobel said "Thank you" sweetly, her heart suddenly singing a paean. Was the woman going, was she really going to leave them in peace? Hallelujah! And was it the house she had called upon? Was that all she wanted of them? The house and her father's money and station? This then was the kind of friendship she had professed so earnestly, this friendship that belonged only to certain fashionable localities and big bank accounts. Well, the Lord had been good to her. Blessed be poverty if it meant that she was thus rid of Mrs. Romayne. No more would the idle gossip of those thieving servants trouble Christobel now, for she could see in the very set of the lady's shoulders as she picked her way disdainfully out of the house, that she would not soon return to disturb the peace of Seneca Street.

Mrs. Romayne's car had no more than turned out of Seneca Street than Maggie hurried around opening all the doors and windows.

"We'll just air it out after her," she explained to the wondering Christobel. "It's not nice that strong scent she uses. We'll get it out of here afore your poppie gets home."

And Christobel smiled assent. She thought the smell of that heavy perfume would always be unpleasant to her.

18

RANNIE sat in the shelter of a thick growth of hemlock filing away at the last link of his fetters when he heard the humming sound of a plane again. His heart beat wildly, and he began to pray, "Oh God, help me! Show me what to do!"

He stole into the depth of a great pine tree and climbed up a little way staying close to the trunk where he would be hidden by the piney plumes, and watched.

He had come down the mountain quite a

326

distance when he first left the cabin, before he had stopped to use his file, and now as he looked to the sky he saw the airplane circling low over the tops of the trees at a distance above him, about where he thought the cabin must be. But he was not near enough to see any numbers on the wings of the great bird. He could not tell if it might be a passenger or mail plane, or some derelict privately owned. He could not even hazard a guess as to whether it might be friend or enemy. There was just one thing certain and that was that some one was suddenly interested in that cabin and was watching it.

He began to speculate as to what he should do. If it was true that the police were on the trail, ought he not perhaps to go back to the cabin and wait until they had a chance to come and find him? On the other hand, if he went back his captors, knowing far more than he did of the movements of the enemy, might find it safe to return and he would be only a captive again.

Of course now he was unshackled and had a gun, but he wasn't much of a shot, and the people who had blackjacked or sandbagged him before might find it easily possible to do it again, and might have more shackles in place of these lost ones. There was also the question of food. If he returned he had only the can of tomatoes and the crust on which he was munching now. He could not hold out indefinitely with hunger in the house. There was no time to be lost. He must get somewhere. Of course a casual survey from his present eminence gave no sign of human habitation in any direction, and it stood to reason that kidnappers would hardly hold him in a very accessible place; nevertheless the quicker he got on the sooner he would come to something, a house or a town or at least a highway and the possibility of meeting a car and catching a ride.

He must get started before another plane came snooping round. A plane couldn't land here anyway, there were too many trees. They were only spying, and until he knew whether they were friends or enemies he preferred to get out of the neighborhood. He had no doubt that he could get home, ƒ ve him time and a free course.

So he slid hurriedly down his tree and went to work violently on the last link between himself and freedom. He made short work of it, and with one wistful look toward the tomato can, for he was very thirsty, he picked it up and went on his way. The file he put away with the gun in his one pocket.

It was wonderful to get away from those nasty chains. His ankles and wrists were sore with their continual chafing, and there were almost tears in his eyes, tears of gladness that the shackles were gone. So carrying his tomato can for baggage he plunged down the mountain, worming his way beneath the undergrowth, through the gloom of the deep deep woods, till the sun went lower and lower and he knew that night was coming on.

His limbs were aching cruelly, and trembling. He wondered at his shaken feeling. Would just a few weeks in confinement do that to one who had been as fit athletically as he had been? But he plunged on down and down and down.

There were no landmarks to tell him which way to go. He might be going straight into Spike's territory. "Oh God, help, help! Show me!" he kept repeating softly.

Then he came to a place where there were rocks, and one quite sheer. It was so dusky now that he slipped on the pine needles with which it was strewn and fell, rolling off into space. He brought up eventually, shaken and bruised on a leveler bit of ground quite surrounded by trees, and almost pitch dark. He caught his breath in horror for his tomato can had been knocked out of his nerveless grasp and for a moment he lay where he had fallen too spent to realize what had befallen him, till the echo of its metal, hitting against rocks and stones as it still rolled on down the mountain brought him to his feet again. He must not let that can of tomatoes go. It was his only hope of safety. He was starved and thirsty. He must find it.

So he sprang after it with great bounds, fairly flying over the descending ground, not pausing long enough on either foot to fall, just carried on down by his own momentum even as the food he chased was being carried. And so finally he began to catch up with it. It seemed a miracle, for it had been so dark when he had fallen. But out here now there was more light and he could see the wicked gleam of the top of the racing can as it caught the fading light.

And now suddenly the ground rose up before them both and the can came to a bump, hesitated and rolled back again down the slope to his very feet, and he was so excited about it that he fell to his knees for all the world as if he were tackling his man in football, and grappling the can in his arms he rolled over and over triumphantly.

When he had recovered his breath he sat

up with the can, got out his file, reached for a stone, and stove a sizable hole in the top of that can. Then he lifted the jagged edge of the tin to his lips and drank.

Such nectar he had never tasted. He drank and drank again until the juice seemed all exhausted.

By this time the sun had disappeared and a great darkness had descended upon the whole land. It was black night suddenly and wholly. There seemed no twilight. He decided that the time had come to rest. There was little likelihood that anything but a bear or some wild thing of the woods would find him here, and he must have rest before he could hope to go on.

So he felt around till he located a bed of pine needles and flung himself down. It was cold now that darkness had fallen, and his shabby clothes were thin, but he was too weary to care. He gave one look upward as he settled his head on a soft place among the pines, and there he saw a great star looking down upon him like a friend. He gave it one long grateful look.

"Oh God," he murmured, "I thank you!"

The first sunlight wakened him, laying lacey fingers on his eyes and forehead as it sifted through the pines, and there before

him as he sat up, glimpsed through an opening in the trees, lay a picture the splendor of
which filled his whole soul.

Strange. He had never thought a thing
about God before till he read that little red
book, but now this panorama spoke of God
with a thrill of joy to his starved lonely soul.

He thought of the little book, was lonely
for it, wondered if he would ever be able to
locate another copy. Oh, surely a thing like
that would not go out of print! He had left
of it only scattered remembered phrases, and
those three verses that he had memorized,
John three sixteen, seventeen and eighteen.
He said them over to himself, then bowed
his head and said:

"Oh God, I guess you know what's best
for me to do next. Please show me."

After that he knocked a larger hole in the
tomato can and finished its contents.

"You can't get away from me any more,
that's sure," he said to the can as he finished
the last bite of tomato, and wished he had
some good bread and butter to eat with it.

Then he picked up the empty can, thinking it might come in handy as a drinking cup
if he came to a stream, and went on his way.

He came to a valley at last, wooded closely,
but with a winding stream, and here in a

sheltered place he had a refreshing drink, and took a dip into the water himself, his first bath since he had been stolen away. It was wonderful! But he dared not linger. The sun was getting higher, and he must get to a highway somehow. How he hated to put on those dirty tattered clothes again. It seemed worse than anything else he had to endure just then. The thought of them was revolting to him, but there was nothing else to be done of course.

His feet were sore with the journey, and the old shoes with which he had been supplied were worn through on the sole. If he had only had a bit of paper or a smooth piece of cloth it would have saved his feet, but he had nothing but a file and a gun, and after an hour more of walking over rough ground he found that the file had worn its way through the ragged pocket and left him, its work done. After all, what more need had he of a file? And the gun was only a burden. He had only three cartridges left, why should he carry that extra weight?

But something told him to keep the little that he had, and he plodded on as nearly south and east as he could judge by the sun. If he was still in America he thought that he would eventually arrive in a region that he knew.

He followed the stream down the valley keeping as much in the edge of the woods and under cover as possible, skirting the mountain on which he had been a prisoner, and at last sighting in the distance a little weather-beaten farm house on a stony little farm.

He trudged on, hope giving wings to his feet, and arrived finally only to discover that the house must have been long uninhabited, that every pane of glass was gone, and the doors taken off the hinges. Even the door-steps had rotted away. No hope from that house.

Dismally he started off again, reflecting that those kidnapers of his were clever men. They knew that he would not easily be found by any of his friends in this vast wilderness of mountains.

That afternoon he walked miles, his feet sore, his head aching, his back feeling as if it would break.

The sun gave a grateful warmth to his chilled body, and he hurried on, rounding the foot of another mountain, and yet another, walking on with his eyes heavy with sleep, and wondering if he were not just going around and around the foot of the same mountain.

But just as the last rays of the sun were streaking across the valley, touching with bright colors the little winding stream which he had been following so long, he saw a group of buildings in the distance, down near the stream, and two cows standing by a barn.

He was almost afraid to reach those buildings lest they should turn out when he reached them to be empty like the last house he had seen, but he argued that no cows would stand around empty buildings in a lonely wilderness. So he walked on more slowly now, for his legs ached unbearably, and the distance seemed to stretch out interminably. But at last he reached the place and saw smoke coming out of the chimney. Surely smoke could not come out of a chimney of an unoccupied house by itself.

When he drew near to the house he saw a man milking a cow, a gaunt stern man in overalls, over by the barn. But as Rannie tried to hasten his weary footsteps toward him a great fierce dog rushed bristling out of the barn door and made for him, and for the first time in his life Rannie felt afraid of a dog. For the dog made it all too apparent that Rannie was ill dressed and ill-smelling in spite of his bath in the stream that morning, and that Rannie was on premises where he had no right to be.

"I'm all right," said Rannie, halting with the dog baying in his very face. "I'm not coming any farther. I just wanta ask a question."

He tried to give his impish grin to the farmer, but he felt so weak and tired that it failed of its usual winning charm. The farmer turned around and eyed Rannie suspiciously.

"You better not stand there," said the man. "That dog's trained t' drive folks away from here. We don't want no tramps around these premises."

"Oh, sure!" said Rannie obligingly, "I don't blame ya. I do look sorta like a tramp, don't I? But I'm not one really. I'm just a kid that's somehow got turned around and lost. Wouldya mind telling me where I am and how far it is ta the next town?"

"Seven miles ta Salters, an' ya better make tracks, fer when I git done this yere milkin' I sets the dog free an' if you hang round these here premises he'll make hash outta ya."

"Oh yeah?" said Rannie with a touch of his old braggadocio. "Looks as if he might. Wouldn't mind sa much ef you'd save some o' the hash fer me. They don't seem ta have many hot-dog stands around these mountains. You haven't got any work around you would want done in exchange for supper havya?"

"No I ain't," said the man rising with a menacing look and a full pail of foaming milk. "We don't keep no road house. I calcalate ta do my own work, an' I ain't got any more chores ta-night 'cept ta feed the pigs. Ef you ain't outta my lane by that time I'm comin' out with my shot gun an' turn my dogs loose. I got another one in the house."

"Say, now," said Rannie cheerfully turning his weary game young grin on the man, "don't get sore. I gotta gun myself when it comes ta that but I wasn't planning ta use it just now. Don't worry yerself. I couldn't be persuaded ta stay ef ya paid me for it. I gotta beat it. Sorry I can't stick around and help ya out in some way but I guess it wouldn't be healthy fer either of us. Thank ya jes' the same. I'll be going on. Goo'night!" and Rannie lifted an imaginary hat and tried to walk away with dignity on his sore feet with the furious dog snapping and snarling at his heels.

Slowly down the road he passed once more,

and out into deepening shadows of the dusk. Seven miles! It looked to Rannie like seven hundred. It seemed to him that he could not walk another step. He was sure that just as soon as he was out of sight of that crabbed old farmer he would drop in his tracks, no matter where it was.

So he moved slowly down the rough half-broken road till the road turned around the foot of another mountain, and then he crept aside into the dusk and stumbling up a steep bank wandered, half drunk with sleep and weak with hunger, toward a great stark barn standing in sight as far as one could see in the deepening darkness. Stealthily he slipped inside the open door and peering about swung himself up a rude ladder which was only cleats of wood nailed to the wall, and crept into a corner where a few armfuls of hay still remained in the dusty loft. He dropped down upon it and almost at once was asleep. There were no stars to watch his sleep, or remind him of a heavenly Father, but as he closed his eyes he began to repeat in his mind those wonderful words, "For God so loved the world—"

Quite early in the morning, just at daybreak Rannie came sharply awake. Something soft and furry was sniffing about his face. A lean gray cat stood beside him regarding him with suspicion. Perhaps she did not like his garments either. Quite close beside him in the hay he found there was a nest of kittens. They were tiny tots just getting their eyes open, and when they saw their mother they began to swarm over him to get to her.

Rannie got up hastily and descended the ladder. Cats and kittens spoke of men not far distant. There was likely a house near by that he had not seen in the dark. He had better be moving on. He was dizzy with hunger and must be looking for a job before he could hope for breakfast. Somehow he could not bring himself to beg it. And there were yet nearly seven miles between him and the nearest town.

So he hurried down the road.

19

IN the first house of the little straggling village the woman was in the kitchen cooking ham and eggs. The smell of coffee floating out the kitchen door made him faint and dizzy. He swayed and almost fell, but caught at the door. Perhaps the woman pitied his white tired young face, for she told him if he would pile up a lot of wood neatly that had been dumped in her back yard she would give him breakfast for it, and Rannie went to work with all the will he had in him. He was slow and awkward at it for he had never done such work before, but it was not anything that needed a skilled hand, and he presently had about half the wood in order when she called him in and gave him a delicious breakfast on a kitchen table covered with neat white oilcloth, and then she gave him a pair of half-worn shoes.

"They are better than those you have on if you can wear them," she said looking at his own.

Rannie thanked her and went grimly out to finish piling up the wood, reflecting on the strange revolutions of existence. Rannie Kershaw, cheerleader of his school, stacking wood for his breakfast and a pair of half-worn shoes! And then he grinned and wondered what his old friends would think.

Rannie felt better with the new shoes on his feet and a whole breakfast inside. He walked down the quaint little village street to the railroad station whither the woman had directed him when he asked for a telegraph office.

The station was just opening as he got there and he asked for a telegraph blank. He borrowed a pencil and began to write.

"Dear Dad, don't pay a cent of ransom to anybody. Jesus Christ has ransomed me and I'm out and free. Don't worry. I'll be home hitch-hiking as soon as I can earn a new suit. Rannie."

"Send that C.O.D.," said Rannie handing the telegram to the agent.

The young man took the yellow paper and read it through, then turned to look at Rannie from head to foot taking in every detail of his disreputable appearance.

"Say," he said eyeing Rannie eagerly, "you ain't a relative of that Kershaw guy are you? You ain't that Randall Kershaw kid that got kidnaped a couppla weeks ago are ya?"

"Sure thing," said Rannie nonchalantly. "Just got away. Couldn't make it any sooner. Get that message off quick as ya can, buddy, will ya? The folks might be worrying."

"They sure are worrying, all right!" said the agent settling down on his high stool before the telegraphic instrument, "the papers are full of it, got yer picture in every day, broadcasted twice a day. Folks all over the continent and some in Europe lookin' fer ya."

"Good night!" said Rannie.

"Come ta look at ya," went on the excited agent, "I believe I'd a known ya from yer pictures. There is a lotta resemblance, only the description of yer cloes don't exactly fit."

Rannie looked down at himself and then grinned.

"Ain't it the truth?" he answered. "But say, buddy, get that message started won't ya? I wantta get that off my chest and go out an' hunt a job so I can get me some cloes an' go home."

"Sure thing," said the agent turning back to his instrument and clicking out the address to Randall Kershaw's father.

"I guess you're gointa put our little old town on the map ta-day, ain't ya?" he said looking up delightedly. "I might even get inta the papers myself, sendin' this first message. But say, there's a guy in an airplane here been scourin' the mountain fer ya fer two days back. I don't know if he's round this mornin' ur not, but he's stayin' at myant's. Myant she keeps boarders. Him an' the other guy, the pilot, puts up there, an' they keep their plane out beyond town in a field. My little cousin went up with 'em yestiday. Say, you better go down to myant's

342

an' see if they're still there. They wanted ta find ya bad."

"Name of what?" said Rannie with narrowing gaze. Were these friends or enemies who were after him?

"Name of Harper," said the eager agent.

"Oh, gee!" said Rannie, suddenly a little eager boy himself. "Not Phil Harper. What kind of a looking guy is he? I wonder if my dad sent him?"

"Sure he did!" said the agent. "You wait till I send this message an' get the mail bags on this down train an' I'll take ya over ta myant's myself."

Rannie slumped into a station seat, his shoulders drooping wearily, and listened to his message being ticked out on the instrument, wondering if his journey was very nearly at an end or whether he would have to hike it back home again, and wondering how far he was away from home anyway.

Just then the station door opened and two young men in flying clothes walked in without looking toward him and went over to the little ticket window.

"I want to send a message immediately," said the tall one.

And then Rannie felt himself get weak all over, and the tears crowd into his eyes. For a minute he couldn't control himself, couldn't make his legs lift him to a standing posture, couldn't make his voice speak. For he knew who these must be, and it was just too much for him coming all at once this way.

Then he heard the agent, clicking out the last word of his own telegram, call triumphantly:

"Say, is that yer man settin' out there? He says he is an he's jest sent a message ta his folks. Ef he ain't the one he's got his nerve. I was just gonta bring him over ta have ya give him the once over."

Philip turned sharply and looked at Rannie, and Rannie managed to stumble to his feet and flash on his wicked young grin, the same grin that was in all his football pictures that had been broadcasted through the land in all the newspapers. It was unmistakable. Philip had not seen Rannie since he was a baby, but that grin, together with a certain appeal in the brown eyes that reminded him of Christobel, made Philip Harper certain, and he strode across the room and literally took the poor dirty forlorn boy in his arms.

"Aw say," protested Rannie, "lay off me till I get a scrub. I'm filthy dirty. Y'll get all messed up!"

But the tears were running down Rannie's poor thin face and he was grinning with all his might. A great weakness was upon him. He felt he was never going to be able to live down these tears but somehow he didn't care.

"Say, old man, how did you get here?" asked Harper after they had all talked at once and all slapped Rannie on his slumping shoulders till he felt if they did it again he would collapse.

"Walked," said Rannie laconically and grinned again through his tears.

"What became of your captors?" asked Philip.

"I didn't wait ta see," said the boy. "They heard a posse was coming an' they lit out, so I thought I'd just file off my bracelets an' take a little stroll on my own hook."

"Could you find your way back?" asked the other flier.

"Not if I know myself," said Rannie with a feeble wink. "Boy! I've seen all of that little old cabin I wantta ever see."

The faces of the two young men kindled as they exchanged pitiful glances.

"Perhaps it won't be so bad from the sky," said Philip.

"Oh boy! Are we going in a plane?" exclaimed Rannie sighing wearily. "It's okay with me then, only lead me to a bath an' a full meal first. Don't happen ta have any extra cloes with ya, do ya?"

"I sure do," said Philip eagerly. "Your sister packed some of your things in my suitcase for you. Come on back to our room and get a bath and some food and then we'll talk. But—first I've got to send the glad news."

Rannie went out to the waiting car with the other flier while Philip stayed behind to send his messages. Soon they were driving the few blocks through the pleasant town to the boarding house.

Nothing was too good for Rannie when "myant" heard who he was, the lost found. She prepared a bath and her best towels and set out a luncheon fit for a king, which Rannie ate ravenously after he was arrayed in his own garments.

"I needta go ta a barber," said Rannie after he had eaten all he could hold.

"That's all right, brother," said Philip, "but that will keep. We've got to hear the whole story and get on our way. We don't want those birds to get away from us, you know."

Rannie looked sober.

"I don't know as you need bother," he

said half anxiously. "The boss of course was a tough egg and woulda finished me if he'd had his chance, but the fella called Bud was white. I wouldn't liketa see him get time ur anything. He really saved my life."

And Rannie told in a few characteristic words of the last few days of his imprisonment. The story of the little book figured vitally in the tale, only Rannie didn't mention what the book was. He just called it a little red book, said it was great and that he hoped he could get one like it some day.

Philip's face kindled at the story, and he smiled gravely.

"Well, Rand," he said, "we'll see what we can do for Bud when the time comes but this thing is connected with one of the most notorious thugs in the country and we're bound to get them if we can. Sorry, but I guess you've got to come with us for a little while and tell us all you know."

So Rannie in a good warm overcoat and sweater underneath it, was put into an automobile and driven swiftly to a field where rested a splendid plane, into which to his great delight they hurried him. The entire village of Salter was assembled to see them start, and as the great bird lifted itself from the earth a sober cheer arose from the village throats as they moved on into the sky, and then quickly away out of sight.

One thing that Rannie could not understand was that Philip, instead of burning up the old suit that he had worn during captivity had carefully done it up and sent it parcel post to police headquarters to be used as evidence in the search. And the gun that Rannie had been so proud to own because it had been left him by Bud, they took away and wrapped carefully for further examination.

They sailed away into the blue sky that was so clear and wonderful, and within just a few minutes it seemed to Rannie, there they were circling around over his own mountain and looking directly down upon the roof of that little log cabin where he had been a prisoner for so many long days and nights.

Rannie's face was very sober as he looked down, and then gave a sweeping glance over the wild empty scenery in every direction.

"Gee! I was pretty far out from everything, wasn't I?" he said lifting startled eyes. "No wonder it took me sa long ta get anywhere. How ever did ya find out where I was?"

"We didn't," said Phil. "We just followed a clue and it led us here. God did the rest."

Rannie's face lightened.

"Yeah, I guess none other!" he said solemnly.

A look of surprise and joy flashed into Philip's eyes but he said nothing more just now. He did not want to spoil that solemn reverence in the boy's eyes.

"You see this has been a former haunt of crime," said Philip.

"Oh yeah?" said Rannie wondering. "Then how come I found a book like that little red fella hid away in the wall?"

"That may be another story too," mused Philip. "You'll have to tell me more about the book. Perhaps we'll get on the track of some other prisoner who needs our help."

"It was a great little old book," said Rannie. "It's changed me inta a different lad."

"That's great," said Philip. "But now, we'll have to get through this and hurry you home to your people. We're going first to land down in that valley and get up that mountain a little way. We want to identify that cave you spoke of if we can. We'll maybe find some of your captors there yet. The roads below have been pretty well watched. I don't quite see how they could have got away."

Rannie gave another startled look.

"Got any guns?" he asked. "They're pretty tough eggs. I don't know as two of you—, at least three of *us*—can handle 'em alone."

"We're not going to," said Philip. "We've got a posse of police down there waiting for us."

And sure enough when they landed there appeared from out a sheltered road where they had been in ambush, a car load of policemen, and two motor cycles. There was another car there for Philip's party and they put Rannie in, attending him every step as if he were something too precious to trust alone even for a moment, and then the cars began to climb up a winding rough trail till looking out Rannie could see far down in the valley again.

After a climb of an hour or two they all got out and walked, keeping Rannie well covered in their midst, and walking for the most part silently, with careful tread, till all at once they stood in a sheltered bit of pine growth, with great rocks cropping out all about and above. Rannie could hear the rushing of the falls, and looking down he saw the deep, dark pool with the cliff just beyond, the cliff where the boss had planned to shove him off to death.

Rannie shivered in his warm overcoat and sweater, and turned a white face toward Philip.

"There's your old cabin up there," pointed Philip.

Rannie looked up and there it was, just showing a corner of the roof and the little high window that had been his. Rannie shuddered again.

"And right about here, somewhere, ought to be that cave you heard about," said Philip studying the rock, and moving on around a jutting of the stone. "We sighted a place from above that might have been the opening to a cave. Yes, here it is, at least—why there's a big stone in front of it!"

But the police officers were already rolling the stone out of the way, and revealed to sight an opening wide enough for a man to go in.

Just inside was a box of provisions, some canned goods and a loaf of bread, as if hastily thrust in, and beside it lay a man.

They all stepped back, not expecting to find their quarry so easily, and yet as they stood there they saw he was no longer a living man.

Rannie catching sight of a can of tomatoes exactly the counterpart of the one he had carried with him on his flight, stepped nearer to look, and there he saw Bud lying, all in a huddle, his hard face white in death. So that was the shot that Rannie had thought he heard! Then the gun the boss carried had not been noiseless after all!

Rannie stepped nearer, his young face drawn in horror. So this was the price poor Bud had to pay for saving Rannie! This was more of his ransom. Two men had had to die to save Rannie Kershaw—the God-Man,—Christ Jesus, and poor Bud who had helped to kidnap him but who had refused to shove him off the cliff, and had left his own gun for his protection.

But Bud believed, Rannie was sure, for there in his folded hand lying across his breast was the little red book held tight and one finger in the page at John three sixteen, "For God so loved the world—"

So, the boss had shot Bud, and kicked him into the cave before he was even dead, had hastily filled the mouth of the cave with stones and fled! Rannie stooped over and took the book gently from the stiff cold fingers, as gently as Bud had removed the book from his own limp hand two days ago. The book had done its work. Bud needed it no longer. Rannie would keep it all his life to remind him what had been the price of his ransom.

Philip hurried him away after that, leaving the policemen to deal with what was left behind, and to gather the evidence they had been sent to get.

All the solemn ride down the mountain Rannie was growing up. He would never be the same carefree youth again. It seemed to him that he saw life from birth to death in a new way and caught a new meaning of what it meant to live on this earth, and be ready for the life that was to be that would never end.

Later while they were waiting for the pilot to do some trifling tinkering with his engine before they started homeward Philip and he had a talk, and he showed him the little book.

"Oh, John's Gospel," said Philip with a light in his eyes. "I love that more than almost any other book in the Bible."

"The Bible?" queried Rannie. "Is this a piece of the Bible? I didn't know the Bible was like that. I'd uv read it before if I had."

Then Philip opened his heart to Rannie and they had a few minutes sweet converse, and Rannie told how he had read the book aloud and what Bud had said about believing.

"I think he meant it," said Rannie thoughtfully.

"He surely did," said Philip, "and he was saved before he died. I'm quite sure from what you tell me that he must have been born again."

"Born again," said Rannie, "that was another thing it told about in the story of Nicodemus. I didn't quite understand what being born again meant, but it seemed to be connected with believing."

"The moment a soul believes on the Lord Jesus as his Saviour he is born again and becomes a child of God."

"Oh, boy!" said Rannie dreamily, "that's great isn't it? I wonder why nobody ever told me before."

"Perhaps you wouldn't have listened," said Philip thoughtfully. "Perhaps God had to let you get kidnaped to be willing to listen to his call."

"Oh, d'ya think so?" said Rannie turning a bright face toward Philip. "Then I'm glad. It's worth it!"

"Your sister will be glad. She has accepted Jesus Christ, too."

"Oh, say! Some home I'm coming to!

Chrissie saved too. And what about my Dad? I wonder!"

"Perhaps God will let you help him find the way. Prayer does wonderful things you know. We can all pray."

And just then the mechanician announced that the plane was ready for flight, and Rannie, with a radiant look at his new friend Philip, settled down in his place to fly home with a great wonder upon him. He felt that the former things had passed away and all things had become new.

20

WHEN the telegrams arrived at Seneca Street it seemed that the world was almost too full of joy.

So many telegrams and letters had been arriving that Mr. Kershaw hardly gave much attention to them any more. He was obsessed with the idea that his boy had been slain, and they would never see him any more. He had sold everything he had, and gathered together all the money he could get or borrow, and it was waiting ready in the bank, the highest sum that so far had been demanded and yet no definite means of getting together with the kidnappers had developed. Only these maddening letters that kept arriving with bits of blue neckties, often of different patterns. Rannie's father did not believe in any of it any more. He thought that God, if there was a God, had taken away Rannie in this awful way to punish him for having neglected his own children so long.

So when Christobel brought him the telegrams, he lay back in his chair and only said, "What's the use? You open them."

Christobel opened Philip's first as it happened, and could hardly believe her senses.

"Oh, Father!" she exclaimed in a tone of gladness that called Maggie from the kitchen. "Read it! 'Rannie found, alive and well. Home soon! Philip.' "

"What?" said Mr. Kershaw sitting up sharply. "Philip said that? Oh, my God! It is too good to be true."

"Here's another, Father," said Christobel so excited that she could hardly open the envelope. "Oh, Father dear! It's from Rannie himself. Just listen!

" 'Dear Dad don't pay a cent of ransom to anybody. Jesus Christ has ransomed me and I'm out free. Don't worry. I'll be home hitch-hiking as soon as I can earn a new suit. Rannie.' "

She had to read it over twice to the bewildered father before he could take it all in, and then he asked, still puzzled, "What does he mean, 'Jesus Christ has ransomed me'? What could that mean? You don't think he's lost his mind, do you Chrissie?" The father looked at her piteously, his eyes so weary, his own mind almost crazed by the strain he had been through.

"Oh no, Father!' He's found it," caroled Christobel. "Why Father, he's somehow found God wherever he's been. He means he's been saved by Jesus Christ and there isn't any ransom to pay likely because God in some wonderful way got him out away from those people without their having anything to do with it. Oh, Father, isn't it just too wonderful?"

Then such a baking and brewing as Maggie carried on in the kitchen, her cheeks blazing with joy, her blue eyes dripping happy tears all day long.

But Rannie's father wouldn't even wait for lunch. He had things to do quickly and he hurried out, saying he would telephone every few minutes to see if there was further word. And a little while later there did come another telegram from Philip saying when they would likely arrive at the flying field, and Christobel relayed it to her father.

He came back to the house presently with a shining new car, one of the latest models, and took Christobel down to the flying field. Maggie refused to go. She said it wasn't fitting and anyway she had to stay and have the dinner hot. But she watched them away with pride in her eyes. Rannie was coming back again. That was enough for Maggie.

It seemed to Christobel as at last she watched the great silver bird of a plane come floating down into the flying field, that her heart would burst with joy. Her two wonderful men Rannie and Philip coming back to her again. And Rannie had found the Lord Jesus. That was best of all.

In spite of Mr. Kershaw's best efforts somehow the secret had leaked out, and a great crowd of friends and strangers and newspaper men and camera men and small boys and girls and business men and everybody was down on the flying field to greet them when they landed.

Rannie got out looking white and thin, but still with his same old twisted grin, and there arose such a shout as it seemed to Christobel that the whole earth could hear. Then the reporters rushed up with their note books, and the camera men in circles all about the plane took pictures of Rannie and Philip and the plane and the other flier. Finally they all got away and Mr. Kershaw led them to the car.

Rannie paused and looked at it with admiration.

"Oh boy! That's some car!" he said. "Somebody loan it to ya? Whose is it, Dad?"

"Yours, Rannie, that's the one you are going to take back to school with you!"

Rannie grinned. He thought it was a joke.

"You forget, Dad, I'm fired from school," he said.

"No, you're not fired any longer," said his father smiling. "Your dean has rescinded the action and they want you to come back and take another try. They have forgiven the whole class for your sake. They've been great, son; they even wanted to give a large sum toward your ransom."

"Say, that's great," said Rannie thoughtfully, "but all the same, Dad, I can't go. I'm gonta get a job an' help you out, and you're not gonta go any further inta debt gettin' me cars, that's a cinch. You failing in business and all!"

"That's all right, Rannie," said his father smiling, "the business is holding its own, and we'll make out. You're going back and you're going to have this car. And as for you, Philip," and he half turned around in the seat and looked back where Philip and Christobel sat hand in hand without seeming to be in the least embarrassed, "You may ask what you will to the whole of my kingdom, for all you have done for me and my boy."

"Well," said Philip, with a twinkle in his eye and a glance at Christobel, "I certainly appreciate that. It's too soon to ask what I want, I know, but I'm serving you notice that some day I'm going to ask you for Christobel to be my wife."

The father cast a quick, happy, surprised look at the two in the back seat, saw the starriness of his daughter's eyes and smiled with a great sigh of relief.

"It's all right with me," he said with a tender look at Christobel, "if you can make her see it that way go ahead."

"She does," said Philip joyously. "We haven't said much about it to each other. There hasn't been any chance, but she does!"

Then Rannie, who had been driving and hadn't paid much attention suddenly burst into the conversation.

"Say, Dad, what about no ransom? Get

onta that? Isn't that great? You won't havta pay any ransom at all."

"But I don't understand. How did Philip work that?"

"Oh, he didn't work that part, God did that, I guess."

"But how? I don't understand," said the father.

"Well, ya see, I found that little piece of the Bible an' I read it, and it said ya only hadta believe ta be saved. I heard the men talkin' about shovin' me off a cliff when they got scared an' I figured it was time ta get ready fer the next world, an' when I read that little book I found it was dead easy, Dad. Just accept what Christ has done. So I just believed. And then I asked Him ta look out fer the rest an' He did, that's all. Didn't ya read my telegram?"

"Why, yes," said the puzzled father, "but I didn't quite understand."

"Well, ya see I promised Him ef He got me outta there I'd b'long ta Him always after, an' I'd let everybody know right off the bat, so I wanted you ta understand before I got home. *He* ransomed me. *You* don't havta. Ever read John three sixteen, Dad? Ya oughtta read it. It's wonderful! Say, Dad, this car is great. Gee, I'm glad I'm home!

361

You all look good ta me. But I'm gladdest of all you don't havta pay any ransom for a poor old wreck like me."

The publishers hope that this
Large Print Book has brought
you pleasurable reading.
Each title is designed to make
the text as easy to see as possible.
G.K. Hall Large Print Books
are available from your library and
your local bookstore. Or, you can
receive information by mail on
upcoming and current Large Print Books
and order directly from the publishers.
Just send your name and address to:

G.K. Hall & Co.
70 Lincoln Street
Boston, Mass. 02111

or call, toll-free:

1-800-343-2806

A note on the text
Large print edition designed by
Pauline L. Chin.
Composed in 18 pt Plantin
on a Xyvision 300/Linotron 202N
by Tara Casey
of G.K. Hall & Co.